Praise for *New York Times* bestselling author
Vicki Lewis Thompson

"Ms. Thompson always delivers
such a wicked comedy with her romance
that you cannot help but laugh out loud one minute
and feel all hot and bothered the next."
—*Coffee Time Romance* on *Talking About Sex...*

"A wonderful feel-good story that
will leave you with a smile on your face."
—*Fallen Angel Reviews* on
"Surviving Sarah" in *Getting Real*

Praise for *USA TODAY* bestselling author Jade Lee

"Terrifically entertaining..."
—*Chicago Tribune* on "Kung Fu Shoes!"

"Jade Lee's new romantic fantasy
is imaginative and action-packed.... I found it
a lovely way to spend a couple of cold rainy days."
—*Publishers Weekly*, Beyond Her Book blog,
on *Dragonborn*

Praise for award-winning author Anna DeStefano

"A talented author who takes a tale
and makes it shine."
—*LovesRomanceAndMore.com*
on *All-American Father*

"Anna DeStefano's remarkable stories
of the healing power of love touch the heart
with hope. One of the genre's rising stars."
—RITA® Award-winning author Gayle Wilson

ABOUT THE AUTHORS

VICKI LEWIS THOMPSON

is a *New York Times* bestselling author who sold her first book twenty-five years ago. It's been a Black Diamond ski slope adventure ever since. The author of more than ninety books, Vicki is an eight-time RITA® Award nominee and the recipient of a Nora Roberts Lifetime Achievement Award. Vicki doesn't ski, but she sees no reason that should stop her from spending a weekend at a cozy ski lodge.

JADE LEE

is a *USA TODAY* bestselling author who has broken new ground in multicultural romance. As the daughter of a Shanghai native and a staunch Indiana Hoosier, Jade Lee found her own identity somewhere between America and China—in her own head. Her imagination allows her to explore China, dragon power and of course the amazing power of love. Her other joys include playing racquetball, in-line skating and watching her two daughters play volleyball. She loves getting mail from readers, so please e-mail her at jade@jadeleeauthor.com, or visit her on the Web at www.jadeleeauthor.com.

ANNA DeSTEFANO

Nationally bestselling, award-winning author Anna DeStefano lives with her husband, son and four (yes, four) spoiled cats in an Atlanta suburb. She loves romantic winter getaways, passionate reads and cutting-edge fashion. Oh—and writing with incredibly talented women. Partying with her girlfriends at Weekend Pass was the most fun she's had in a long time. To catch a glimpse of her alter ego, check out Anna's award-winning romantic-suspense series from Harlequin Superromance, Atlanta Heroes. You can find out more about Anna on her Web site, www.annawrites.com.

Winter Heat

VICKI LEWIS THOMPSON
JADE LEE & ANNA DeSTEFANO

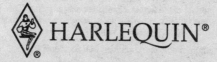

HARLEQUIN®

TORONTO • NEW YORK • LONDON
AMSTERDAM • PARIS • SYDNEY • HAMBURG
STOCKHOLM • ATHENS • TOKYO • MILAN • MADRID
PRAGUE • WARSAW • BUDAPEST • AUCKLAND

Recycling programs
for this product may
not exist in your area.

ISBN-13: 978-0-373-83730-4
ISBN-10:   0-373-83730-5

WINTER HEAT

Copyright © 2009 by Harlequin Enterprises S.A.

The publisher acknowledges the copyright holders
of the individual works as follows:

WEEKEND FLING
Copyright © 2009 by Vicki Lewis Thompson.

WEEKEND TIGRESS
Copyright © 2009 by Katherine Grill.

WEEKEND MELTDOWN
Copyright © 2009 by Anna DeStefano.

This edition published by arrangement with Harlequin Books S.A.

® and TM are trademarks of the publisher. Trademarks indicated with ® are registered in the United States Patent and Trademark Office, the Canadian Trade Marks Office and in other countries.

www.eHarlequin.com

Printed in U.S.A.

CONTENTS

WEEKEND FLING

Vicki Lewis Thompson

* * *

For Marsha Zinberg, editor and friend,
who is one of the main reasons
I've enjoyed myself all these years.

ACKNOWLEDGMENTS:

Many thanks to my trusty partners in crime,
Jade Lee and Anna DeStefano,
for their enthusiasm and good cheer.

Dear Reader,

Welcome to one of my cherished fantasies, a weekend at a ski lodge with a sexy guy. No, I don't ski. You have a problem with that? I don't spend hours swimming when I'm at the beach, either. The difference might be that I actually *can* swim, while I actually *can't* ski. Nor do I want to try. I'm convinced I would break something, and then what kind of weekend do you have, hmm? A weekend of pain!

I've never indulged my fantasy of staying at a ski lodge, maybe because I worry that, not being a skier, I wouldn't be accepted. Nothing's worse than feeling like an outsider, y'know? But neither do I want to learn to ski and risk pain and breakage so I can be an insider.

So I've come up with a plan. I'll make the reservations, buy the clothes, go to the lodge and... arrive on crutches. Instead of a pariah, I'll be that brave soul who can't ski this weekend (sob!) but showed up *anyway*. I think this could work for me. Feel free to steal the idea.

Warmly,

Vicki Lewis Thompson

PROLOGUE

TRACY BINGHAM EMPTIED the last of the beer into her mug and banged the pitcher down on the table. "How are two people who just got dumped supposed to write love poetry?" She glared at her best bud Josh Dempsey, the genius who had dragged them into this.

"The gang at the office is counting on us to contribute something. I think we need more beer." Josh signaled the waitress. "Unless you want to go somewhere else? This might not be the best atmosphere."

"But I like it here." Tracy glanced around at the cozy L.A. bar that she, Josh and their ex-lovers, alias pond scum, had chosen as a regular Friday-night happy-hour spot. "We shouldn't have to give up our favorite drinks place on top of everything else."

"This is my fault. I should have said we weren't up to it."

"It *is* your fault, but I suppose we can't risk looking like pathetic losers in front of the whole office. If the rest of them are writing love sonnets for this contest, we have to write one. Read me your first two lines again. Maybe I'll get inspired."

Josh put down his beer and picked up his notepad. "'I love your eyes, so like the ocean deep, when sunbeams dance on waves that flash with fire.'"

She gazed at him with sympathy. He hated sympathy, but

she couldn't help it. He was a good guy who'd been blind-sided by a bitch. "That's not bad. Were you thinking of Lisa?"

"No. I was thinking of Miss Piggy." His glance dared her to argue with him.

"I can see that. Miss Piggy has beautiful eyes."

"Yes, she does. So you have to rhyme with *deep* and *fire*. That should be easy."

"I accept the challenge." Tracy scribbled quickly on her notepad and read the lines out loud. "'Your lips are juicy as a garbage heap. Behold the rat who's found his heart's desire.'"

Josh chuckled, which made her laugh. No doubt they were getting punchy, between the beer they'd consumed and the stupid situation they were in. First of all, their lovers had left them for each other. In a sense, she and Josh had been the matchmakers for Lisa and Brian.

Right on the heels of that disaster, the ad agency they worked for, Innovations, Inc., had lost the promo bid for an upscale Colorado ski resort to Innovations' arch rival in Los Angeles, A-List Productions.

When the resort had advertised a promotional love sonnet contest with the top prize being a vacation for two during the resort's opening weekend, the Innovations team had vowed to field several entries so they could win at least one of three trips offered. They were counting on Josh and Tracy, the office's creative duo, to write one. The A-List execs would croak if somebody from Innovations won the contest. Despite recent dual breakups, Josh and Tracy felt honor bound to give this a shot.

It was pretty damned funny, all right. Tracy couldn't seem to stop laughing, and then she got the hiccups.

"Don't hurt yourself over there." Josh put down his beer and started writing.

"I'm developing a taste for black humor."

"Then you'll like this." He continued to write.

"Let me see." Tracy tried to grab the notepad, but he jerked it out of reach.

He placed the last period with a sharp jab of his pen and started reading. "'You are so sweet that I would love to be, a big mosquito landing on your chest. I'd shove my stiff proboscis into thee, and suck up all your lusciousness.'"

She whooped in approval. "Hey, I do believe my muse is waking up!" She quickly wrote two more lines. "'I love to run my fingers through your hair, cascading down like draining motor oil.'" She pointed her pen at Josh. "Go."

He pursed his lips and gazed at the beamed ceiling. "Okay, got it." He read the lines as he wrote them. "'You say your skin is blotchy. I don't care. I love your nose. I even love that boil.'"

"Brilliant. Now we need the big finish. The last two lines have to rhyme."

Josh smiled an evil smile, which made his dimple flash. "I'll do the first one."

Tracy had to admit Josh had a killer dimple. His curly dark hair and gray eyes weren't bad, either, especially like now, when he was presentable. But she knew things could get really ugly when he was on deadline.

In the three years they'd worked together at Innovations, they'd seen each other at their worst. An ad campaign often meant pulling all-nighters, which led to a generous helping of foul language and bad hygiene. After a few of those sessions, she had no illusions about Josh Dempsey.

She doubted he had any about her, either. She could be quite unpleasant during a forced march at work. On one memorable occasion she'd threatened to shove her computer monitor up his ass. She'd also purposely doused him with water a couple of times, and once with a Starbucks mocha frap.

They'd come through the tough periods still friends, and she treasured that. She'd especially appreciated his friendship during the past month, after they'd discovered that when they'd worked late several nights in a row, Lisa and Brian had amused themselves playing hide the salami.

Tonight's brainstorming session, one she'd sort of dreaded, was turning out to be more entertaining than she'd expected. "So what's your line?"

Josh looked smug. "'You've taught me, dear, that I'm not really gay.'"

Tracy burst out laughing again. Nobody was less gay than Josh, which made the line even funnier. The next line popped right into her head. Creatively, she and Josh had always been in sync. "'So be my love until we rot away.'"

"Yeah." He grinned at her. "That's a wrap." He poured them each more beer. "We're done here."

Tracy picked up her mug. "We can't submit that, you know."

"Why the hell not? It's freaking iambic pentameter. It has the right number of lines. It's a veritable Shakespearian sonnet."

She lifted her mug in his direction. "You're right. We satisfied the requirement. Here's to us."

"To us." He clicked his mug against hers. "I mean, we're only doing this so nobody can accuse us of being slackers. It's not like we really want to win."

She looked into his gray eyes. They really were nice eyes. "You're right. Us winning the trip would be ridiculous."

CHAPTER ONE

JOSH GLANCED AT TRACY sitting across from him in the limo transporting them up the winding, snow-packed road to Weekend Pass Resort. "I can't believe we won with that lame, crazy sonnet."

"Who knew they'd find it 'refreshingly zany'?" Tracy had been to the salon, and her red hair was a little shorter today than it had been yesterday.

Josh thought the chin-length style was cute. Deceptively cute, considering this was a woman capable of pouring liquid on him when she got in a snit.

She'd decked herself out in designer jeans, sexy-looking boots with four-inch heels and a white turtleneck. Over that she wore a white parka with a blue wool scarf draped around her neck. Dark had fallen long ago, and he couldn't see her face very well in the dim interior of the limo, but he'd noticed in the airport that the scarf exactly matched her eyes. She had great eyes, better even than Miss Piggy.

Tracy had never seemed to care about her clothes before, but she'd gone out shopping with a couple of women from the office a few days ago. They'd probably twisted her arm to dude herself up for the occasion, considering there would be media all over the place. Josh didn't care if he appeared on camera wearing a four-year-old jacket, but women worried about stuff like that.

"You should have taken my suggestion and come up here with Marcy. You like Marcy." Tracy set her champagne flute in its holder so she could unwind the scarf from around her neck.

"I barely know her, and besides, she doesn't deserve the trip. You do. You could've found somebody to go in my place. I offered to bow out."

"That wouldn't have been fair. Entering was your idea."

"And writing something snarky was yours." Josh raised his glass in a toast. "If I do say so myself, we rock. The A-List people were furious that two people from Innovations won."

"Yeah, I'm happy about that. They're such an obnoxious bunch. Still, this trip is so wasted on us."

"Except for the complimentary champagne and the limo ride." Josh took another swallow. "I could get used to that part."

"You know what I mean. It's supposed to be a romantic getaway to Telluride. The way the limo driver closed his back window, I'm positive he expected we'd make out on the way up the mountain."

"Yeah, he probably did. I've always wondered what that would be like."

"Embarrassing, that's what it would be like. He might not be able to hear anything, but he has a perfectly good rear-view mirror."

"Are you saying you'd never make out in a limo, then?"

Tracy shook her head. "Not this chick. I prefer privacy."

So she wasn't particularly sexually adventurous. He wondered how she'd react to the topic he'd been mulling over for days. "According to the Internet, the place is crawling with singles ready to party."

Tracy picked up her champagne flute and sank against the leather upholstery with a sigh. "I have to admit A-List has people talking about Weekend Pass Resort. Have you seen Maddy Lov's blog?"

"I read a couple of entries. I'm surprised she's the guest celebrity this weekend. When we were bidding on the job, I got the sense the owners were on the conservative side. Did you see the video for her last hit?"

"The one where she was practically naked? I think everybody with a TV has seen it. For this gig I was expecting Dick Van Dyke, Angela Lansbury, somebody like that."

Josh finished his champagne and reached for the bottle. "Wouldn't it be sweet if A-List messed up by contracting with Maddy?"

"I've been thinking the same thing. If A-List and Maddy are setting a tone the owners don't like, we can be right there with our business cards."

"See, then it wouldn't be a wasted trip. The Innovations brass would love us to pieces." Josh held up the bottle. "More champagne?"

"No, thanks."

"Don't mind if I do, then." As the limo rounded another curve, he concentrated so he didn't pour champagne on himself. He might not worry about fashion, but he'd rather not arrive smelling like booze. "So what do you think of that idea going around the office?"

She hesitated. "What idea?"

"That we use this weekend to hook up with someone."

"Oh, that idea." She sounded less than enthusiastic.

"Personally, I think it's worth considering." In his opinion, he and Tracy had grieved over their respective breakups long enough. They might not be ready for long-term commitments, but they should at least get back out there and score some sex.

Her chin lifted a fraction. "Does that mean you intend to hit on women while you're here?"

"I've always hated that expression, but, yeah, I might check out the possibilities." The temperature in the limo dipped a few degrees. "You got a problem with that?"

"It's none of my business, really." Her voice was getting frostier by the minute. "But we'll be sharing a room. You should probably give me a signal, like hanging your Jockeys on the doorknob."

"Oh, for crying out loud. I'm not going to hang my Jockeys anywhere. I wouldn't use our room. That would be gross." Then he had an unsettling thought. "Of course, if *you* thought you might use the room for that, maybe we could work something out, but I really think—"

"Don't trouble yourself. I'm not planning to have sex this weekend."

"And you don't think I should, either, do you?"

"I did not say that." Icicles formed on each word.

"You didn't have to. It came through loud and clear by the way you said, 'I'm not planning to have sex this weekend,' like you had a stick up your ass."

"I resent that! Just because I don't feel like falling into bed with some virtual stranger doesn't mean you shouldn't. Go for it! Be my guest! Screw your brains out this weekend."

"If I get the chance, I sure as hell will. It'll be good for what ails me. And judging from that outburst, I'd say you could use a dose of the same medicine."

"What?"

He was glad she hadn't accepted another glass of champagne because right about now he'd be wearing it. "Trace, it's been six months. I can't speak for you, but solo sex is getting old. We have a weekend with no specific work obligations, and—"

"We're here."

"So we are." Josh peered through the tinted windows as the limo glided to a stop in front of the main lodge, a massive two-story structure of wood and stone. Despite the building's size, it nestled in a stand of snow-covered blue spruce as if it had been there for generations. Golden light from large windows spilled onto pristine snowdrifts.

Josh had always thought he liked the ocean better than the mountains, but a place like this could change his mind. "Gorgeous." He glanced at Tracy, expecting a response. Instead she sat rigidly upright, like a condemned prisoner perched in the electric chair. Obviously his willingness to troll for sex this weekend had freaked her out.

He lowered his voice. "Trace, if it'll make you uncomfortable, I'll give up my little plan, okay?"

"I wouldn't dream of interfering in your sex life."

"Aw, don't be like that. Look, I promise to keep my fly zipped. I'll—"

A bellman in a navy parka sporting a Weekend Pass logo on the sleeve opened the limo door, and Josh could only hope the guy hadn't heard that last part.

"Welcome to Weekend Pass." Cold, crisp air tinged with wood smoke wafted into the limo as the bellman held out a gloved hand to help Tracy out.

"Thank you." Tracy unbuckled her seat belt and picked up her oversize hobo purse from the floor. "We'll talk later," she murmured to Josh as she moved toward the limo door.

"Right." Josh half rose to follow her and found himself crouched with his face inches away from her temptingly curved backside. Must be the designer jeans in operation, he told himself. Sure, he might be feeling a tad deprived these days. But no way was he getting a sexual zing out of staring at Tracy Bingham's butt. No way.

TRACY COULDN'T IMAGINE what was wrong with her. She'd acted like a bitch, when all Josh wanted was a little action, for which she couldn't blame him. He was a normal, red-blooded male with a strong sex drive. She had no good reason to stand in his way, and she'd apologize once they had a moment alone.

The resort looked beautiful so far. The shadowy bulk of the mountains hovered above the lodge, and runs for night skiing glowed along the steep slopes. Tracy had never skied, but if she ever planned to try, this would be the place, where lessons, equipment and lift tickets were free for contest winners.

As the bellman handed her gracefully out of the limo, a good-looking guy with dark-blond hair came forward and introduced himself as Tony Rossi. His black leather jacket looked expensive, and Tracy was glad she'd splurged on a few clothes for the trip. She recognized Rossi's name from all the e-mails they'd exchanged about details for the trip. She hadn't been able to figure out if he was with A-List because he didn't look familiar, and she knew most of the rival agency's people.

"Nice to meet you at last," Tracy said, shaking his hand. Cameras flashed, reminding her about the media coverage she and Josh had agreed to in exchange for this weekend. They'd had to send in photos of themselves along with the sonnet, and Tracy was sure that winners had been partly chosen because they were promotable. To her left, a guy with a camcorder was taking footage of their arrival.

Josh came to stand beside her, and she introduced him to Tony, putting a little extra warmth into the introduction because she was feeling guilty about her behavior in the limo.

"Welcome to Weekend Pass," Tony said as he shook hands with Josh.

"Thanks." Josh returned the handshake and then tucked his hands in his pockets. "I guess we're in the same business as you. Tracy and I are with Innovations, Inc."

Rossi nodded. "I'm aware of that."

"Are you with A-List? Because I don't think we've ever met, and I know most of the A-List people."

Tracy ducked her head to hide a smile. She'd been trying to think of a polite way to find out Tony's role, but good old Josh cut right to the chase.

Tony stiffened. "No, I'm not with A-List. The Walkers hired me to…to manage the opening weekend for them."

"Interesting." Josh paused, as if contemplating that fact. "I would have thought A-List would be doing that."

"The agency's handling a few things. They have a couple of their people on-site."

"Who's that?" Tracy asked.

"Evelyn Jacobs and Samantha DeWitt." He spoke the names in a neutral tone, as if to give nothing away. "But I'm overseeing the operation. If you have any problems, it's best to come and see me." He displayed very white teeth in a diplomatic smile. "Not that I expect you to have any problems. You'll both have a great time."

"I'm sure we will." Tracy guessed that Tony wasn't on good terms with Evelyn and Samantha. Tracy didn't blame him. They were a couple of twits. "Anyway, we're thrilled to be here," she said.

"Great." Tony glanced over her shoulder. "Your luggage is onboard, so if you'll both climb in with Mark, he'll take you to your cabin."

Tracy looked over at the little electric cart that now held their luggage. "Aren't we staying in the lodge?"

"That was the original plan," Tony said, "but the Walkers and I decided you and Josh would have more privacy in one of the luxury cabins instead of in a room at the lodge."

Tracy suddenly pictured being all alone in a secluded cabin in the woods sucking her thumb and feeling lonely while Josh… Well, she didn't want to think about what Josh would be doing…or sucking on. "But we don't need privacy," she said. "A room at the lodge would be fine."

"Just enjoy yourselves," Tony said. "The cabins are the best we have to offer. I like them better than the celebrity suites."

"But—"

"We appreciate it," Josh said. He took her arm and propelled her across the icy drive to the cart.

"The welcome reception's at seven-thirty, dinner's at eight-thirty," Tony called after them. "There will be a map in your cabin, or call for a cart if you want a ride back here."

"Thanks!" Josh helped Tracy into the cart, which was a good thing because the four-inch heels didn't navigate too well on ice.

"I'm being a pain, right?" she said under her breath.

"Kinda."

She wanted to apologize right then for her comments about his weekend plans, but she knew he wouldn't like having her broadcast his business to their driver, so she stayed silent.

Well, as silent as she could be when she was nervous. "It's cold," she said. As if to corroborate that, her breath made clouds in the air.

"It's warmer during the day," Mark said. "And when you're involved in physical activities, you barely notice the cold."

Tracy immediately thought of Josh involved in a physical activity—boinking some woman he hadn't met yet. Was that safe? She wondered if he worried about STDs. "It's pretty dark back here." She peered through the shadowy, snow-covered pines and saw lights glowing from windows as they passed cabins spaced fairly far apart.

"Follow the path lights and they'll take you right back to the lodge," Mark said. "Or I can come and get you if you'd rather ride."

Josh settled back in his seat. "I'm sure we can find our way."

Tracy could well imagine why he'd want to learn the route. Then he could navigate it after his rendezvous with some snow bunny. "This looks like bear country," she said.

"It is," Mark said, "but they're hibernating."

"Oh." She tried to think of some other reason that would make walking around after dark a dangerous thing to do. "How about rattlesnakes?"

"They're underground, too," Mark said. "In winter you might see a fox or maybe a snowshoe rabbit. Deer and elk show up now and then. Coyotes are around all year, and the wolves are coming back."

"So you could be walking along this path, and a pack of wolves would suddenly surround you—"

"Nope." Mark turned and smiled at her. "Wolves don't attack people. They're magnificent, though, so you'd be lucky if you glimpsed one."

"That's all the more reason to walk the path," Josh said. "Maybe we'd see something exciting."

"Maybe." Tracy suspected Josh would be the one wearing a rut in the path. She'd be the one holed up in the cabin, reading the books she'd packed.

"Trace, you're jiggling your foot."

She stopped immediately. "Sorry." He'd reminded her about it several times during the trip. She'd accidentally kicked him when they were on the airplane.

"You didn't used to jiggle your foot."

"You just didn't notice it before." But he was right. She'd fallen into the habit around the time they'd discovered they'd won the contest, and people in the office had started mentioning this would be a great time for each of them to have a weekend affair.

"With all the time we spend together, I would have no-ticed," Josh said. "You realize that's supposed to be a form of self-stimulation."

"Josh, for pity's sake."

"Just an observation."

She lowered her voice. "You think I'm repressed."

"I didn't say that."

"Well, I'm not," she muttered.

"If you say so."

She didn't like that he thought she was repressed. She wasn't repressed. She was...still healing from a bad ex-perience. Maybe her confidence wasn't completely rebuilt. Although she'd told herself a million times that Brian falling into bed with Lisa had nothing to do with her own inadequa-cies, her ego hadn't quite bought the story.

Apparently, Josh didn't have those self-doubts. He'd been dumped, too, yet he was ready to party. They'd had the same amount of time to get over the split, so if he was ready, she should be, too.

"This is your cabin." Mark parked the cart in front of a one-story log cabin with a front porch.

It appeared to be at the end of the lane, which should have made it seem even more isolated, but lights shining from the curtained front windows canceled that impression. The cabin looked incredibly cozy and inviting, a haven from the stresses of the world.

"This was the first structure built at Weekend Pass," Mark said as he helped Tracy down. "The Walkers stayed here while the rest of the lodge and the other cabins were con-structed."

"So they've taken a real interest from the beginning," Josh said.

"Absolutely." Mark climbed the stone steps, crossed the

wooden porch and opened the front door. "It's been their dream for years. They have a beautiful home on the grounds now, but they've mentioned that sometimes they miss this cabin. They say it has good vibes." He motioned them both inside.

Tracy stepped into the lamplit room and sighed with pleasure. The furniture—a sofa, round coffee table and two easy chairs—were grouped in front of a stone fireplace. Everything was upholstered in soft denim and accented with colorful pillows that coordinated perfectly with the large braided rug covering the wood floor. The light came from two floor lamps that looked as if they'd been carved from tree branches. Wildlife paintings hung on the wall and a fire was laid in the hearth, ready for a match.

Josh let out a little whistle of approval. "Nice."

"Go ahead and explore," Mark said. "I'll bring in your luggage."

Tracy turned to Josh. "I thought we'd be in some anonymous-looking hotel room. I never expected it to be so…"

"Perfect?"

"It is perfect. Too bad we're not—" She caught herself before she said the first thing that came to mind—*a couple*. No telling why she'd even thought such a thing. "—staying longer," she finished, hoping she hadn't sounded like an idiot.

"I know," Josh said. "I've never had a vacation in the mountains, but this is really appealing."

"It is." From the corner of her eye, Tracy could see through the door into the bedroom, but she decided not to be the first one to venture in there.

Until this moment, she hadn't truly appreciated what being roommates would mean. She'd asked for two double beds, thinking that would do the trick. After all, she and Josh had spent whole nights together, but they'd been slaving away at the office, immersed in a work environment. Sometimes one or the other of them had caught a quick nap on the office sofa, and she had thought this wouldn't be all that different.

Big mistake.

"Let's see what the bedroom and bathroom look like." Josh the Intrepid walked right in.

She had no choice but to follow, unless she wanted to come across as a scaredy-cat. The secret to this weekend might be to pretend this cabin was the equivalent of the office. Therefore she should bring up some work-related topic.

She started into the bedroom. "I'd say there's no love lost between Tony Rossi and the A-List people. We should be able to make inroads into— Omigod." She stared at the bed, the only bed, in the room.

Tony hadn't been listening to her when she'd made her sleeping arrangement request. Instead of two doubles, he'd given them a king. And what a king. The canopy bed was big enough for Paul Bunyan, and the type of thing he might have built, too, if he'd been so inclined. Peeled logs gave the frame a massive look, but the sheer masculinity of the bed was softened with a fluffy yellow comforter and mounds of snowy pillows.

"I…I asked for two doubles." Tracy glanced at Josh to see how he was reacting to this bed, which seemed made for having lots of good sex.

He wore a dazed expression.

She could only assume he was imagining getting his groove back in this particular bed and was awestruck by the prospect. If that was what he wanted, she'd see what she could do about it.

"Tell you what," she said. "I'll have Mark take me and my luggage back to the lodge. I'll bet they have a spare room I could have."

He gazed at her. "What're you talking about?"

"You have plans for this weekend, and I apologize for my

first reaction. I wholly support you." She gestured toward the bed. "And this is exactly what you need to…to bring those plans to fruition."

"Tracy—"

Mark came through the bedroom door pulling both their suitcases. "Ah, I see you've found the best part of this cabin. The woodworker who made that bed put it together inside the room. The Walkers loved it so much they had him build them a duplicate for their house, although no two will ever be alike."

Tracy turned to Mark. "Unfortunately, gorgeous though this bed is, it—"

"Don't worry, Trace." Josh stepped over to retrieve their suitcases. "I already checked the mattress, and it's plenty firm. You won't have a problem with it."

"But that's not the only issue. We—"

"The pillows are hypoallergenic, too."

She recognized that he was trying to get her to shut the hell up, so she did. Maybe they needed to work this out quietly with Tony, later on. That was fine.

Josh handed Mark some folded bills. "Thanks for everything. We'll take it from here."

A tip! She'd been so focused on this awkward situation that she'd completely forgotten they needed to tip their driver.

Mark smiled at them. "Thank you, and enjoy the place." Then he left.

After the door closed behind him, Tracy let out a sigh. "Thank you for getting the tip. How much did you give him? I want to pay half."

"Forget about the tip. What was that nonsense about you moving out of this cabin?"

"You need to have it all by yourself."

"You would move out of this incredible cabin and take

some standard room at the lodge, so that I could get some action?"

"Yes, and my first response was unforgivable. You're my friend, and I want you to be happy. I want you to find somebody this weekend." She felt a twinge when she said that, but she barreled on. "In fact, I'll *help* you find someone. When you do hook up, and I'm sure you will because you're an amazing guy, then you need that bed."

He continued to stare at her, and slowly a bemused smile replaced his puzzled expression. "I don't think I ever understood before how generous you are."

"So it's settled, then. We'll work it out with Tony at dinner, and he can send someone to transfer my suitcase."

"No, it's not settled. This is a great cabin, and we both won it, so we're going to share, like we planned. The bed's not a problem. You can have it and I'll take the sofa. I've always wanted to sleep next to a fire anyway."

She had to admit that she didn't like the idea of them completely separating. Then who would she talk to about stuff? "You might not be using the sofa anyway. You might end up in someone's room."

He waved away that possibility. "Maybe not. It was just an idea."

"It's a good idea." She took a deep breath. "In fact, I'm looking like a wuss compared to you. I've decided that I…I'm going to go for it."

He frowned. "Don't push yourself into something you're not ready for."

"I'm ready."

"You don't look ready. You looked scared shitless."

"Okay, maybe I am, but what about this? We'll help each other find someone, and in the process, we'll watch each other's back. What do you think?"

"I guess we could try it."

"Great! Now let's check out the bathroom." She put on what she hoped was her jaunty, confident face and walked into the bathroom.

Of course it was perfect, too, with a large walk-in, multijet shower in travertine marble, a separate room for the toilet, dual sinks and mirrors everywhere.

Tracy couldn't hold back a little *wow,* but she was determined not to stand there like some starstruck hick from the sticks. Instead she walked over and began rummaging through the amenities in the basket on the counter.

She shouldn't have been surprised by what she found in addition to the requisite lotions, shampoos and conditioners, but she was. She needed to become more sophisticated if she expected to have the kind of weekend Josh envisioned. That sophistication could begin right now.

"Oh, look," she said brightly. "Condoms!" Fanning them out in her hand, she turned back to Josh. "We can divide them up!"

CHAPTER TWO

THE WALK BACK UP to the lodge gave Josh a chance to think about whether he'd royally screwed himself. He was the genius who'd championed this hookup plan, and to be honest, he'd concentrated mostly on his own activities. Vaguely he'd realized that it worked both ways and that Tracy might be scouting out partners, too. He'd been fine with that.

Or so he'd thought.

Maybe he'd been secretly pleased with her reaction in the limo. He'd had to give her grief for it, because they always gave each other grief, but, yeah, he'd been relieved that she didn't plan to shag some guy while she was up here. He could handle a weekend affair, but Tracy…Tracy would get involved. She wouldn't be able to go to bed with a guy one night and leave him the next.

But thanks to him, that was her plan. He thought she was headed for disaster, but he couldn't very well say that when he'd encouraged her to take this step. When he'd made that idiotic statement that she *needed* some good sex, he'd been projecting his own problems on her.

No question he was feeling seriously deprived. If he wanted any proof of that, he should look no further than his current sexual attraction to Tracy. With every minute he spent in her presence, he became more obsessed with things he'd never paid attention to before.

For example, she had a tiny freckle on the left side of her mouth. He'd developed a fascination with it, which had led to a fascination with her mouth in general. She had a Kewpie-doll mouth, curved just right for kissing. How had he missed that in the three years they'd known each other?

Sure, she'd always been dating other guys and he'd dated other women, and then they'd both ended up with Someone Serious, or so they'd thought. She'd never been available, and they'd gone the friendship route, treating each other the way you'd treat a brother or sister.

Well, she was available now, and in a few minutes she'd be scanning the crowd looking for a bed buddy. He tried to tell himself that was just as well. Assuming she found some-one, and the way she was looking tonight that was a distinct possibility, then he wouldn't have to battle this ridiculous fixation he'd just developed.

Because he sure as hell couldn't act on it. That would be the stupidest cliché in the book, the old friends-to-lovers schtick. Besides that, they worked together. They worked so well together that he wasn't sure he could do his job without her as a brainstorming partner. Mucking that up with an affair could play havoc with their careers, and with the economy like it was, neither of them needed to be job hunting.

"Did you remember to bring your poem to read?" Tracy's question fogged the air as they walked.

"Yeah." They'd been warned they'd be asked to read their winning poem during dinner, and they'd convinced Rossi to let them bring a more sincere, less snarky one.

Josh had volunteered to handle it because he had a poem he'd written for a girlfriend a couple of years ago and because Tracy hated speaking in front of a group. He'd minored in drama, and public speaking didn't faze him. Tracy fazed him, though. She'd changed into an ankle-length black cashmere sweater dress for tonight's function, along with a different, dressier pair of boots.

When she'd walked out of the bedroom, dangly silver earrings peeking through her red hair, he'd been lucky that she wasn't a mind reader. His thoughts had moved into X-rated territory the very second he noticed how the dress clung to her breasts and hips. *Shall I compare thee to a mid-summer night's wet dream?*

For the walk to the lodge, she'd put on a black velvet coat and the blue scarf that so perfectly matched her eyes. He wondered if she had any idea how great she looked. He should tell her, but he was afraid the comment might betray him and she'd figure out his thoughts weren't so platonic anymore.

Compared with her, he felt underdressed. A white turtleneck, wool slacks and a sport coat had seemed okay when he'd left L.A. But he didn't own a topcoat, so to keep from freezing to death he'd had to put on his quilted jacket over the sport coat. Not a good look. He'd ditch the quilted jacket once they were inside.

"I think we need to strategize," she said.

"You mean about meeting Samantha and Evelyn?" At least he hoped that was the topic, and not her new interest in the singles scene.

"No. Samantha and Evelyn won't be a problem. We need to strategize about how to check out the available people we might hook up with."

Just as he'd feared. "What do you have in mind?"

"You talk to the guys, and I'll talk to the women."

"Sounds like a junior-high dance."

She made an impatient noise. "What I mean is, you scope out good candidates for me, and I'll do the same for you."

"And then I come over and whisper that Johnny likes you, and you give me a note to take back to Johnny?"

"Josh, be serious! This could work."

"No, it couldn't. You have no idea what attracts me to a woman. I can't have you picking out my date."

"I know more than you think, smarty-pants."

That made him grin. He hadn't been called smarty-pants in twenty years, ever since he'd learned that cool guys didn't advertise their brain power. About that time he'd taken up surfing. Nobody dared call a surfer dude *smarty-pants*.

"Oh, yeah?" he said. "What's my type?"

"For one thing, you like blondes, and I'm not saying that because Lisa was a blonde. Your other previous girlfriends were blondes, too."

He found it interesting that she'd noticed. "There are a lot of blondes in Southern California. It's the dominant hair color for women under thirty. Hair color isn't a biggie for me." He was developing a fondness for red, though.

"You like women with a nice set of twins."

He laughed. "There's a no-brainer. What man doesn't?"

"I once heard a man say he liked small-breasted women."

"So he was more evolved than the rest of us. But I promise you, the size of a woman's breasts is not a deal breaker for me. Look, I'm a guy, so I notice if a woman's pretty or not. I notice her figure. But that's all superficial."

"I'm glad to hear you say it. All right, you also want a woman who has a few brain cells to rub together."

"True."

"A woman who can stand on her own."

"True again. I hate clingy and dependent." That's why he got along so well with Tracy. She never expected special consideration because of her gender.

"See? I could so choose someone for you."

"You've missed the most important thing."

"Sex appeal? I could gauge whether someone would turn you on."

If that were true, she'd be blushing right now, because he was incredibly turned on. All this talk about his preferences had brought him to an unavoidable and shocking conclusion. She had it all. But she was Tracy, his work buddy. Getting sexual would change everything, and if the affair went sour… He didn't even want to contemplate the ugly fallout.

"I'm not talking about sex appeal," he said. "Although maybe, in a way, I am. If a woman makes me laugh, I find that very sexy."

"So that's your number-one requirement? That she makes you laugh? I never thought of Lisa as being very funny. She must have been funny in private."

"Well, yeah, she…" He couldn't lie to Tracy. He'd never been able to do that. "You know, she wasn't funny at all. That's a hard thing to admit, that I was thinking of marrying someone who didn't make me laugh."

As if giving him time to digest that, Tracy walked along beside him without saying anything. Nothing broke the stillness other than their footsteps crunching along the packed snow.

At last Josh broke the silence. "I've spent a lot of time hating Brian's guts for stealing Lisa, but maybe I should thank the guy." The last bit of sadness melted away from his memories of Lisa. "The only times Lisa and I laughed together were when we had drinks with you and Brian." And Tracy had been the one making him laugh, but he decided not to mention that.

"As long as we're giving true confessions, Brian didn't make me laugh, either," Tracy said. "And that's important to me, too, but I ignored it because he was generous and prompt and all sorts of good things that are difficult to find. But he was crushingly dull. The most interesting thing he ever did was cheat on me with Lisa."

Josh chuckled and then instantly apologized.

"No, go ahead and laugh. It's funny. I thought he had no imagination whatsoever. I mean, even in bed— Whoops! I didn't mean to say *that*."

Still laughing, Josh reached an arm around her shoulders and gave her a quick, sideways hug. "Poor Trace. I think Lisa and Brian did us each a huge favor." He made sure it was a catch-and-release hug, so she wouldn't think anything of it. He'd hugged her like that a hundred times, at least. No big deal.

This time it was a big deal. This time he registered a spicy perfume and the softness of her body as he pulled her close. She felt damned good close to him like that, even if it was only sideways and not a full-body hug. Had he ever given her a full-body hug? If he had, he must have been too drunk to notice how wonderful it was. He distinctly remembered them leaping together in a full-body slam after two days of hard work had paid off with a big contract for Innovations. But a body slam didn't count.

By now she was giggling. "We should send them thank-you notes, don't you think?"

"That depends on what you plan to say in the thank-you note. 'Thank you for leaving because you were lousy in bed' might not give him warm fuzzies."

"Spoilsport. Okay, no thank-you notes. I'd be tempted to say something nasty. Hey, we're almost there, and we still don't have a strategy. Obviously you think my idea sucks."

"It has some basic flaws. You haven't taken into account pheromones."

"You're right! And you know what? I believe in that. I stopped taking birth-control pills because they're supposed to mess with your ability to detect pheromones."

"When did you do that?"

"A couple of months ago. It's supposed to take a while for

your body to readjust, but my pheromone detector is probably working great right now."

That depressed him. Perverse as it might be, he wanted her to be as attracted to him as he was to her. But she'd shown no sign of it, which meant that pheromonewise, they weren't meant to match up. In the long run, that was a good thing, so he should just forget about it.

"So I guess we're on our own, right?" She glanced at him as they approached the main entrance to the lodge.

"For the initial contact," he said. "But feel free to ask for help if you run into trouble."

"I will. And you're welcome to do the same. Let's go get 'em."

So there it was. He'd set the stage for Tracy to have herself a fling. She'd insisted they each take a couple of the condoms with them tonight, and he hadn't had the heart to tell her he already had some packed in his suitcase. Anyway, the message was clear. He could have a fling, too. Whoopee.

FROM THE MOMENT Tracy walked into the lobby, she felt like a star on the red carpet. People holding drinks turned and waved, calling out her name and Josh's. Magically, someone came to take their coats. She wondered how she and Josh had morphed into the next Brad and Angelina, and then she saw the posters, one for each winner and his or her companion, mounted on easels over near the registration desk. That explained why they were suddenly famous.

"Darlings, you're *here.*"

Tracy found herself looking into a tabloid-familiar face. "Hello, Ms. Lov."

"Heavens, call me Maddy! Aren't you the lovely one." She air-kissed Tracy on both cheeks before turning her high beams on Josh. "Joshua Dempsey! How is it that you're not my next MTV video costar? I'm calling my agent *tout de suite* to complain, you cutie-pie." She grabbed him by the ears, which were now red with embarrassment, and nuzzled her nose against his. "Great eyes, Joshua. Maybe I won't ask for you, after all. You're liable to steal the scene."

When she released him, he staggered backward and glanced frantically in Tracy's direction. When he spied her, he grabbed her arm. "Maddy, have you met Tracy Bingham? We work together. She's—"

Maddy poked him in the chest. "You're too cute. I met Tracy five seconds ago, but I excuse you for not remembering. That happens a lot when I'm around." She lifted her arm and snapped her fingers. "Drinks! These folks need drinks!"

Tracy fought the urge to laugh. Maddy was a force of nature. Tracy had been prepared to dislike her, but how could you dislike someone so full of energy?

"Are you two a couple?" Maddy asked. "You look like you should be a couple."

"Actually, no." Tracy pulled her arm from Josh's death grip. "We're—"

"Ah! Perfect. Chocolate martinis." Maddy grabbed two from the tray and handed them to Josh and Tracy. "What do you mean, you're not a couple? What's that about?"

"We're good friends." Tracy cradled the martini in both hands. "We collaborated on the poem, which was entered in both our names, so that's why we're both here." Then she took a sip of her drink. Heaven. This celebrity business wasn't so bad.

"I remember!" Maddy pointed a red lacquered nail at Tracy. "You two wrote that hysterical one about the rat and the mosquito and the draining motor oil. I almost peed my pants! Evelyn and Samantha weren't sure the Walkers were right to let you win, but I said, hell, yeah! These two are twisted, and I love that."

"Are Samantha and Evelyn here tonight?" Tracy hoped to find out if they were in the doghouse. Whatever their situation, Evelyn and Samantha weren't staying in a cute little cabin for the weekend and they wouldn't be slurping free chocolate martinis, either.

"I'm right here." Evelyn, her blond hair in an updo and her curvy body in a silver, shape-hugging dress, sashayed forward with the fakest smile Tracy had ever seen. "Congratulations, Josh and Tracy. What a coincidence, huh? Two people from Innovations winning a spot."

"Quite a coincidence." Josh seemed to have recovered himself. "How's everything going, Evelyn?"

"Couldn't be better." Evelyn fiddled with the glittery necklace that dangled into her well-displayed cleavage. "Sam's upstairs in a crisis with the hair dryer, but she'll be down any minute. And you've met Maddy. Isn't she fabulous?"

Maddy rolled her eyes and tossed her famous blond curls. "I'll bet you say that to all the stars."

"Of course not, silly."

Maddy's eyes narrowed slightly but her laugh was bright. "You wouldn't be calling me silly, now would you, darling?"

"Why, no!" Evelyn paled slightly under her makeup. "Oh, look! Here comes Sam."

As yet another blonde pranced over wearing stilettos and a fire-engine red dress, Tracy began to see what Josh meant about the blonde ratio in Southern California. Out of four women from that neck of the woods, she was the only nonblonde.

She had a horrible thought that Josh might be attracted to either Evelyn or Samantha. She hoped not. They were both too self-absorbed to have a sense of humor. Under Josh's stated criteria, neither of them would qualify. Besides, he couldn't date somebody from A-List Promotions. He'd never live it down.

Maddy had flirted with him, but Tracy couldn't see anything happening there. The quality of Maddy's attention reminded Tracy of a scattergun—spraying compliments everywhere with no particular aim in mind. But Tracy was pleased that tension seemed to exist between Maddy and Evelyn. All might not be rosy for A-List.

"Excuse me." Tony Rossi headed in their direction. "I'd like to borrow Josh and Tracy for a minute."

Both Evelyn and Samantha stiffened. Samantha stepped in front of Tony. "If you're planning to take them over and introduce them to the Walkers, Evelyn and I would prefer to do that."

"I'm sure you would, but the Walkers have requested that I handle it." Tony stepped around her and smiled at Josh and Tracy. "I see you have drinks. If you'll follow me, I'll take you to the people who made this all possible."

"We know a little about them," Tracy said as she wound her way through the crowd behind Tony. "Our company, Innovations, Inc., bid on the PR contract. We lost to A-List."

"That's…unfortunate." He changed direction, led them over to a small alcove and turned to face them. "Maybe we should have a quick discussion before you meet them. I'm going to guess you entered the contest as a dig at A-List."

"They're a rival company," Josh said. "We're not good losers."

"I get that. You might as well know that the Walkers aren't thrilled with the way A-List has handled the promo for this weekend. They wanted somebody like Tony Bennett or Julie Andrews, and instead they got Maddy Lov. Her blog, which the Walkers didn't find out about until recently, has billed this place as a swinging singles destination."

"We saw that," Tracy said. "And our impression of the Walkers was that they're fairly conservative."

"They're not old fogies, by any stretch, but their dream was a romantic getaway for couples. I've been hired to put that spin on the opening. They weren't prepared to fire A-List, because then they'd have no celebrity at all, but I'm supposed to do what I can to tone things down. This is my specialty, to come in and save a PR situation from disaster. I don't take long-term contracts."

Tracy exchanged a glance with Josh. This could be good for them.

"I can tell what you're thinking," Tony said. "And I'd like you to hold off on any pitches for your company until the weekend's over."

"That would be the gracious thing to do," Josh said. "No problem."

"I have another favor to ask." Tony scrubbed a hand over his face, as if he'd had a very long day. "I need for the Walkers to believe that at least one of the winning couples fits their idea of what this resort is all about. Liz Song is coming alone, so she won't work. I've met Felicia Gallo and Willard Chambers. They're…well, they won't fit the Walkers' image, either. That leaves you two."

Tracy swallowed a sip of her martini. "But we told you we weren't a couple."

"I know. Just don't tell the Walkers. They wanted you to stay in their cottage. Let them believe that it's a love nest for the weekend. Can you do that?"

Tracy looked at Josh, who was looking right back at her. "You know how I feel about lying," she said to him.

"I know," Josh said quietly. "But this is obviously important to these people. They've put a lot of money and effort into their dream."

Tracy took another drink from her martini. Why did everything have to be so complicated? She turned back to Tony.

"The thing is, Josh and I each had a painful breakup about six months ago, and we thought this weekend might be a good time to look for someone—"

"That's fine. Just be discreet," Tony said. "The Walkers go to bed early. After ten at night you can do whatever you want, but I'd really appreciate it if you'd act like a couple the rest of the time. These folks have enough to worry about. Their son was supposed to handle security for Maddy Lov, and he's stuck in bad weather in Chicago."

Tracy smiled. "Maddy looks like the kind of girl who can take care of herself."

"Oh, I'm sure, but we still need security. It's the right thing to do. Liz Song is held up in the same storm, and if Felicia and Willard hadn't flown through Dallas instead of Chicago, they wouldn't be here, either."

Tracy knew how it felt to have all your plans put in jeopardy. She'd begun picking out china and looking at houses in the months before Brian cheated on her. She completely understood that sick feeling of disappointment when all your expectations went up in smoke.

"Okay," she said. "We'll do the best we can. That is, if you're okay with it, Josh?"

"I'm fine with it, Trace."

So she was off the hook, at least until the Walkers retired for the night. By that time she could use jet lag as an excuse to turn in herself. For now, she didn't have to worry about hitting on some guy, and that was a huge relief. She was only doing it so she wouldn't look like a lightweight compared to Josh.

Instead, she'd get to pretend that she was actually *with* Josh. That might confuse someone he tried to hook up with later, but those were the breaks. She couldn't get herself to feel upset about it.

He was looking very appealing tonight in his turtleneck and sport coat. Pretending to cozy up to Josh would be no hardship. If she didn't know better, she'd say her pheromones were kicking in and steering her toward Josh, of all people. Now wouldn't that be inconvenient?

CHAPTER THREE

DURING THE WELCOME reception and dinner, Josh tried to keep the players straight in this crazy drama. Evelyn and Samantha were definitely on the outs with the Walkers. The older couple did everything possible to avoid the A-List women, although Evelyn and Samantha had managed to plop themselves on either side of them at the dinner table.

The Walkers were polite about it, but they didn't look very happy with the seating arrangement. Now that Josh had met them, he could understand.

They were open, genuine people who'd done well financially and wanted to turn that wealth into something special. Tom carried himself with military bearing from his years in the service, and Alice had the ruddy complexion of a woman who enjoyed plenty of time outdoors. They were both avid skiers. When they were first married and Tom was still in the military, they'd used every weekend pass during the ski season to hit the slopes somewhere. Naturally they'd named the resort Weekend Pass, in honor of those romantic getaways.

How the Walkers had ended up with A-List mystified Josh, except that he knew A-List had a habit of promising the moon and delivering a pile of shit instead. Tom and Alice weren't savvy in the ways of PR companies and might have been sucked in by all those glittery promises. Innovations didn't tend to make wild claims, and sometimes it cost the company business, but working for them meant Josh could sleep at night.

At least usually. Sleeping on the sofa while Tracy lay in that bed designed for sex wouldn't be easy. But it was the right thing to do. For now, though, with the Walkers keeping an eye on them, he was supposed to act like an eager lover.

To that end, he put down his fork and leaned over to murmur in Tracy's ear, which gave him a whiff of her spicy perfume and consequent heart palpitations. He struggled to remember what he'd planned to say. Oh, yeah. "The Walkers are looking, so maybe you should quit shoveling in the Stroganoff and give me a soulful glance."

"Mmf." Still chewing, she turned so they were almost nose to nose. Then she crossed her eyes.

Fortunately, he didn't have a mouthful of food like she did, because he would have choked on it when he started to laugh. As it was he had to cover his mouth with his napkin so he wouldn't draw too much attention to himself.

Tracy swallowed her food and grinned at him. "Sorry," she said softly. "Couldn't resist."

Josh kept his voice low, too. Maybe the Walkers would think he was murmuring sweet nothings. "At this rate the Walkers will think they've given their favorite cabin to Lucy and Desi."

"I think we're okay. They seemed to like us well enough. Can I go back to eating now? This food is amazing, and I want to finish before the dessert arrives."

"Knock yourself out. I like a woman who enjoys her food." Chalk up another point for Tracy. He'd never thought about it before, but she didn't get all hinky about calories. He was sick of dates who analyzed everything before putting it in their mouths. Yet Tracy had a terrific figure.

"I wouldn't be enjoying this food half as much if I had to

recite the poem afterward," she said. "Thanks for that. Oh, look. Chocolate cake for dessert. Yum."

"I was just wondering. Do you work out?"

She glanced at him. "Is that a hint that I should pass up the cake?"

"No. God, no. Eat the cake. It's just that you seem to love food, and you're not fat, so—"

"Thank you." Her blue eyes twinkled.

"That didn't come out very well. What I'm trying to say is, you look…great."

"Josh, are you giving me a compliment?"

"Um, yeah. Guess so."

"No need to be all embarrassed about it."

"I'm not embarrassed."

"Yes, you are. Your face is red."

He sighed. Normally he was better at conversing with women and giving them compliments. But this whole thing with Tracy was weird. She was his buddy, yet he was becoming sexually attracted to her. He had to fight that, but in the meantime he was supposed to be acting like her lover for the Walkers' sake. No wonder he was off his game.

"What do you think about Felicia and Willard?" Tracy said in an undertone.

Happy to change the subject, Josh glanced to the far end of the table where the other winning couple sat with Maddy and Tony. Liz Song still hadn't shown up. "I know they're supposed to be together, but I just don't see them as a couple."

"Neither do I. She's got all that Italian heat going on, and he's much cooler and more sophisticated. Plus, I'm probably wrong, but is something going on between Felicia and Tony?"

"I didn't catch anything." But then, he'd been completely absorbed in watching Tracy move through the evening in that slinky black cashmere. He'd gone so far as to imagine that she must be wearing a black bra and panties underneath. He had *never* fantasized about Tracy's underwear before.

"I'm probably imagining things."

"I hope so, for Tony's sake. His job is tough enough without adding something like that. I wouldn't want to be in his—" Josh stopped speaking as Tony stood and clinked his spoon against the side of his water glass.

"The Walkers have requested that we have the poetry reading prior to dessert. Felicia and Josh, are you each prepared to read?"

"Absolutely." Josh pulled a slip of paper out of his jacket pocket, but it was only for a quick reference. He'd memorized the poem. "Ladies first."

"No, no." Felicia looked a little nervous. "You go first, Josh. Please."

"All right." He'd thought this would be easy, but his heart was pounding as he stood. Too late he realized that with the situation changed, he was nervous about how Tracy would react. It was, after all, a love poem, and the Walkers would expect him to present it to her with feeling. He wondered if she'd look into his eyes and see the desire that he'd tried so hard to hide.

Probably not. She knew he'd written it for another woman. Sure, it mentioned gazing into her blue eyes, and Tracy had blue eyes, but so did a lot of women. Tracy deserved to have some guy write a poem for her and recite it in public, so she'd feel special. Unfortunately, he might be the wrong guy at the wrong time.

Nothing could change that now. He took a deep breath and shoved the paper back in his pocket. He'd do this right.

Gazing into Tracy's eyes, he repeated the words of love he'd written. And suddenly his nerves disappeared. The poem was perfect for Tracy, with her dreamy blue eyes and her fair skin dusted with golden freckles.

Somehow in the past few hours she'd become a heroine, his heroine, and he could tell her so under cover of this command performance. He didn't expect her to take it seriously, which was a bonus. When it was all over, she'd probably have trouble controlling her laughter.

TRACY KNEW PERFECTLY well that Josh had written this poem for someone he'd dated a couple of years ago. Her name had been Helen, or maybe Heather. This poem wasn't about Tracy at all. So why was she becoming so emotional hearing it?

Jealousy, that's what. No man had ever been so smitten with her that he'd written her a poem. This Helen, or Heather, rated a wonderful poem that should have made her worship the ground Josh walked on. But according to Josh, she'd moved on. What was wrong with that girl? What was wrong with Lisa, who'd abandoned Josh to fall into bed with Brian?

Tracy battled a very unsettling thought. She was developing a crush on Josh. Having him read this poem as if dedicating it to her made everything worse. She wanted that poem to be hers. She wanted Josh to be smitten with her. What a stupid idea. He was here to get his groove back with some other chick. He'd told her so.

When he finished, the table was silent for a second, before it exploded in loud applause and catcalls. Tracy, however, couldn't seem to move. She was afraid if she started clapping, the tears would leak from her eyes. How embarrassing would that be?

Josh glanced down at her and frowned. Then he sat and took her hand. "Are you okay? I didn't mean to—"

"I'm…I'm fine." She forced herself to smile her brightest smile. "That was beautiful, Josh. Unbelievably beautiful."

"But I've upset you. You're trying not to cry."

"Nope!" She swiped at her eyes. "Just got something in

my eyes, that's all. I think it was when the waiter ground pepper on my salad. It went flying everywhere."

He didn't look as if he believed her, but thankfully he let it go.

"Terrific job, son." Tom Walker stood and reached across the table to shake Josh's hand. "I knew we had the right people in that cabin."

"Lovely." Alice Walker wiped at her eyes, too. "And don't believe that about the pepper, Josh. Tracy was crying out of joy and love, just like I was. She's just not ready to admit it in front of all of us. Wait until you two are alone. I'm sure she'll explain then."

Tracy decided they wouldn't discuss the poem at all once they were alone. They'd be better off having no conversation whatsoever. Anything they said could lead them into trouble, and with every passing second, her urge to melt into Josh's arms grew stronger, so she needed to keep alone time to a minimum.

She didn't pay much attention to Felicia's recitation. She was too busy planning the best way to end the evening. What if Josh wanted to head for the bar and look for women? After all, the Walkers would be going off to bed soon, which meant the charade could be canceled for the time being.

The thought of Josh in the bar being ogled by single women raised Tracy's blood pressure. Not good. She needed to let him do whatever would make him happy.

Before she realized it, dinner was over. She and Josh said good-night to the Walkers and thanked them for a great evening. Tony handed each of them a schedule of the upcoming activities for the next two days and invited them to the bar for a drink.

Tracy had her answer ready. "Thanks for the offer," she said. "But I'm ready to turn in." She held up the schedule. "Gotta rest up for the activities."

"I'll walk you back to the cabin, then," Josh said.

She wasn't about to let him do that. "Don't be silly. I'll bet you'd love to stay for a while. I can find my way back."

"I'm sure you can, but I'm tired. Come on. We'll go back together."

"But—"

"You're not *leaving?*" Maddy bustled up, followed by a group of paparazzi. A single furrow appeared in her otherwise perfectly smooth brow. "The party's just getting started!"

"We're kind of pooped," Josh said.

"I can unpoop you! I'm organizing a salsa contest in the bar, and I'm dying to see your hips wiggle, Joshua." Maddy punctuated her statement with a quick shimmy, and the cameras all flashed.

Tracy tried not to think of Josh's hips wiggling as she gazed at him. "You should go, Josh. It's not every day you're asked to dance by Maddy Lov."

"And that's not all." Maddy preened. "My agent's set me up to be a contestant on an upcoming *Dancing with the Stars*." She turned to the photographers. "Did you get that? And I'm planning to win it." She glanced back at Josh. "Better take me on now, Joshua, because soon I'll be out of your league."

He laughed. "You're out of my league now, Maddy. But I'm flattered. I'm also exhausted. Maybe tomorrow night."

Maddy reached out and pinched his cheek. "You're playing hard to get, aren't you? Either that, or I'm not getting the whole story on you two." She gazed at Tracy. "He put on quite a show with that poetry."

"Yes." Tracy's voice clogged up on her. "Yes, he did."

"See, you sound like you're coming down with something," Josh said. "We really do need to go."

"Well, if you must, you must." Maddy lifted her arm and snapped her fingers, which seemed to be a regal habit she'd developed. "Coats! We need coats for these people! One long black velvet, one sort of ordinary navy quilted job."

Josh winced at the description of his coat.

"It's a perfectly good coat," Tracy said quietly. "We're not movie stars, after all."

"Maybe not, but you look like one."

She took the compliment gladly. Josh was a nice guy, and at the moment, she sincerely wished they didn't have such a close working relationship. She wished he could be the stranger she stumbled upon at this resort.

"If you're both so tired, you should take a cart back," Maddy said. "I can call for—"

"That's okay," Tracy said as she buttoned her coat. "We'll walk. Good night, now."

"Ta-ta, darlings!" Maddy waved them off.

"I'm glad you vetoed the cart," Josh said as they descended the steps and crossed to the path that would take them to their cabin.

"So far that walk between here and the cabin has been my favorite part," she said. "It's so peaceful."

"We're not going to get much peace for the next two days. We're scheduled up the ying-yang."

"And I understand that. The Walkers need to get as much bang for their PR buck as they can. I liked them, Josh. I liked them a lot."

"Me, too. I hope this resort works out for them. I also hope you don't mind this charade we've been roped into."

"I don't mind. And I have to say, you're good at it. Maybe you should have been an actor."

"What do you mean?"

She shouldn't have said that. "Nothing. Never mind."

"Trace, you can't throw out something like that and then do the 'never mind' thing. That's not fair."

It wasn't, she thought with a sigh. "That poetry reading. I know you wrote that for someone else, but anyone in the room would have sworn it was for me. Very impressive."

He was quiet for several seconds. "I guess you think I'm an insincere creep, huh?"

"No! I didn't mean that at all. Tony asked us to put on a show, and you came through in spades. I found myself wondering what was wrong with Helen, or Heather, whatever her name was, that she didn't snatch you up and never let go."

"I didn't make enough money for her."

"What?"

"She was hoping to live in Malibu, and for that she needed a guy in a much higher income bracket."

Tracy blew out a breath, which made a sizable cloud in front of them. "I can't *believe* that. I've heard stories about mercenary women, but I've never heard of one who ditched a wonderful man because she had her sights on Malibu. I'm so glad you didn't end up with her."

"So am I." His steps crunched over the snowy path. "You think I'm wonderful?"

"You know that."

"No, I don't. I can't recall you ever saying to me, 'Josh, you're wonderful.' I can remember a few times when you said, 'Josh, you're a shithead' and poured something all over me."

"That's just work. You know how I get." She turned her collar up against the cold.

"Bitchy."

"Yes, bitchy," she agreed. "Well, we're not working this weekend, and there are no contracts on the line if we don't produce a dynamite PR campaign in the next forty-eight hours, so I'm free to say, 'You're wonderful.'"

"In that case, I'm glad we won this contest."

"I am, too."

"Except…maybe we need to face the dangers in this situation."

A chill ran down her spine. "I thought Mark said there were no bears or rattlesnakes?"

"I'm not talking about critters in the woods. I'm talking about us. Our situation."

"Oh."

"We've never spent this much time together without being involved with something work-related."

She wanted to argue, because she had a feeling where this was going. "This could be called work-related. We're trying to snag the contract away from A-List."

"Yes, but that'll be easy. The Walkers hate them and they like us. We're a shoo-in. We don't have a real challenge there."

She sighed. "I suppose not."

"But personally we have a huge challenge. Okay, I can only speak for myself, but after that 'you're wonderful' comment, I have a hunch I'm speaking for you, too. The danger is we're becoming attracted to each other."

"Horrors!" She couldn't help it. He sounded so damned serious.

"I know it's not exactly the end of the world, but think about the consequences."

"Josh, between us we have enough condoms to last a week. There would be no *consequences*."

"Good Lord. How much wine did you drink?"

"Not enough. Look, I know you're right. Temptation has been thrown in our path, but getting involved would be a disaster. Is that what you're trying to say?"

"In a nutshell."

"I have the perfect solution for you. Get involved with someone else this weekend."

He met that suggestion with silence. And more silence.

"Josh? Wasn't that the plan you had when we arrived?"

"Yeah." He sounded disgruntled.

"So what's the problem?"

He muttered something under his breath.

"Sorry. I didn't catch that."

"I said, 'I don't want to get involved with someone else.'"

"You don't?"

"No. I want to get involved with you. Happy now?"

Actually, she was ecstatic. She couldn't remember ever feeling this happy in her life. But he was right about the mess they could make.

"We need to think about this," she said. "We don't want to do anything impulsive we'd regret later."

"No shit."

They'd reached the cabin, and lights were glowing from inside. Tracy would bet the resort had a turndown service and there were mints on the pillows of that boink-o-rama of a bed. Knowing the Walkers, there could be champagne cooling beside the bed, too.

Tracy kept her gaze on the cabin because she didn't dare look at Josh. "I think it might be a really bad idea for us to be alone in the cabin right now."

"I think you're right." He cleared his throat. "I'll wait here until you're safely inside. Then I'll go back to the bar for a while."

"I hate to make you—"

"You got a better idea?"

"No."

"Then get on in there. And lock your bedroom door."

A thrill of excitement shot through her. He wanted her that much? "I can't lock the bedroom door. You couldn't get to the bathroom."

"I'm a guy. I can pee in the woods."

"It's below freezing out here!"

"Will you let me worry about that? Get in the cabin, please."

More turned on than she'd been in ages, she scurried up the steps, crossed the porch and fumbled with the key. Finally she got the door open. Turning, she looked back at Josh.

He stood there watching her, shoulders hunched and hands shoved in his pockets.

She couldn't bear to think of him hiking back through the cold when he obviously didn't want to. "This is crazy. Come on in. I'm sure we can control ourselves."

"Speak for yourself. Good night, Trace." With that he turned and started back down the path.

As she watched him disappear into the darkness, she wondered what would happen while he hung out at the bar. A couple of drinks might cause him to reconsider his original plan. The lodge was chock-full of single women, and he could easily find a substitute for Tracy. After all, she'd encouraged him to solve the problem exactly that way.

An unwelcome picture of Josh kissing someone else flashed through her mind. That was followed by an image of Josh riding the elevator up to that person's room. Tracy shut down the mental movie with a groan of frustration. No point in torturing herself.

Walking into the cabin, she closed and locked the door behind her. She honestly hadn't seen this coming, and now she was in her least favorite position. No-win.

CHAPTER FOUR

TWO HOURS LATER Josh navigated the path to the cabin with much less coordination than he had earlier. The salsa contest had been in full swing when he'd arrived, and Maddy had been all over him like white on rice. But despite her enthusiasm, Josh could tell she wasn't trying to seduce him. She just loved to have fun.

Once he'd switched to hard liquor, he'd become a lot of fun. He'd dirty danced with her and any other woman who came out on the floor. Although Maddy hadn't propositioned him, several other women had. God help him, he'd made up a story about being in therapy for performance issues. That hadn't always worked, because a couple of women offered to help with that problem, but for the most part he was able to stave them off.

Eventually he'd calculated that he'd been away long enough for Tracy to be asleep, and he'd left the lodge, once again on foot. The cold air had sobered him up some, but he was still pretty trashed. That was a good thing. He wasn't worth anything in bed when he was this blitzed.

He couldn't get over the quiet out here in the woods. His footsteps crunching on the packed snow made the only sound in the stillness. He was used to traffic and construction sounds both at work and surrounding his L.A. apartment, so this lack of noise was almost spooky.

Then he heard something howl. He wasn't enough of an authority to know whether it was a coyote or a wolf, but the lone cry made the hair on the back of his neck stand up. He walked faster, which made his heart rate go up because of all the booze he'd consumed.

Another howl broke the silence, and then a third, followed by yipping noises. Definitely a pack of something. But the cart driver—Mike or Mark or Mick, whatever—had said that wolves didn't attack people. That was a myth, the guy had said.

Josh forged on and tried not to think of "Little Red Riding Hood." Or "Peter and the Wolf." Or that other story he'd read in college about the guy who was surrounded by wolves and had to keep a fire going to ward them off.

But Josh had no fire, not even a flashlight. He could smell smoke, though, so there was a fire going somewhere nearby. Maybe the fire was to scare off the wolves. Except you weren't supposed to have to do that, according to Mike-Mark-Mick.

When he came within sight of the cabin, he started running, although in his condition it was more like lurching. He wasn't sure if the howling had stopped, because his breathing was so loud he couldn't hear much of anything else. The pack could be right on his heels, for all he knew. He wasn't about to look over his shoulder to find out.

Gasping for breath, he stumbled up the steps and fished in his pocket for the key. Dammit, where had he put that thing? He started to swear. God, was that the sound of some animal panting nearby? Or maybe that was him. Yes, it was him, breathing like a freight train.

The door swung open and Tracy stood there in a shaft of light. "Josh? Is something wrong?"

"Wolves." He said it before he could censor himself. It might not be wolves, but now he had to pretend it had been or feel like a complete doofus.

"Wolves?" She opened the door wider. "Come inside, for heaven's sake!"

He didn't need more of an invitation than that. Once he was inside and she'd closed and locked the door, he realized the wood smoke had been coming from the chimney of this cabin. Tracy had lit a fire.

"You saw wolves?" she said again.

"Oh, yeah." He'd stopped shaking enough to notice she was wearing a white flannel nightgown. It looked very soft.

"Where were they?"

"I think they had me surrounded." He tried not to look at her breasts, but the flannel draped them so sweetly, and if he was any judge, which he was, she wasn't wearing a bra underneath.

"That sounds very scary."

"It was." Then he remembered he was supposed to be a manly man. "Not for me, though. But I'm glad you weren't out there."

"Me, too. Take off your coat and come sit by the fire. I found some packages of cocoa. Do you want some cocoa?"

The thought of cocoa made him want to barf. "Uh, no, thanks." His knees threatened to give way, so he headed for the sofa. He'd meant to sit down slowly, but he sort of fell onto the cushions instead.

"Don't you want to take off your coat?"

"Well…sure." But he didn't think he had the strength.

He glanced up to find her standing in front of him looking concerned. Sexy, too. He wanted so much to reach up under that flannel nightgown and touch her soft skin, but his arms didn't seem to be working so well.

"I'm getting you some B-12 and a glass of water. You need to hydrate."

"I'd love to touch your breasts." From the way she stared at him, he figured that might not have been the PC thing to say. "But I won't," he said. "They're your breasts, and you decide who touches them."

Her lips twitched, as if she might be trying not to laugh. "You are so toasted. I'll be right back."

He zoned out for a while and then she was back, handing him a vitamin pill and a glass of water. He swallowed the pill and drank the water before handing her the glass. "Thanks."

"Would you like some help with your coat?"

"Sure."

Kneeling down, she reached for his zipper. "I feel terrible that you had to get loaded to survive the evening."

"I'm fine." He hiccupped. "Peachy."

"No, you're not." She unzipped his jacket. "But I guess I'd rather have you drink yourself into a stupor as opposed to hopping into someone else's bed tonight."

"They asked."

"I'm sure they did." By pulling on one sleeve at a time, she got his coat off.

"I told them all I had performance anxiety."

"Oh." She made a funny sound, as if she might be swallowing a giggle.

As for him, words popped out of his mouth whether he wanted them to or not. "You smell really good. Like pancakes and syrup."

"Thank you. You smell like the bottom of a whiskey barrel." She managed to get him out of his sport coat, too.

"I wish I wasn't drunk. Then we could have sex."

Next she pulled off his shoes. "I thought you got drunk specifically so we couldn't have sex."

"I did, but now I wish I hadn't, because you look like a virgin in that nightgown."

"Are you fond of virgins?"

"Not real ones. You're not a real one."

"That would be a true statement." She stood and surveyed him. "All right, my party animal. I'm going to lift your feet and try to get you horizontal on this sofa. Just move with me, okay?"

"When I'm horizontal, will we have sex?"

"I think not. On three. One, two, *three*." She dragged his feet around, and the rest of him miraculously straightened out and flopped onto the sofa. She dusted her hands together. "There."

"The room's spinning."

"It'll stop in a minute. I'll get you a blanket."

He closed his eyes, but that didn't help with the spinning, so he used an old college trick and put one foot on the floor. Marginally better.

She returned with a fluffy blanket and a pillow and set them on the coffee table. "Your foot's on the floor."

"I know. Better leave it there."

"Okay." She tucked the blanket around him. "We need to find a different solution to our problem. We're spending one more night here, and I don't want you to feel obligated to get drunk again to make it through."

"You smell good enough to eat."

"Maybe we should see about getting a second room, after all." She slipped her hand under his head and lifted it so she could slide the pillow underneath.

Her touch felt like heaven. "Maybe. Your hand feels great. Maybe if you stroked my—"

"Josh!"

"My head. I was gonna say head."

"Sure you were. Try to get some rest." She cradled his cheek in her hand. "You're a good man, Josh."

His conscience pricked him about pretending to be in danger before. "They probably weren't wolves."

"It doesn't matter."

"I want you, Trace. I want you bad."

She gazed into his eyes. "Everything will look different in the morning."

He seriously doubted it. This was going to be a hell of a long weekend.

WHEN THE BEDSIDE phone rang the next morning, Tracy rolled over and glanced at the clock before grabbing the receiver. Almost nine. They were supposed to have another meet-and-greet poolside at nine.

"Just checking to see if you and Josh are on your way," Tony said. "The third contestant arrived late last night, so we have everyone on-site."

"We'll be there as soon as we can. Bye." She hung up and jumped down from the huge bed. If a person fell off this monster, they could break something. Still, it was sinfully luxurious, and she'd slept like a hibernating bear. Ha-ha.

Once she was fully awake, she could see they had a logistics problem—two people who had to shower and make themselves presentable in about ten minutes. One bathroom.

She opened the bedroom door and walked into the living room to find Josh sitting on the sofa holding his head. He glanced at her with bloodshot eyes. "Was that a fire alarm?"

"Telephone."

He winced. "Don't shout."

"Oh, boy." Spinning on her heel, she hurried back to the bathroom and dug around in her cosmetic bag until she located some ibuprofen. She shook out two, filled a water glass and walked back into the living room.

"I want to die."

"I know. Take this."

He gulped the pills and the water. "You go. Tell them I'm dead."

"We can do this, Josh, but we have to share the bathroom. You shave and brush your teeth while I shower. Then you can shower while I get dressed and put on makeup. Come on. Take your shirt off on the way. We can't waste any time."

He followed her into the bedroom like a zombie. Once there, he pulled off his turtleneck and left it in a heap on the floor.

She couldn't worry about neatness now. Grabbing his shaving kit out of his suitcase, she hurried into the bathroom. Then she plopped his shaving kit onto the counter next to one of the sinks and reached into the shower to turn on the hot water full blast.

"You'll be naked in there," he said.

"And you'll be too busy shaving and brushing your teeth to notice." She, however, had observed that he had great pecs and just enough chest hair to make the view interesting. His shoulders looked broader when he was shirtless, and he had decent biceps, too.

Yikes. She was ogling. Mentally giving herself a shake, she pointed at his shaving kit. "Go!"

Obediently he pulled out his shaving cream and a razor, which made his muscles flex ever so subtly.

She clenched her jaw and turned away. She would *not* allow herself to start fantasizing about Josh as a bed partner. He'd gone to a lot of trouble and pain to keep anything from happening between them last night, and she wasn't about to let that sacrifice be for nothing.

But now she had to do the brave thing, the part she'd tried not to think about. Throwing a towel down next to the glass block wall that partitioned off the shower, she whipped her nightgown over her head and jumped under the spray.

With a yell, she jumped back out again and grabbed the towel to cover herself.

Sure enough, Josh had turned to stare.

"S-scalded m-myself," she said.

He swallowed. "Um…are you all—"

"I'm fine." Wrapping the towel all the way around her body, she turned back to the shower and adjusted the temperature. "I'm going to leave it on when I get out, to save time, so you won't have to adjust it." A quick glance over her shoulder confirmed what she feared.

He was still watching her, his razor held in midair, his eyes glazed.

"Josh, shave!" Then she dropped the towel and charged into the shower again.

"You have a great ass!" he called over the sound of the spray.

So maybe he'd only seen her from the back. That was some comfort. She soaped up quickly.

"And great tits, too!" he added.

Okay, he'd seen the full monty. Not much she could do about it now. She knew one thing for sure—they were getting a second room today. She'd explain the situation to Tony and promise him the Walkers would never know.

A room in the lodge would put maximum distance between her and Josh. She'd give Josh the cabin, now that she'd had one night in that fabulous bed. But a second room was a problem to be solved later. At the moment she had to finish this shower in record time.

Fortunately her office buddies had talked her into a leg wax before this trip, because she had no time to shave her legs this morning. Rinsing off, she edged around the side of the glass block wall and snatched the towel from the floor. She didn't dare glance up to find out whether Josh was paying attention as she wrapped herself in it.

When she finally did look, she realized he wasn't even in the bathroom. So he was a gentleman, after all. She'd always thought so.

Then he walked into the bathroom with another of the towels wrapped around his hips and nothing else on. She gulped at the sight of him. The chest she'd already had a chance to admire, but now she was treated to a view of his firm thighs and sexy calves.

They'd been good friends for—was it three years?—and she'd never realized he was hot. Not every man looked good draped in a towel, but Josh was made for that kind of pinup-boy outfit. He could do commercials.

She wasn't about to tell him so. "Your turn." She walked past him, and her toes sank into the thick carpeting in the bedroom. This cleanup plan of hers was working out rather well, except for a couple of small glitches. She should be able to dress before he finished his shower. They could trade places again, so that he dressed in the bedroom while she put on her makeup in the bathroom.

Sure, he'd seen her naked briefly, but it wasn't as if… Then she realized that in order for him to fetch that towel he'd casually knotted around his hips, he would have had to walk over to the rack that was right next to the shower. From that vantage point he would have been able to see into the shower. Easily.

She stalked over to the bathroom door but kept her eyes averted from the opening into the shower. She wouldn't stoop to his level of Peeping Tomdom. "You spied on me while I was in the shower, didn't you?"

"I had to get a towel." His words were punctuated with the slap of a washcloth over his skin.

God, she wanted to look. "That doesn't answer the question. Did you or did you not spy on me?"

"I wouldn't call it that."

"What would you call it, then?"

"Taking advantage of a golden opportunity."

"Josh Dempsey, you are no gentleman!"

He turned off the water. "And unless you walk out of this bathroom right now, you are no lady."

"Don't worry, I'm leaving." But instead of turning away from the shower to go back out the door, she turned toward it. She told herself that was a mental error, that she'd meant to swing around in the other direction so there was no chance that she'd catch a glimpse of... Oh...dear...Lord.

Face aflame, she hurried back into the bedroom. Maybe she'd hoped that he'd have an unimpressive package. If so, that hope had just gone up in smoke, along with all her resolutions about keeping her distance from him.

Instead she started wondering how soon she'd be able to find another job. If she and Josh didn't work together, this cohabitation problem wouldn't exist. So the logical solution was for her to quit.

Then she'd be free to enjoy the bounty of this man who was temporarily her roommate. Lisa had to be the biggest idiot in Los Angeles, to give up all *that*. There was always the chance that he didn't know how to use that top-of-the-line equipment, but Tracy wouldn't bet on it. Josh was smart, and an intelligent man would make it a point to understand the operating system.

Breathing hard, she stood in the middle of the bedroom and tried to remember her name. Why were they rushing around taking showers when they could be writhing on that immense bed and making use of the plethora of condoms provided by the resort? If the resort supplied them, the management must expect them to be used.

"I thought you said we had less than ten minutes to get out of here."

She faced him and struggled to remember what it was they were supposed to do in ten minutes. "I...um..."

His gaze heated. "If that's not true, I have a few suggestions."

"It's true. I just—"

The phone rang again. This time Josh crossed to the bedside table and picked up the receiver. "Yes?"

The ringing phone triggered Tracy's memory. They were expected at the resort. They'd won this trip, but the contest had specified they'd make themselves available for resort promotion. Another promo session was set to start immediately, and they were both still basically naked.

"I think our clocks might be wrong," Josh said into the phone. "We thought it was only eight. You bet, Tony. Sure, send a cart if that makes sense. It'll get us there quicker." He replaced the receiver. "A cart's on the way. We have to make an appearance."

"I know we do."

"Get your clothes and close the bathroom door. I'll dress out here. Meet you on the front porch in five minutes."

She nodded, snatched some things out of her suitcase and dashed into the bathroom. "We have to talk," she said before she closed the bathroom door.

Even with the door closed, she could hear him laughing. "I don't think a conversation is going to do the trick!" he called, making sure she'd hear him.

She heard him, all right. Yep, she might be handing in her resignation Monday morning.

CHAPTER FIVE

As JOSH THREW ON HIS clothes and made sure everything was buttoned and zipped before he headed for the front porch, he had little time to contemplate his most vivid picture of Tracy to date—a goddess standing naked under the shower spray. But he knew the pace would slow down eventually and he'd have to deal with that image.

He was in real trouble now, and it was all his own doing. He could have snagged a towel without looking into the shower. A sensible guy would have done exactly that, but, no, not him. Now he'd had a glimpse of naked Tracy, and he wanted more. Much more.

She wanted to talk. He wanted action. God, how was he going to make it through this weekend without drinking the bar dry? As he climbed into the cart and took the jolting ride to the lodge, he was reminded with every bounce the price he'd pay if he repeated his performance of the previous night.

Tracy jiggled her foot the entire time, and although she kicked him twice, he didn't mention it. If she was in the same state he was in, she deserved to indulge in a little foot jiggling.

The cart got them to the lodge in record time, but they were still abysmally late. The pool area was virtually deserted, and that's where all the action was supposed to have taken place.

"We need to find Tony and apologize," Josh said.

"Blame it all on me." Tracy glanced around, as if expecting Tony to materialize at any moment. "I know what he's up against, and I hate that we might have made his job tougher."

"There you are!" Alice Walker bustled over to them, followed closely by Tom. "You missed the kissing contest, and I'm sure you would have won, hands down."

"Kissing contest?" Josh frowned. "I don't remember that being on the schedule."

"Well, it wasn't," Tom said. "But Maddy Lov is something of a loose cannon, and she had the thing going before anyone quite knew what was happening. Say, have you two had breakfast?"

"Yes." Josh couldn't imagine shoving food into his hungover self.

"Not exactly," Tracy said.

Alice laughed. "So one of you is a breakfast eater and the other one isn't? Tracy, I think we should feed you. Josh can have coffee." She gestured toward the resort's coffee shop.

"Great idea." Josh went along willingly. How selfish of him not to realize Tracy would be hungry. And he could use a cup of coffee, now that he thought about it. A dose of caffeine usually helped with a headache.

As they all headed toward the coffee shop, a phalanx of media folks hurried in their direction. Tom blocked their progress and spoke quietly to them until they dispersed.

"Thank you, dear," Alice said. "I'm sure these young people could use a break from swimming in a goldfish bowl."

"It's not so bad," Tracy said. "It's a small price to pay for such a lovely weekend."

"I know you agreed to it," Alice said. "But you deserve to have breakfast in peace. In fact, I deserve to have breakfast in peace. We wouldn't be able to talk if we had them hovering around. Ah, I see the waitstaff has cleared our favorite table."

Josh began to see the advantage of hanging out with the Walkers. They were seated at a booth with a spectacular view of the slopes. Framed by the window, the scene looked like a ski resort diorama, with toy action figures zipping down the slopes and riding back up on miniature lifts. A waitress took their order immediately, and coffee appeared like magic.

"I have to say I'm proud of this place." Tom settled back against the leather cushions of the booth. "I wasn't prepared for Maddy Lov and her brand of publicity, but I doubt she can ruin everything in one weekend."

"She's generating quite a bit of excitement," Alice said. "I suppose that's good, but I'm not sure the publicity we're getting is the kind we intended."

Josh longed to point out that she and her husband wouldn't have these problems if they'd hired Innovations instead. But that would be an obnoxious thing to say in the face of the Walkers' gracious invitation to breakfast. He and Tracy would make their pitch when it was more appropriate.

"The resort is gorgeous," Tracy said. "That will come through in the footage, and it'll be obvious guests are having fun. People will be dying to book reservations."

Tom nodded. "Reservations have been flooding in, but I worry that they're all generated by the singles crowd we have here this weekend. When we dreamed up the poetry contest, we thought it would attract—"

"Wait a minute," Josh said. "The sonnet contest was your idea?"

"My idea, actually," Alice said with a smile. "I majored in English in college, and I think love poems are a dying art."

"We thought it was A-List's concept," Tracy said.

"Goodness, no." Alice unfolded her cloth napkin and settled it in her lap. "They tried to talk us out of it, but we insisted this would set the tone for the resort."

Josh put down his coffee mug. "Now I feel guilty about the poem Tracy and I entered. It wasn't very romantic."

Tom chuckled. "No, but it was funny as hell."

"And you more than made up for it with the one you recited for Tracy last night." Alice beamed at them. "I wasn't at all surprised you slept in this morning."

Josh felt like a first-class jerk for not contradicting the Walkers' impression that he and Tracy were committed to each other. But he'd promised Tony they'd keep up the charade. He had no idea what to say.

Fortunately for him, Tracy knew exactly what to say. "It's a wonderful cabin. I'm honored that we're allowed to stay there."

Josh sent her a look of gratitude. "So am I."

"I had a feeling about you two," Alice said. "That crazy poem told me you shared the same sense of humor. That'll take you farther than sex, although sex is nice, too."

Josh had a bad feeling he might be turning red, and he didn't dare look at Tracy. They desperately needed a change of subject. "The skiing looks great out there. Do you have snow-making machines?"

"You bet." Tom launched into a detailed description of his beloved snow machines that made Alice roll her eyes but saved Josh and Tracy from having to talk about themselves for the rest of the meal.

"I hope you're both planning on skiing this afternoon," Alice said as they left the coffee shop. "I'd hate to think Tom made all that snow for nothing." She winked at her husband.

"When it comes to skiing, I'm a rank beginner," Josh said, "but I'll give it a shot."

"We have great instructors," Alice said. "Treat yourself to a lesson."

"I sure will. But I can't speak for Tracy."

"Oh, I'm up for a lesson, too." She seemed excited by the

prospect. "Since the afternoon's somewhat unscheduled, I'd love to take advantage of our free rentals and lift tickets. Thank you so much for providing that."

"Yes, thank you," Josh echoed. Once again, Tracy had saved him from coming off as an ingrate.

"I'm afraid you'll have to put up with photographers invading your privacy," Tom said.

"It's not a problem," Josh said. "Like Tracy mentioned, it's a small price to pay for this terrific weekend."

"I'd advise you to go over to the ski shop and rent your gear now," Tom said.

"We will." Josh held out his hand. "Thank you for everything, including breakfast."

"Our pleasure." Tom's handshake had the firmness of a man used to being in charge.

"Absolutely," Alice said. "It's fun to finally meet you two." She gave Tracy a hug and then moved right on to hugging Josh, too.

In that moment he allowed himself to imagine being exactly who Alice thought he was—Tracy's devoted and romantic boyfriend. It wouldn't be so tough to take.

TRACY HELD HANDS with Josh as they left the Walkers. He'd initiated the connection, and after the first shock of it, she'd known he was only doing what the Walkers expected of them. She tried not to like the contact too much, but Josh was good at this maneuver. He laced his fingers through hers in a warm grip that she could get used to in a hurry.

The Walkers had pointed them in the direction of the ski shop, which was accessible by going outside through a set of double doors and across the pool area. The morning air was brisk as they stepped through the doors, but the sun kept the temperature pleasant.

Once Tracy was fairly sure the Walkers couldn't see them anymore, she pulled Josh to a stop and slipped her hand free. "Before we rent our stuff, we need to make a quick detour. Or at least, I do."

"Bathroom?"

"No, registration desk."

"For what?"

"I'm going to book a room at the lodge for tonight."

He gazed at her. "Look, if that's the solution, then let me do it."

"That's not fair. I had the benefit of the fireplace while you were gone, and I got to enjoy that big bed. You should have a chance to—"

"Do you really think I'd have a good time by myself in that cabin?"

"So invite someone to go home with you."

He cleared his throat. "This is going to sound strange, but I couldn't do that. It's our cabin now. Inviting another woman to stay in it feels wrong."

She couldn't help smiling. "That's so weird, but it makes me feel good. Thanks, Josh."

"Can't help it." He shrugged. "It is what it is."

She was dying to ask exactly what *it* was, but they probably couldn't afford to have that discussion. "Then we'd better get you a room at the lodge, so you can invite someone up if you want."

"We can see about getting the extra room, but don't count on me getting it on with someone else this weekend."

Her traitorous heart leaped for joy. Still, she had to argue the point. "If you went to bed with someone else, that would solve everything."

"Contrary to popular belief, guys can't simply will themselves into a sexual encounter."

"But yesterday, in the limo, you were perfectly willing to fall into bed with the first attractive woman you found."

He looked into her eyes. "That was yesterday."

"And now you've seen me naked."

"Okay, that's part of it."

She laughed. Guys really were predictable.

"Hey, let me finish before you judge me. I was having problems with my seduction plan before I saw you naked. My plan started to crumble the minute you stuck your nose in the air and said you wouldn't be having sex this weekend."

"But you got mad at me for saying that!"

"I got mad because you were so damned self-righteous and cute, and even though I wasn't aware of it at the time, I began thinking of you in ways I never have before. Some switch got flipped during that exchange in the limo and I don't know how to switch it back."

"So what do you want to do about it?" Earlier today she'd considered leaving her job. She held her breath, wondering if he'd suggest leaving his so they wouldn't have the potential danger of working together if things fizzled.

"I don't know."

She exhaled slowly. Obviously quitting her job to open the way for them to have sex would put her in the very-needy category. He certainly wasn't willing to suggest it for himself, so she wasn't about to admit her willingness to throw her career in the Dumpster on the off chance they'd find something wonderful together.

"Then let's go see if we can get you a room for tonight," she said. "My conscience can't stand seeing you go on another bender."

"First I'll make sure the Walkers aren't anywhere in the vicinity." He walked back to the double doors, opened one and peered down the hall. "I think we're safe."

Back inside, she walked briskly beside Josh, their footsteps muffled on the deep carpeting of the hallway. What looked like original Western art lined the walls, punctuated by accent tables holding large vases of fresh flowers. "This is an incredible place."

"It is," Josh agreed. "Listen, if anyone sees us at the registration desk, what will we say?"

"We're asking for a friend who thought he might join us here for the weekend."

"Perfect. Your brain is working a lot better than mine this morning, Trace."

"That's because you pickled your brain last night. But I'm not casting blame. You did it for a noble cause, and I appreciate that."

They turned a corner and headed toward the main desk. Fortunately the registration area was almost empty. The contestants' pictures still graced the lobby, but a new easel had been added advertising Maddy Lov's autograph party this afternoon for her autobiography *Lovin' on Maddy Lov.*

Josh pointed to the sign. "Do you want to get one of those books autographed today?"

"We probably both should. We could sell them on eBay for a bundle."

"What, you wouldn't keep it for your grandchildren?"

Tracy grinned. "The woman is thirty-three, and she's writing her autobiography. Doesn't that seem strange to you?"

"Not if some publisher's willing to pay her to do it. Fame is fickle. If she waits until she's sixty, her star might have faded and she'd lose her chance to cash in on being a celebrity. I think there's a smart cookie lurking under all that blondeness."

"Yeah, I kinda like her, too. I didn't want to, but I do." Tracy glanced around. "Looks like the coast's clear. Let's see what kind of vacancy they have."

Moments later they left the registration desk empty-handed.

"I guess it's the bottom of a bottle for me," Josh said.

"I can't believe every single room is booked." Tracy shook her head. "You have to give A-List credit. They might not be following the Walkers' vision, but they've turned this place into a howling success."

"Which means we're stuck with each other."

Tracy tried to ignore the zing of sexual excitement that shot through her. They'd be together in the cabin again tonight. "I don't want you getting drunk again," she said.

"Then give me an alternative. Wait, I know. You can tie me up."

He was teasing, so she decided to tease him right back. "I had no idea you liked that sort of thing."

"Not the S and M brand of tying up! Now you've added a new image to my growing list of fantasies."

"Sorry." But she wasn't *very* sorry. She'd never felt so desirable in her life. Josh was suggesting that he found her irresistible. True, he'd recently seen her naked, and men were programmed to automatically want a woman they'd seen naked, but still…she liked being lusted after.

"I need ideas, Bingham." He opened one of the double doors for her and they stepped out into the sunshine. "Solid ideas. We've brainstormed a hundred PR campaigns together. We should be able to brainstorm this."

Tracy gazed up at the dazzling white slopes and the skiers whizzing down them. "What if we wear ourselves out?"

"In bed? That's from the frying pan into the fire! But I like it."

"No, Dempsey, not in bed. We'll go skiing for the rest of the day. It'll be a lot of work, because we don't know how to ski. By dinner we'll be exhausted."

"Maybe." He sounded doubtful. "It might work for you, but don't forget I'm a surfer. I'm in shape."

She could vouch for that. She'd forgotten about his surfing, but that explained his yummy muscle definition. She'd never seen him surf and why would she? The only social activities they'd shared were during their ill-fated double-dating days, which only had involved happy hour and the occasional dinner.

"Okay, I'll be exhausted and you won't," she said. "But unless you enjoy shagging a limp dishrag of a woman, I'd be no fun for you."

"I can't picture you as a limp dishrag."

Where he was concerned, she couldn't, either. One touch from Josh and any hint of limp dishrag would disappear. He could pump new life into her, literally. Oh, baby. Now that was an image.

"There's a dance tonight," she said. "We'll go. I won't be up to dancing after spending the afternoon on the slopes. In fact, by tonight I may have broken something vital, considering how nonathletic I am."

"Maybe you shouldn't ski. This isn't *Fear Factor.* If you think you really might hurt yourself, then—"

"Hey, we get free skis and lift tickets. I'm doing it. That comment about breaking something was for extra drama. I probably won't, but I will be wiped out. You, however, Mr. Totally-in-Shape, will be ready to rock and roll at that dance. You'll meet all the women in the place, no doubt. You might even find one you really like."

"I already have."

That brought her to a dead stop. Her pulse raced at the implication of his words. They had to settle this, once and for all. She turned to face him. "Josh, you can't say stuff like that."

He closed his eyes and took a deep breath. "You're so

right." He opened his eyes and looked at her. "I need to shut the hell up and go with your plan."

"Exactly. And if you found another woman to be interested in, so much the better." The thought made her physically ill, but unless he was ready to go for broke, quit his job and sacrifice everything for their relationship, she should encourage him to find someone else. Her life would be less painful that way.

"You should look for someone else, too." He said it grudgingly, as if his heart wasn't in it. Yet he'd said it, which was a far cry from staking his claim to her.

"You're right." Her heart cracked right down the middle. "I should."

CHAPTER SIX

JOSH DIDN'T MIND a bit staying on the bunny slope, using the tow rope and helping Tracy master the basics. Being near her was good enough for him. But she became defensive about her lack of skill and sent him to the next level.

"I know I suck at this," she said. "And you don't. I don't want you getting bored hanging around with the beginners. Honestly, Josh, I'll probably do better when you're not around."

That stung. He'd thought he was helping her learn, but apparently not. "All righty, then. See you back at the lodge." He stomped over toward the lift.

Once on the ski runs, he progressed rapidly. The balance he'd learned on a surfboard served him well, and he should have been thrilled with his progress. Instead he missed Tracy. Women flirted with him, but he didn't have the inclination to flirt back.

Bottom line—he couldn't relax and have fun when he was worried about how Tracy was doing. She might have sent him away, but he suspected she was trying to put some distance between them to reduce the sexual tension.

Just because she'd told him to leave didn't mean she could navigate this strange new world on her own. She'd admitted that she wasn't into sports. She'd even joked that she might end up breaking something critical.

He'd known she was kidding, but he couldn't get the possibility out of his head. What if she had hurt herself? What if she was in an ambulance right this minute headed for the E.R. in Telluride?

Josh returned to the bunny hill, but she wasn't there. The instructor said she'd decided to try one of the easy slopes, although the instructor wasn't sure she was ready. Fighting panic, Josh made the rounds of the lifts.

He asked people in line if they'd seen a redhead, about five-six, wearing a white jacket, blue scarf, black ski pants and a white knit cap. Nobody remembered seeing her. He pictured her buried in a snowdrift, her ankle broken, her shoulder dislocated…or worse.

With her lack of coordination, she could have plowed right into a tree. He thought about alerting the ski patrol, but if it was a false alarm, she'd never forgive him for embarrassing her. Finally he decided to ski all the easy slopes and keep his eyes peeled.

As he rode the first lift, he wondered if she'd given up and gone back to the lodge for a cup of cocoa or something stronger. Somehow he doubted that. She might bitch and moan when she encountered a challenge, but she wasn't the type to cave. He had to believe she was still on the mountain…somewhere.

An hour later he was halfway down the third run he'd investigated when he spotted her. She'd obviously fallen and lost both poles in the process. A blond guy had stopped to help her to her feet.

Josh had no reason to interfere. He had every reason to leave her alone, in case the guy appealed to her. To hell with that.

Digging his poles into the snow, he cut across the run toward the cozy twosome. Maybe Tracy wouldn't welcome his presence. If so, he'd ski on down to the bottom and call it a day.

In other words, he'd make himself available in case she needed backup, but he wasn't there to chaperone...exactly. He wouldn't mind finding out a little more about this ski bum, though. No yahoo was going to get close to Tracy until Josh had a chance to check him out. The world was full of weirdos.

When he reached them, he created a rooster tail of snow as he swerved to a stop. His arrival might have been a tad dramatic, but so what? The guy needed to know who he was dealing with.

"Josh!" Tracy pushed her goggles up on her forehead, as if to see him better. "I'm so glad you're here. This is Dirk. He was kind enough to stop and help me up."

Her expression told him everything he needed to know. She was caught in a vulnerable position and didn't know how to get out of it. But she was clearly unwilling to entrust herself to this Dirk person unless she had to.

That warmed Josh's heart. "Thanks for the help, Dirk. I'll take it from here."

The guy kept his goggles on as he glanced at Josh. "You're her boyfriend?"

"That's right."

"So why weren't you skiing with her?" He still hadn't released Tracy's arm, and he'd positioned himself between Tracy and Josh. "She could use some help."

"We got separated," Tracy said. "Totally my fault. I won't take off like that again, Josh, I promise."

"We had a misunderstanding, that's all," Josh said. "Anyway, Dirk, thanks for helping my girl out of a snowdrift." He stuck out his hand in a gesture of friendship, thinking good manners would force the guy to let go of Tracy and shake his hand.

Dirk ignored Josh's gesture and turned toward Tracy. "In

case you have any more *misunderstandings* with your boy-friend, I'm in room 246. I guarantee I can give you a better time than he can."

Josh heard a low growl and realized with some surprise that it had come from him. Some primitive instinct took over as he reached out and grabbed a fistful of Dirk's jacket. "Stay away from her."

Dirk sneered at him. "Poor girl. She'll never know what she missed." Letting go of Tracy and wrenching free of Josh, he shoved off down the slope.

Josh and Tracy were thrown off balance and fell together in a tangled mess of skis, arms and legs.

Josh sighed. "Wow, that was graceful."

As Tracy struggled to a sitting position, she looked at him lying next to her in the snow and began to laugh.

Watching her laugh and seeing the sparkle come back into her blue eyes made him grin like an idiot. He sure did like Tracy a lot. Although he hadn't thought about it much, he'd have to say that being with her gave him a real high.

Come to think of it, she was the reason he loved coming to work every day. He'd thought it was the creative atmosphere of Innovations, but, no, it was Tracy.

Her laughter died away. "What is it?"

"What do you mean?"

"You were smiling, and then you got this really serious expression on your face. Is something wrong?"

"I just realized how special our friendship is."

She nodded. "I know. Believe me, I've given plenty of thought to that subject."

"Did you watch *Seinfeld* when it was on?"

"Never missed it. I even watch the reruns." She scratched her nose with her gloved hand. "Why?"

"There was this episode where Jerry and Elaine wondered if they'd have a good time in bed, so they tried it. Remember that one?"

"Yes." She gazed at him. "Somehow they kept being friends, even after the sex didn't work out." She hesitated. "But if you're suggesting that it might happen like that for us, that we could maintain the friendship, I don't… The thing is, I'm not sure that we could…"

She was only confirming what he knew in his heart to be true. "It's okay, Trace. I don't think we could stay friends, either. At least not the close friends we are now. And that would be a shame."

"It would." She held his gaze a moment longer. Then she smacked the snow next to her. "I guess we'd better untangle ourselves and go ski some more!"

TRACY SKIED UNTIL she thought her arms and legs would fall off, but she wasn't sure that would be enough to keep her from grabbing Josh once they were alone. Who could resist a man who came to your rescue when you were struggling to fend off a slimy guy like Dirk? Soon after he'd stopped to help her, she'd realized he probably looked for women having trouble on the slopes and offered to improve their skills.

His hands had been everywhere they shouldn't have been, and she would have kneed him in the groin, but a woman wearing skis she couldn't control was at a disadvantage. If she'd tried to defend herself, she would have fallen down, making her even more vulnerable.

Then Josh had come along, and she'd wanted to kiss him. She still did, no matter how much she'd exhausted herself trying to maneuver her poles and skis. Eventually Josh convinced her they should end the torture.

"You'll be really sore as it is," he said as they turned in their equipment. "We should probably hit the hot tub before going back to the cabin."

"Ixnay on that." She could imagine how the soothing bubbles in a hot tub shared with Josh would stir her libido to action. "I have a better idea. We'll go back to the lobby. You take a cart to the cabin and get cleaned up for the dinner buffet and dance, while I wait in the lobby. When you're almost ready to come back here, call me on my cell. I'll take another cart, and we won't have a repeat of this morning's shower-sharing episode."

Josh hesitated, as if his brain had stalled on the image she'd conjured up. She wouldn't be surprised. She was tripping out on the picture of him wearing nothing but a towel.

"Okay," he said at last.

"I have another suggestion," she said as they traversed the carpeted hallway toward the lobby. "I can't picture the Walkers hanging out at this dance. I'm betting the band will be loud and not their style of music. That means we don't have to act like a committed couple."

"Unless Dirk shows up."

"Thank you for that intervention, by the way. If I hadn't been hampered by skis and boots and stuff, I could have handled Dirk. But he had the advantage, and I didn't like how the encounter was going."

"Did he do anything obnoxious? Because I have his room number, and I can always punch him out retroactively."

Tracy smiled. That was what she lo—uh, *liked* about Josh. He laced his chivalry with humor. Couldn't get a better combo than that. "While he was helping me up he copped a feel, but—"

"That's enough reason. Why don't you shower first and I'll go locate Dirk?"

"No. It's not worth causing a scene over, especially because it would probably end up in the media. I don't want the Walkers to have to deal with that, do you?"

"I guess not, but it would be lots of fun to put a dent in that square jaw of his."

Tracy laughed. "I had no idea you had a violent streak."

"I had no idea, either. I haven't issued an ultimatum like that in…years. Not since high school."

She touched his arm. "Just so you know, I'm honored that you threatened him on my account. I can't remember when a guy has ever done that for me. It's thrilling, in a Neanderthal kind of way."

"Is that a compliment? Because it doesn't quite feel like one."

"It is."

"You never told me your suggestion, by the way."

"Oh." She almost hated to make it, although it was the most logical way to handle the evening. "Because we won't arrive at the dance together, we can each go our own way. We might meet someone."

"So you're still on that kick."

"It's a solution, Josh. All we need is for one of us to find someone we like, and they'll create the barrier we need to preserve our friendship."

"I hate it when you're right."

"Then it's a plan?"

"It's a plan." He sighed heavily. "I'll be glad when we finally get back on that plane to L.A."

She couldn't say that. In spite of everything, she'd loved the time she'd spent with him. She was willing to take a chance on ruining their friendship, but he'd made it clear he wasn't willing, so she'd help him maintain the status quo.

As they entered the lobby, she noticed the sign advertising Maddy's autograph party was still up. "I wonder how the book signing went. We completely missed it."

A bellman on his way to the elevators paused and glanced at them. "Did you want one of Ms. Lov's books? We have a ton of them upstairs. I think they're planning to sell them at half price tomorrow, but I could probably get you a discounted one now, if you want. You could have her sign it at the dance."

Tracy shook her head. "That's okay. We can get one some other time." But the PR professional in her was curious. "You have a lot of books left over? Why is that?"

"Nobody came to the signing. Well, a few people came, but not the crowd we expected. Ms. Lov wasn't very happy."

"I'm sure she wasn't." Tracy hated to see a failed publicity event, even if she wasn't the one in charge.

"I'm surprised," Josh said as the elevator doors closed behind the bellhop. "I would have thought she'd be mobbed."

"Except that they scheduled this in the middle of a Saturday afternoon," Tracy said. "Resort guests are mostly young and single. They might like Maddy, but they'd still rather ski than go to an autograph party. For this demographic, A-List should have had the signing at the dance tonight."

"You're right." He gazed at her in admiration. "You and I could have done a dynamite job if we'd won this contract."

"Yes, but then we'd be working all weekend instead of enjoying the good life."

He seemed about to say something, as if he might like to argue whether they were enjoying the good life.

"Never mind, Josh. Go find yourself a ride back to the cabin."

"Yeah. Don't get into trouble while I'm gone." With a small salute, he walked out the front doors.

The desk clerk seemed confused that Tracy had stayed behind. "May I help you with something, Ms. Bingham?"

She wasn't used to being recognized by the hotel staff, and she had to remind herself that her picture was staring the clerk in the face.

"No, thanks. I'm waiting for a friend." That would explain why she'd plopped into one of the comfy leather armchairs. Once there, her tired muscles reminded her of exactly how much she'd abused them today.

"One more day," she murmured. "I can last one more day." Then she'd be back in her normal routine, back in her own apartment with Josh back in his. They would interact at work, and eventually the image of him coming out of the bathroom with the towel draped around his hips would fade. They'd return to their status as work buddies.

At least, that was the theory.

Evelyn walked into the lobby, saw Tracy and acted as if she'd like to slip out again. But they'd made eye contact, so she couldn't quite do that.

"How's it going?" Tracy asked out of politeness.

"Great!" Evelyn flashed her perfect white smile in Tracy's direction, but her gaze didn't quite meet Tracy's. "Perfect." She adjusted the lapels of her black business suit.

Tracy should have let it go, but a devilish urge made her press the point. "I heard there were a lot of books left over from the signing."

"Oh, *that*." Evelyn rolled her heavily made-up eyes. "Maddy was completely off her game. She'd counted on the security guy being there—you know, the Walkers' son, Matt—because Maddy can't concentrate on bringing in good energy if she's worried about stalkers and stuff."

"I suppose."

"But Matt was nowhere to be found. I heard he took off with some Asian chick, and Maddy was left defenseless. When you're worried about a lack of security, you can't be open to all your fans. Of course they sensed that negative energy and stayed away."

"Makes sense." Tracy worked hard to keep a straight face.

She'd heard a lot of BS in her public relations career, but this might take the blue ribbon for audacity. She could hardly wait to tell Josh. He'd split a gut laughing.

Except she wasn't supposed to be yucking it up with Josh tonight. She'd brilliantly suggested they spend the evening with other people, in hopes one of them would find a partner and squelch the whole attraction problem they had going on.

"Well, gotta go up to the penthouse suite." Evelyn flashed another fake smile and held up a tube of lip gloss. "Maddy admired this on me last night, so I'm letting her use it tonight."

"See you later." Tracy was just settling back in her chair when her cell phone played the salsa tune she'd assigned to Josh. She dug it out of her purse and answered it. "You're done already?"

"No. What's the dress code for tonight?"

"I'm wearing a cocktail dress."

"Somehow I don't think that'll work for me."

She smiled. "I meant you should choose whatever a guy wears when the women have on cocktail dresses."

"Trace, I'm not even clear on the definition of *cocktail dress*."

"Go look in the closet."

"Okay." There was a muffled sound of footsteps and a sliding door opening. "I'm looking in the closet."

"It's the emerald-green one."

"Ah." More rustling.

"Does that help?"

"Isn't this cut a little low in front?"

She'd said exactly the same thing to her buddies the other day when they'd gone shopping with her. They'd insisted she looked wonderful in it, and that she would need something completely different from the black sweater dress she'd worn the first night.

"It's no more revealing than the one Evelyn had on last night," she said.

"She was practically falling out of that thing! I'll bet you can't wear a bra with this."

"Josh, you sound like some overprotective big brother. Don't worry about my dress. Do you have something appropriate to wear or not?"

"I brought a black silk shirt."

"Nice." And she wouldn't be touching it. Nope, not even a little bit, not if she planned to keep this relationship platonic.

"Do I need a tie?"

"I don't think so." She had a sudden insight. This conversation was the kind married couples had, and she and Josh had fallen into it automatically. In some ways they were as comfortable with each other as two people who had been married for years.

But when it came to certain topics, like for instance, *sex,* they were clueless about each other. She'd never even kissed him. Maybe she should at least find out what that was like before they left the resort. One kiss wouldn't ruin everything, would it?

Maybe tonight, during the dance, she would find an opportunity to kiss him. That would be safe territory, because they couldn't do anything wild and crazy when surrounded by a bunch of other people. Unfortunately, she'd told him they should keep away from each other all night, which made stealing a kiss problematic.

"Tracy? What do you think?"

"About what?" If he'd asked her something, she had no idea what it was.

"You're not falling asleep there in the lobby, are you?"

"No, just thinking about something else. What was your question again?"

"I asked if I should wear the sport coat."

"No. The silk shirt makes enough of a statement." And she was already imagining running her hands over it when she treated herself to one kiss. "Josh, I know I said we should stay away from each other tonight, but let's meet up after the first hour or so and have one dance, just to compare notes on how it's going."

"Great idea. Anyway, go ahead and find somebody to bring you out here. I'm ready to head back. I'm going to walk."

"Watch out for the wolves."

"The what?"

She'd suspected he wouldn't remember much about last night. "Just kidding. So the plan is that an hour after I get there, we'll find each other and dance one dance. Right?"

"That's the plan. Listen, maybe you should wear the black dress again. That looks good."

"I'm wearing the green dress, Josh. Bye." She snapped her phone closed. If she didn't know better, she'd think Josh was worried about her attracting guys in that low-cut dress. If she didn't know better, she'd think that Josh was acting like a jealous boyfriend.

CHAPTER SEVEN

JOSH NURSED A MARTINI and watched the door. All around him the party was in full swing. The band, complete with strobe lights and smoke effects, wailed away on a raised platform at the back of the room. The dance floor was packed with writhing couples, so Josh had avoided that area. He wasn't in the mood.

Tracy had been right that the choice of music would probably drive the Walkers away. Josh had looked for them on purpose, but they were nowhere to be seen. He was pretty sure he'd spotted their son, Matt, though.

He was a younger version of Tom in build, but he had Alice's eyes. He also had Security Guy written all over him. Maddy Lov stuck to him like glue, and Josh thought there was more than security on her mind. For the first time this weekend she seemed serious about nabbing herself a man.

Long buffet tables piled with food lined the left and right sides of the room, and round, linen-draped tables surrounded by chairs filled the rest of the space. Josh had already munched his way through a plateful of finger food, so he wasn't starving to death anymore. Skiing all day had given him an appetite, but once that hunger eased, a different ache clamored for attention.

He wanted to be with Tracy.

More significantly, he wanted to be *alone* with Tracy. He

couldn't stop thinking about how she'd fill out that green dress that looked wicked draped on a padded hanger in the closet. He could only guess the effect once Tracy was zipped into it.

After their wild morning sharing a bathroom, he had all the visuals he needed to picture her routine. He knew exactly how she'd look in the shower, and that alone was enough to get him hard. He didn't need the added image of Tracy drying herself with one of the fluffy resort towels and smoothing scented lotion over her body. The image came to him whether he needed it or not.

Next she would put on panties, which were black in his fantasy, but no bra. He knew enough about women's clothing to understand that a dress like that wouldn't accommodate a bra. Finally she'd slide into the dress. A pair of glittery stiletto heels had been sitting on the closet floor, and she'd no doubt wear those.

He could predict his reaction when she walked through the ballroom door. Unfortunately, if he had that reaction, so would every other guy in the room. He would want to station himself by her side and never leave. But he'd agreed to back off.

Obsessed as he was, he didn't know if he could honor that agreement. It was the dress. If not for that damned dress, he'd still be in control, but the dress had put him over the edge.

He'd examined it thoroughly before leaving the cabin. He'd run the zipper up and down several times and satisfied himself that it worked smoothly. The hook and eye would be a no-brainer. In essence, he knew exactly how to get the dress off. A man who'd vowed not to take a certain woman to bed tonight should not be figuring out how to get said woman out of her clothes.

But he had a one-track mind and couldn't seem to— *There*

she was. He nearly choked on his scotch. His imagination hadn't done her justice.

Through some kind of magic only women understood, she'd turned her normally smooth hair into a mass of soft curls that begged a man to touch them. But that wasn't all a man would want to touch. The neckline of the sleeveless green dress plunged nearly to her waist, giving a tantalizing view that stopped just short of being scandalous.

Josh had seen her naked breasts during their brief morning encounter in the bathroom, and that experience worked to intensify his already out-of-control lust. He knew what was under that draped fabric, and he wanted all of it. Now.

The loose skirt of the dress caressed her bare knees, and the silver do-me heels were almost overkill. Once Josh managed to tear his gaze away from her, he quickly scanned the room to see if all male eyes were riveted on Tracy.

Not all of them were, but sure enough, a couple of guys had noticed that an unescorted, hot-looking woman had arrived. As they started in her direction, Josh hesitated. He and Tracy had made a bargain.

Then he spotted Dirk, the lecherous skier, heading from the other side of the room toward Tracy, and all bets were off. Setting his drink on the nearest table, Josh mumbled apologies as he shoved his way through the crowd. He made it over to Tracy ahead of the other two guys, but Dirk beat him there.

Josh ignored him and grabbed Tracy's hand. "I thought you'd never get here. Let's dance."

"Hold on, buddy." Dirk tapped him none-too-gently on the shoulder.

Josh pretended not to notice. "The band's not bad," he said to Tracy as he started toward the dance floor. "I think you'll like—"

"I said, *hold on.*" Dirk clamped a hand on Josh's shoulder.

Tensing, Josh released Tracy's hand and shrugged off Dirk's grip before turning to face him. Dirk had seemed about Josh's height when they were all on skis, but now he was a couple of inches taller. Josh wondered if the guy wore lifts.

In the process of confronting Dirk, Josh also became aware of a couple of paparazzi lurking nearby, digital cameras at the ready. He'd rather not have this turn into an incident that would cause the Walkers grief. "Look, she's with me. Can we just leave it at that?"

"No, we can't. I'm tired of you butting in." His speech was only slightly slurred, but it was obvious he'd had a few drinks.

"And I'm tired of you trying to steal my girlfriend."

"I say she's not your girlfriend! You weren't skiing with her today, and just now she came in alone and you made no move toward her. Now back off and give someone else a chance."

From the corner of his eye, Josh could see the paparazzi raising their cameras. Wouldn't they love to see this degenerate into something physical? Dirk seemed to be spoiling for it.

Tracy stepped up beside Josh and wrapped her arm around Josh's waist. "I *am* his girlfriend."

Josh reciprocated by wrapping his arm around Tracy; the close contact sent his pulse rate into the stratosphere. "So that's it, then, Dirk. See you around."

"I think you made it all up so you could look good for this dumb contest," Dirk said. "I've never even seen you kiss each other."

Tracy turned more fully into Josh's arms. "Let's fix that, shall we?"

Before he knew what hit him, she'd pulled his head down. His mouth had dropped open in shock when she started the maneuver, and she took full advantage of that to French the hell out of this kiss. Considering they'd never mutually enjoyed a lip-lock, her boldness caught him completely off guard.

But not for long. In no time he'd caught up to her, and soon he was the one angling his head and seeking deeper penetration. He poured all the sexual frustration of the past twenty-four hours into the kiss. Digging his fingers into her soft curls, he used his tongue to tell her exactly what was on his mind.

From her response, she might have some of the same ideas. She matched him thrust for thrust, and her breathing was as labored as his. Dimly he realized that this was a first kiss, which was supposed to be more tentative and filled with sweetness rather than lust.

Not much to be done about that now. The kiss had started out at level ten and moved right off the charts. It could only end one way, with both of them naked and horizontal. Cancel that. Vertical would work, too. All he required was an unyielding surface to brace against.

"All right, all right. You've made your damn point."

What point? Josh didn't remember trying to make a point. And what kind of jerk would interrupt him in the middle of the most excellent kiss of his life?

Tracy groaned and pulled away.

He urged her to come back to him, desperate to recapture his prize. "Don't go," he whispered hoarsely.

Her voice wasn't much steadier than his. "We have…a crowd."

"Huh?"

"People." She held his head and turned it to one side.

A flash nearly blinded him. When he looked back at Tracy he couldn't see her very well because of the black spots in front of his eyes. But now he remembered where they were.

Clearing his throat, he stepped away from Tracy. Despite

the black spots, he could see that she wasn't quite as pulled together as she had been when she'd walked in. Her hair was tousled as if she'd just climbed out of bed, and although her mouth still had lipstick on it, it was a flat pink instead of the glossy shine she'd had before.

He rubbed his fingers across his mouth and they came away with pink smears, so he was probably wearing some of that pink shine. He couldn't bring himself to care about that, or to worry about the embarrassment of kissing someone so passionately while surrounded by gawkers. If Tracy was willing to kiss him in public, he was more than willing to let her.

Now that the show was over, though, the crowd drifted away, leaving him standing facing the woman he most wanted in the world. He swallowed. "Nice dress."

"Thank you." She smoothed out the wrinkles he'd put there. "Nice shirt."

He looked down and noticed his shirttail was coming out of his slacks. He didn't bother to tuck it in. Instead he glanced up and looked into her eyes. "We agreed that sex and friendship didn't mix, right?"

"Uh-huh." She held his gaze. "Are you ready to start circulating?"

"No."

"What are you ready to do?"

"End this friendship."

THEY DIDN'T TALK DURING the cart ride back to the cabin. Tracy wondered if the driver, who thankfully wasn't anyone they'd met before, suspected their motive for the abrupt departure. Probably. As she and Josh sat holding hands and gazing at each other, the air crackled between them. It wouldn't take a genius to pick up on that.

The ride seemed endless, and although Josh's grip on her

hand remained firm, she wondered if the delay would make him change his mind. She'd already decided to go for broke. If sex really did ruin their friendship and working relationship, she'd find a different job. It was worth the risk. The alternative was never making love to Josh, and she couldn't bear the thought.

Still, as the cart driver accepted his generous tip and drove away, she turned before climbing the porch steps. Josh should get one more chance to back out. "We've been friends a long time, and—"

"Don't chicken out on me now, Bingham." He tugged her gently up the steps while he fumbled in his coat pocket for the key.

Her heart pounded so loud she thought he might be able to hear it. "I thought maybe you might chicken out, Dempsey."

"Not a chance." He slid the key card into the slot, but the door didn't open. He tried again, and the light still flashed a stubborn red. He muttered a few choice words under his breath and pushed the key in again. This time he wiggled it. No green light.

Maybe it was nerves, but she started to laugh. "What's the matter? Door not responding?"

"Don't take this as an omen. I'm usually very good at inserting things and getting the green light."

"I'm sure you are." In fact, she could hardly wait to find out.

"It's just that I'm a little…ah—finally!" He shouldered the door open and dragged her in with him. "There." Kicking the door shut, he pulled her into his arms.

"You're just a little what?" she asked as he started unbuttoning her coat.

"Eager." And his mouth came down on hers.

She lost track of the progression of events after that. They left a trail of clothes between the living room and the bedroom, and the undressing part went much faster than she would have expected. He pulled his shirt over his head without unbuttoning it, and he was very quick with her dress, as if he'd rehearsed taking it off.

The maid had been in during the day, so the comforter was pulled up and the pillows neatly stacked against the head-board. Josh flipped on a bedside lamp and threw back the comforter. Pillows scattered.

Wearing only her black panties, Tracy vaulted onto the big bed, bouncing with the impact. "You could practice gymnastics on this bed."

"Let's do that." Shucking his briefs, Josh climbed in after her.

She might have seen him naked, but she hadn't seen him naked and aroused. "That's quite a handle you have there," she murmured.

He stretched out next to her. "Feel free to grab on."

She started to reach for him, but then she pulled back.

"Hey, you were the one who nearly made me come with that first kiss. Don't turn shy on me now."

"I'm not shy. It's just that…" She glanced from his impressive cock to his intense gaze. "Once I touch you there, everything changes."

"News flash. It's already changed." He cupped her face in both hands. "I'm going to kiss you, Trace, and I'd love for you to do whatever comes naturally at moments like this."

As his lips met hers, she discovered that she naturally wanted to explore all the uncharted territory laid out before her, and she could hardly miss the most prominent part of it. When she tried to close her fingers around his equipment, her fingers didn't touch. What in hell had Lisa been thinking?

"That's good," he murmured against her mouth. "Don't stop. I'm just going to…" He trailed kisses down her throat.

She anticipated his direction, and her already tight nipples began to tingle. She prayed he knew how to do this and wasn't a pounce-and-suck lover. Not every man knew how to treat a woman's… Oh, but this one did. He ran his tongue slowly around the rigid tip.

When she was ready to beg him to take the next step, and not a moment sooner, he drew her nipple into his mouth. The easy, almost lazy way he did it created the first contraction of her womb. In reaction, she clutched his penis tighter and his groan of pleasure reminded her that he had needs, too. In her ecstasy, she'd nearly forgotten.

She stroked him in rhythm with the movement of his mouth at her breast. Then his hand invaded her very damp panties and searched out her drenched vagina. Before long they had an entire symphony going on.

Her control slipped away as she writhed on the sheets. He was right—solo sex was *nothing* like this. A climax that would put all her recent ones in the shade threatened to descend on her at any moment.

Then he paused and lifted his head. "Let go."

She pushed against his fingers buried deep inside her. "I will. Any second now."

"No, I mean let go of *me*." He sounded hoarse, a desperate man.

She released him immediately. No telling what she'd done in the throes of lust. "Did I hurt you?"

"God, no. But you're going to make me come, and I don't want to. Not yet."

"But I'm ready to—"

"That's the idea." He turned his attention to her other breast and found her clit with his thumb.

She hoped everyone was at the party, because she began to holler. She was afraid she cried out embarrassing things like *more,* and *faster,* and *right there!*

Josh followed directions beautifully, and when her orgasm arrived, it was something to behold. She arched off the bed and grabbed the sheets in both hands while she gasped and shouted out her pleasure. As she trembled in the aftershocks, Josh kissed her all over, paying special attention to the dewy spot between her thighs.

In the process he removed her panties. Good. They were only in the way. But she didn't fully understand his long-range plan until his tongue began to work. Dear heaven, he expected her to do this again. "Josh, I can't."

"We'll see."

"No, really. That was… I really don't think…" She couldn't even form words. She was sated, spent, wrung out…or not. A miracle was taking place, because she was responding to his moist caress with the same spiraling tension she'd felt moments ago.

Unbelievably, she was going to come again. The promise was there, the oncoming wave about to crash over her. He was showing her things about herself she'd never suspected, never dared hope could be true.

Abandoning all hope of modesty, she lifted her hips to give him greater access. He had the most talented mouth in the universe. She could write a whole poem about his mouth, and another one about his tongue and his fingers, which had come back into play and were pumping steadily, stroking her G-spot until— Yes! Yes, yes, yes! She exploded into a million pieces while her cries of delight and gratitude rained down upon him.

But this was becoming a little one-sided. Struggling out of her daze of sexual satisfaction, she opened her eyes to find him watching her. She had to lick her lips and concentrate before she could say what was in her heart, but eventually she managed it. "Tell me what you want."

His breath caught. "Do you mean that?"

"Anything. I'll return the favor you just gave me. I'll lick your toes, your knees, whatever erogenous zone is your favorite. Point me there."

He shook his head. "None of that. But ever since I saw this bed, I've had a fantasy."

"Name it. Want to tie me up? I'll even do that. I'm putty in your hands."

His gray eyes grew hot. "All right." He sat up. "Kneel on the bed and hold on to that post." He pointed to the one at the end of the bed.

Her pulse, which had started to slow, picked up again. "Facing away from you?"

"Yes."

"That's so cavemanesque."

"I know. You don't have to."

She reached out and stroked his penis, running her thumb over the tip, where a bead of moisture had gathered. "I want to. Suit up."

His gaze burned into hers. "Don't worry. You're safe with me."

She knew that, which was why he could suggest anything and she'd go along. She trusted him as she'd never trusted a man before. Although logic told her it was impossible to suddenly fall in love with someone you'd known for three years, she was beginning to wonder if that explained this whole crazy weekend.

Maybe it wasn't so sudden. Maybe she'd been in love with him all along and never been willing to admit it to herself, let alone to him. Besides, he'd never mentioned the L-word, and that would be so embarrassing, if she blurted it out and they weren't in the same book, let alone on the same page. For now she'd keep her mouth shut.

Wrapping both hands around the peeled log that formed

the corner post of the bed, she lifted her hips and angled herself the way she imagined he wanted her. "Like this?"

"Like that." His voice rasped in the stillness. The snap of latex was followed by the movement of the mattress as he came up behind her.

She was so excited and ready for him that her thighs were slick. Trembling, she waited for him to touch her, to thrust inside as if they were two animals mating.

But first he kissed the soft skin of her backside. "You're so beautiful." He nipped her gently. "How could I have missed knowing that?"

"We…we were friends."

"And now we're lovers." He caressed her, molding her with his hands, separating, exploring. His fingers slid so easily inside her that he had to know how excited she was.

She arched her back, which lifted her hips even higher.

He stroked her with his fingers. "You want this, too."

"Yes."

"I didn't expect—"

"Do it." Her muscles clenched around his fingers. "Take me, Josh!"

He groaned. In a split second his fingers were replaced with the tip of his penis. He eased in slowly, letting her adjust to his size.

"More."

With a primitive sound that rumbled deep in his chest, he thrust deep inside her.

In that moment she knew—this was the man she'd waited for, her forever-after guy. But the glitch was, she might not be his forever-after girl. If she wasn't, how would she ever bear the pain?

CHAPTER EIGHT

JOSH'S FIRST THOUGHT was *She's perfect.* His second thought was *Oh, shit, she's perfect.* He wasn't ready for that. He'd been willing to risk the friendship to find a bed partner. Beyond that, he wasn't prepared to go.

Lisa's defection had made him doubt the whole concept of permanence. Maybe he'd believe it again some day, but for now, he wanted an F-buddy, as his friends referred to their casual girlfriends. Sometimes those relationships went on for a year or two.

The secret was not to care too much. Keep it light and breezy. Laugh together, but don't cry together. Considering Josh's previous friendship with Tracy, he'd thought they could pull that off.

And then he'd made this incredible connection. Worse yet, it wasn't only his dick feeling the love. His whole body was ready to party down, because Tracy was…perfect. Too intense, way too intense.

Couldn't help it. Couldn't help it now. Her body called to him—*finish it.* His body demanded release. With both hands he stroked from her hips forward, sculpting in at her waist, out at her ribs. Leaning over her, he cupped her breasts.

At this point, an animal would surge forward and bite his mate's neck. Josh had the same impulse, but he restrained himself. That was about all he could restrain.

Kneading her breasts, he began to pump. He closed his eyes in an attempt to regain some measure of control, but it was useless. He thrust faster, the front of his thighs slapping the back of hers, her breasts jiggling in his grip.

His breath came in harsh gasps, and each time he pounded into her, she cried out. With superhuman effort, he held himself still. "Am I hurting you?"

"No! Keep going!"

That eliminated all hope of caution. He increased the pace, moaning in ecstasy as she tightened around him, increasing the friction. He wanted her to come, too, but at some point he ceased to worry about that. The need to spill his seed into her became too great, and he sought the angle that would give him release.

There. Oh, dear heaven, *now*. Now! With a roar, he flung himself into her and erupted with such force that he envisioned blasting through the tip of the condom. Her cries echoed his, and he sank against her, glad she'd made it, but knowing he wouldn't have been able to hold back another second to accommodate her.

He'd never had sex this good. Although he didn't want to think about it, especially when his mega orgasm had temporarily fried his brain, he suspected that the good sex had to do with deeper feelings for Tracy. Damn. He had no idea if she felt the same or whether she was simply looking for an F-buddy, too. He could be headed for Lisa, Part Two.

He'd be wise to end this tomorrow before he got into really big trouble. And he would end it. But that left several hours and a generous supply of condoms. He might burn in hell for wanting to enjoy Tracy until the sun came up. So be it.

As SUNLIGHT FILTERED through the curtains of the bedroom, Tracy reluctantly opened her eyes and stared at the beamed ceiling overhead. Time to face the music. She'd had more sex, and really good sex at that, than she'd ever had in one night. Josh was a terrific lover, and he'd complimented her extravagantly on her response, her beauty, her creative play in bed.

But he'd never admitted to any special feelings for her. Consequently she'd kept her feelings secret, too. She had to believe he didn't want anything deeper than this. All the evidence indicated that Josh was hoping for a happy-go-lucky bed partner, and that would be enough for him.

Therefore she had a decision to make. Was it enough for her? If so, they could continue as before, working together at the office and sleeping together in their off-hours. She could hope that he might eventually consider more of a commitment, but she had no guarantee that would ever happen.

Several of her friends had gone that route—agreeing to unlimited sex that they secretly hoped would lead to love and rings on their fingers. In most cases, it hadn't. The relationship had drifted along until the woman called a halt and moved on. Tracy contemplated that kind of slow death and shuddered.

Then again, maybe she was wrong. She glanced over at him. He lay on his side facing her, eyes closed and his arm tucked around her waist. Maybe he'd wake up, look at her and tell her he loved her. It could happen.

His lashes fluttered, and he opened his eyes. A smile touched his bristly morning face. His erection nudged her hip. "Morning wood," he murmured by way of explanation. It definitely wasn't an apology for being aroused the moment he was awake.

"I've heard of the syndrome." And though she could feel fatigue in nearly all of her muscles from the combination of skiing and sex, she grew damp thinking of having that morning wood deep inside her.

"We have condoms left. If I promise not to give you whisker burn, would you consider—"

"I might." She returned his smile.

"Music to my ears." He rolled away from her, grabbed a condom from the stash on the bedside table, and was back in seconds with his little raincoat on. "We need to give the bed one more workout."

"It's been a good bed."

"You've been an even better lover." Moving between her thighs, he braced himself on his outstretched hands. "Help me in, Trace."

She grasped his latex-sheathed penis and guided him into her warmth. He felt so good there, so right.

Once he had his bearings, he pushed in until they were locked tight. "I love how we fit."

"Me, too."

"I'm not going to kiss you. Not before I've shaved. You'd look all red in the countless pictures they'll be taking this morning."

So he did care about her. But worrying about whisker burn wasn't exactly planning a future together. "I can do without the kiss, if you'll make me come."

"I fully intend to do that." He began a slow, steady rhythm. "We haven't talked about…what happens next."

"Mutual orgasms."

"After that."

"Amateur snow sculpting."

"We'll miss it." He stroked her steadily.

"Then there's a brunch."

He shifted his angle slightly, paying more attention to her G-spot. "Forget the resort. I mean in L.A."

"What do you want?" She was giving over control, and she knew it. But this feeling was so right, so good.

"I want to keep seeing you."

"Having sex with me."

"Oh, yes." He shuddered. "You turn me inside out, Trace." He pumped faster. "I don't want to give you up."

As her climax drew near, she knew what her decision would be. "I don't want to give you up, either."

"Thank you." He stroked her with exactly the right angle and pace to guarantee that she'd explode any second.

"My…pleasure." With a cry, she arched upward and rode the wave of her orgasm.

"And mine." With a groan of satisfaction, he buried himself within her, his body racked with the tremors of his climax.

She'd made her bargain. She'd agreed to share his bed with no promises, no protestations of undying love. It would have to be enough.

THE BRUNCH WAS SERVED buffet style, and Josh ate everything in sight. He couldn't remember ever being so hungry. Tracy surprised him, though. She wasn't eating much, and she hadn't had any dinner the night before, so she should be famished.

"You need to try the eggs Benedict," he said as he brought another full plate back to the table they were sharing with the Walkers. "It's tough to get them to taste right for a buffet, but the chef has done it."

"You should have some more food, Tracy," Alice said. "I hope you're not feeling sick."

"No, not at all. I feel fine. And the food's wonderful. All the excitement must be getting to me."

Tom reached over and patted her hand. "I can tell you're not used to being in the spotlight. Soon you'll be able to go back to your normal routine. A few quiet evenings with Josh and you'll be right as rain."

Josh paused with his fork halfway to his mouth. The Walkers must assume he and Tracy lived together. He wondered if Tracy would correct that impression.

She didn't. "You're right," she said. "This weekend has been far more intense than the kind of schedule Josh and I are used to."

Josh was fine with letting the matter slide. No reason to disillusion this nice couple by telling them the truth, that he and Tracy didn't consider their relationship anything more than a fun sexual release.

Maddy Lov came over to the table, a mimosa in one hand. "There's the happy couple! You two disappeared early last night." She winked. "But that's okay. We all understand, don't we?"

"They are a couple of lovebirds," Alice said. "You know, I just had the best idea! What if we had your wedding here, at the resort?"

Fortunately, Josh didn't have a mouthful of food, or he would have needed the Heimlich maneuver. "That's...uh... quite a concept," he stammered.

Tracy looked equally stricken. "What a wonderful idea," she said. "But I don't know if Josh and I could afford—"

"Oh, for Pete's sake," Tom said. "You wouldn't *pay* for it. We'd do it as a favor. And I'm sure the publicity would help us, so we'd all benefit."

Josh felt his chest tighten. "We haven't exactly set a date."

"Then set one!" Maddy gestured with her champagne flute. "It's not every day you have a chance like this."

Tracy pushed back her chair. "Excuse me a minute. I seem to have something stuck in my throat."

Josh thought she sounded sort of choked up. He stumbled to his feet. "Tracy? Can I do something?"

"No, it's okay." She backed away from the table. "I'll be fine. Don't make this more embarrassing than it is."

"Oh, dear." Alice started to get up. "Want me to come with you? I know first aid."

Tracy waved her away. "I just need a minute to do some unlovely hacking and coughing. Seriously, don't worry about me. I'll be back before you know it."

Josh decided to follow her anyway. Something was wrong, and he wanted to know what it was. But as he started after Tracy, Maddy blocked his way.

"I'll go," she said. "You wouldn't be welcome in the girls' bathroom anyway."

"I don't care. I want to—"

"Cool it, Josh. I'll take care of it." Maddy set her glass on the table and hurried away.

Alice touched Josh's arm. "I don't mean to pry, but she's not pregnant, is she?"

"No." Josh gazed in the direction of the bathrooms and struggled with how to respond to that suggestion. "We haven't… We're not ready to consider that option, yet."

Tom was quick to respond. "And there's nothing that says you should. That's a purely individual decision."

"But your children, if you choose to have any, would be beautiful," Alice said.

They would. Josh had a sudden image of a kid with carrot-red hair. Or maybe they'd take after him and have dark hair, but blue eyes like Tracy's. She would be a great mother, with her sense of humor and her— Good God, what was he thinking?

They'd just agreed to have a no-strings sexual relationship once they returned home. It was a single guy's dream, and he had it: a dynamite woman in his bed who wasn't making any demands. He didn't need to be thinking of the kids they could make together.

Alice came to stand beside him. "I hope I didn't cause a problem by suggesting you have the wedding here. You may have some other spot in mind. It's just that you two are so much in love, and I selfishly wanted to be part of your plans. Forgive me."

In love? She thought he and Tracy were in love? He wrestled with that as he turned to her. "There's nothing to forgive. You and Tom are two of the most generous people I know. Thank you for making the suggestion." He couldn't think of anything more to say that wouldn't make a bigger mess than they already had going.

"Keep it in mind." She squeezed his arm. "The offer's good anytime."

Josh had the sensation that he'd stepped on a roller coaster and he had no choice but to stay put, hanging on for dear life, until the ride was over.

Tom brought him a mimosa. "Here, son. At moments like these, I've discovered a little booze can't hurt."

"WHAT DO YOU MEAN, he doesn't love you?" Maddy stood like an avenging angel in the women's bathroom.

"Just what I said." Tracy grabbed a paper towel as she fought tears. "We've been friends for three years. Now we've had sex, and it was great, so he wants to be friends with privileges. He's had a bunch of opportunities to say he really cares about me, but he hasn't taken those opportunities. He wants carefree sex, and I…I thought I could give him that."

"No, you can't."

Tracy looked at her through swimming eyes. "You're right. I thought I could, but once Alice started talking about a wedding, I folded."

"So tell him. Give him an ultimatum, that it's happily ever after or Splitsville."

"I'll lose him." Tracy blew her nose on the paper towel.

"No big loss, if he's not willing to risk anything."

Tracy stared at her. "That's what this is all about, isn't it?

I thought I was the chicken, but he's a bigger chicken than I am. He doesn't want to take a chance that I'll break his heart like Lisa did."

"I don't know who Lisa is, but I can guess. And, yeah, he's got a yellow streak a mile wide down his back. Call him on it, Tracy. You have more self-respect than to give yourself away for nothing."

"Thank you." Without thinking, Tracy hugged her. To her surprise, Maddy hugged back. Tracy moved away, feeling self-conscious. "I'm sure you don't like people invading your personal space like that."

"Hey, that's what girlfriends are for. Now go out there and tell that man of yours how the cow eats the cabbage."

Squaring her shoulders and tossing the paper towel in the trash, Tracy walked out of the bathroom. She could swear the *Rocky* theme was playing in the background. When she reached the table where Josh sat with the Walkers, he got up immediately and came toward her.

"Are you okay?" Taking her by the shoulders, he looked into her eyes. "You look upset. Maybe we should go back to the cabin so you can rest before the flight home."

"I am upset, and it's because of you, Josh Dempsey."

He looked as if she'd slapped him. "Me?"

"I'm an amazing catch, and yet you're willing to use me as a temporary distraction, some open-ended entertainment until something better comes along. Josh, I love you, but if you aren't willing to get married and love me back, with all your might, then we're through." By the end of the speech she was breathing hard, but she felt great.

He gulped. "You…love me?"

"Yes. Lucky you."

It took him a moment, but eventually the grin started, and then the laughter. "I love you, too!" He practically shouted it, so several people turned around to stare. "But you had the courage to actually say it, and for that I'll worship you forever."

"You will?"

"I will." He drew her into his arms. "Marry me, Tracy. Marry me and have my babies. Grow old with me. I think we have a shot at celebrating our fiftieth, and I want to take that risk."

Her heart felt so full, she wondered how it would hold all the joy. "Me, too, Josh," she murmured. "Me, too."

And just before Josh kissed her, she caught sight of Maddy Lov giving her two thumbs-up. She wrapped both arms around Josh, and in the process gave Maddy the V for victory sign. That woman was definitely getting an invitation to the wedding.

* * * * *

WEEKEND TIGRESS

Jade Lee

* * *

My heartfelt thanks to brilliant editors
Stacy Boyd and Marsha Zinberg!
Thank you so much for inviting me to play!
And to playmates Anna and Vicki: You're the best!

Dear Reader,

A few years ago I was visiting my cousin's wife, Rosie. She's a kindergarten teacher and a dynamo in all the best possible ways. And do you know what? She was fascinated by my tigress novels about Chinese Tantrics. The more we talked, the more intrigued we both became. I could not fathom a life surrounded by six-year-olds. Who would choose such a thing? And she wanted to know more and more about exotic women who openly explored sex as a way to a spiritual heaven.

Later I wondered what would happen if sweet Rosie suddenly decided to chuck it all to become a sex goddess. But wait! Why couldn't she be both? A kindergarten teacher by day and a sex goddess by night? How exactly would other people react? Add in one hyperparanoid government agent, and I had a story worth writing.

Talk about fun! I do love torturing my hyperparanoid heroes!

Jade

CHAPTER ONE

"I'M SITTING NEXT to an exotic male dancer!" Liz Song whispered into her cell phone. It was a lie. She sat between an elderly man in his seventies wearing teal argyle socks, and an exhausted mother of four. The O'Hare Airport waiting area was overstuffed with people delayed because of the terrible winter storm booming overhead. Liz was currently killing time her own way by lying to her best friend. "He wants me to take him along on my fantasy ski weekend."

"Is he blond?" Sarah asked.

"Bleached," Liz answered, unable even in her lies to have a full fantasy.

"Then you're better off dumping him. You deserve only the hundred-percent real thing."

Liz laughed, but her voice must have sounded strained because her best friend abruptly turned serious. "Are you really all right? Was the funeral awful?"

"I'm fine," Liz answered, wondering if it was a lie. "I'm about to go on a free ski weekend. What could be better?" She kept the melancholy out of her voice. First her mother's best friend Marta had died from a stroke, then her aunt Ting Wu—who was supposed to be joining her on this fabulous free ski weekend—became ill and had to cancel. That left Liz sitting in O'Hare feeling lost and alone, hence the elaborate fantasy of exotic male dancers willing to run away with her.

"Are you wearing the dress your aunt sent?" Sarah asked.

Liz grimaced as she shifted in the tight silk. "I don't know why I specifically had to wear this thing while I'm flying."

"Because you look fabulous in it?" Sarah shot back. "Exotic male dancers don't just hit on anybody, you know."

Liz smiled and tried not to tug at her ornate hair comb shaped like a tigress and dragon at play. "I don't think Auntie Ting meant for me to wear this in an airport waiting area. Do you know what trouble I had getting the comb through security?" Another lie. In truth, the jade comb was stone and so hadn't even raised eyebrows.

"She said your energy connected to earth, wind and whatever, today."

"My qi was in full blossom," Liz corrected. "It means I'm extra sexual today and—"

"And guys are going to flock to you like horn-dogs!" Sarah shot back with glee.

Liz grimaced at the image. "Yeah!" she said with false enthusiasm. She didn't add the extra instruction from her aunt. Even Sarah didn't know what Liz was supposed to *do* with whatever man hit on her today.

"Well, whatever," Sarah continued. "It's your own fault that you didn't fly out a day early to take full advantage of the outfit at a fancy resort."

"I had to teach this morning."

"The kindergartners would have survived without you."

"Actually," she confessed into the phone, "I feel very strange in this outfit. It makes me feel—"

"Beautiful? Sexy? Exciting?"

"Deceitful," she answered.

"Go on with your bad-girl self!" Sarah squealed.

Liz rolled her eyes. "It's just so different from my usual

jumper with big pockets. It's like I'm in the world of a real adult again, but I haven't a clue what to do."

"It's like riding a bike, Liz. Just give it a shot."

Liz twisted awkwardly in her seat. Did she tell? Did she confess that she was toying with more than a return to sensual adulthood? That she was, in fact, exploring something a great deal bigger? A total career, total personality change from a boring kindergarten teacher to a sexual goddess the likes of which few men or women understood?

"Um, Sarah, have you ever heard of tigresses?"

"You mean like female tigers?"

"I mean like the Asian sexual goddesses who live on a remote island of Hong Kong."

"Squee!" Sarah laughed. "Is this some book you're reading?"

Liz swallowed and looked out the window at the blustering snow. "Um, yeah," she lied. The truth was that these women were real, and her aunt was one of them. The very same aunt who had sent her the outfit, the comb and the strict instructions to get down with the first man who intrigued her today. "Well, you see, there's this girl—woman, actually—and she wants to make a big change in her life. She wants to become—"

"A sex goddess! Oooh, this is you, Liz. All the way, you just have to do it!"

"Yeah, but can you imagine doing it for real? I mean sex with a stranger, seduction as an art form?" She still couldn't believe that her aunt was a modern-day geisha even though she'd learned the truth years ago. "But it's more than just sex. It's Tantrism and I don't know—"

"You're overthinking Liz. Funerals always do that to me, too. Just do it, Liz. All of it."

And right there was the crux of the matter. Could she throw over everything she'd ever believed she was in order to become so much more? Maybe. For a weekend at least.

"All righty, then," she said, her courage growing. "As of this moment, I'm leaving crayons and dinosaurs behind. I'm a tigress!" Or a cub, which was what novices were called.

"You go, girl!"

"I'm a wild woman. And now I'm going to strut my stuff with that dancer!"

"Go! Go! Go!"

"Bye!" She clicked her cell phone off and stood up to go strut her way…to the bathroom, then maybe the bookstore. Yeah, she thought dryly, she was in for a wild, happening weekend.

MATT WALKER BLINKED as the tigress wandered through the bookstore. It couldn't possibly be true. Why would the practitioner of an ancient Chinese Tantric cult be here, wending her way through an O'Hare gift shop?

Then again, why not? Though tigresses lived on a remote island of Hong Kong, they had to get men somewhere, didn't they? And a tigress could be caught in the middle of a winter storm just like anybody else. He just never expected to see one face-to-face. They were notoriously reclusive. Their beauty and their sexual skills made them a target for every horny man and woman who'd ever heard of the sexual goddesses.

He wandered deeper into the bookshop, giving a casual wave to the clerk. There were hundreds of TSA agents working in O'Hare, but he was higher up on the food chain that most. And he was certainly the only high-level manager who frequented the bookstore, so he was well-known here. Meanwhile, his gaze followed the sensual Chinese woman as she strolled idly through the narrow aisle.

She fit the legend, all right: long silky black hair, flawless skin and a silk *chong san* that hugged every curve. She didn't move like a walking seduction, and the huge purse she carried didn't fit the image, but she was still beautiful. There was an expressive innocence in the way she smiled while scanning the children's section, an unstudied serenity that surrounded her as she knelt down to pick up spilled picture books.

It was all an act, of course. According to legend, these women studied sexual personas like a compulsive gambler studied the racing stats. Her innocence, wrapped in an exotic Chinese package too beautiful to ignore, was designed to snare men like him who were drawn to mom-and-apple-pie women.

He curled his lip, uninterested in a mirage, no matter how beautiful. He was about to turn away when she stood up and he caught a flash of the comb in her hair. He narrowed his eyes. She couldn't really be advertising here, could she? With a second look, he saw it: a tigress and a dragon locked in carved copulation, the sign of a tigress on the prowl. He studied the woman's face. She didn't look like a seductress, like a woman looking for a "man to milk," and yet…

He caught her eye. It was a brief look, a casual exchange of glances between strangers. He saw a flash of flirtation, a whisper of daring and something else. Longing? He stared harder, but then she turned away. She didn't move fast, but she was definitely leaving.

He followed her without thought. "Excuse me, miss," he said.

She turned and looked at him slowly, her dark eyes revealed by micromillimeters through exotically slanted lashes.

"I'm Matt Walker, TSA agent." He flashed his badge out of habit. She didn't even look at it. "I'd like a word with you, if I may."

"Is there a problem?" She looked vaguely flustered. Even knowing that it was an act, his groin thickened. The way her skin took on the slightest rose tone and her lips parted was tailor-made to stir a man's lust.

He kept his tone professional as he ushered her out of the bookstore. "This way, please." He wasn't sure what he intended. He did want to talk to the woman. A real live tigress in Illinois? What were the odds? The opportunity to learn about her religion and culture might never come again.

For example, how could a cult of sexually promiscuous women survive in a repressive Chinese society? Not only survive, but thrive for centuries! Did they really believe that taking a man's sexual emissions were akin to taking their yang energy—their male power? If she mixed it with her female yin, would it lead to immortality?

His questions were endless. Most of what he knew of tigresses was gossip and rumor from when he lived in Hong Kong. And yet as he watched her walk beside him, his thoughts were far from academic. His hands itched to stroke the soft silk that shaped her breast. The span of her hips was slender, and yet wide enough to cradle a man. How had she managed to turn his thoughts down that route with just a single sidelong glance?

"In here, please," he said, ushering her into the most secluded place he knew: an interrogation chamber in a currently unused area of Terminal 4. Thankfully, it wasn't far from the bookstore. The room was stark with only two chairs and a table, the walls an intimidating scuffed white. Even worse, he pushed a button that shuttered the window so that it was just him and her. If he meant to seduce her, this was the least-romantic place in the world. If he meant to relax her, to talk to her as a friend so that he could learn about her history and her beliefs, this was the exact wrong approach. So what exactly was he doing? It wasn't like him to act so illogically.

He gestured her to a seat, his attitude bordering on cold. As her eyes widened in shock at their location, he abruptly realized what he was doing. He was going to interrogate her. Why? Because despite her appearance, he really couldn't believe that a Hong Kong tigress was on the prowl in O'Hare.

It wasn't anything she had done—exactly. It was more a gut feel that went all the way to his bones. She was not a tigress. She was not a sex goddess, if such a thing existed, and yet when he looked at her, every thought in his mind turned to lust. Something was very wrong here, and that made it his job, as head of TSA security in this terminal, to find out exactly what.

He started by pretending kindness. "Please, take a seat. Can I get you something to drink? Tea, maybe?"

"Am I in some kind of trouble?" Her voice wavered with anxiety as she delicately settled in the chair.

His groin tightened. He couldn't stop staring at the way her silk skirt outlined her bottom while the side slit split open right up her thigh. He swallowed, feeling unsettled by his own reactions. So he slipped into what he was most familiar with: suspicion and interrogation. He smiled with false reassurance. "If you give me your flight information, I'll make sure you don't miss boarding."

She frowned. "My flight's been delayed by the storm. Why am I here, officer?"

The tigress showed her claws. He smiled. "That's a beautiful comb in your hair," he said slowly. "Rather provocative, don't you think?"

He watched her eyes widen and her hand lift—presumably to touch the comb—but then she froze, her gaze slipping around the room. "You're not really a TSA agent, are you?"

"Yes, ma'am, I am."

"You're not dressed in any uniform."

He pulled out his badge, set it on the table and tapped on his full title. Then as she picked it up, he strolled behind her, looking at her from all sides. Up close, her comb appeared every bit the real thing. On sudden impulse, he reached out and plucked it from her hair. She gasped in surprise as her black hair tumbled down her back.

"What—"

He stepped around her, holding the comb directly in front of her eyes. "I know about tigresses," he said, his voice dropping low into his throat. "I know what this means." He twisted the comb in just the right way. If this comb was a fake, he'd break it in half and he would owe this woman a huge apology and a new jade comb. But if he was right...

With a barely audible click, the tigress and the dragon slipped apart, separating neatly into two pieces. It was the real thing, but was she a real tigress? The idea still felt too off, especially as she stared at the comb with every appearance of shock.

"How did you know?" she whispered.

He smiled slowly. "Like I said, I know about tigresses." He held the tigress half out to her. "I know that this comb in your hair means you're on the prowl for a green dragon— an untrained man. And that any man who captures your comb will, um, get the benefit of your expertise." He arched his brow in challenge.

She took the tigress from his hand, but he didn't release it. Instead, he held it still as her tiny hand fluttered against his. Was she nervous? Or just playing nervous? Her expression seemed mixed halfway between wonder and fear.

Then she abruptly smiled. "You're a real blond, aren't you?"

He blinked, thrown by the non sequitur. "One hundred percent," he answered as he released her half of the comb. "Looking to expand your yang store with a blond? I have heard that tigresses like to experience all types of male energy in all types of ways."

She arched her brow in challenge. "You're the expert on tigresses. You tell me."

He leaned forward far enough to smell her hair. He scented an exotic mix of lavender and spice that went straight to his groin. He ignored his reaction and instead searched her face, watching closely for clues. "I think you're a liar," he said coldly.

She flinched, but to her credit, she didn't run. Instead, she lifted her chin. "I was in a bookstore minding my own business. You're the TSA agent who dragged me in here, broke my comb—"

"It's not broken—"

"And now you're calling me names. I think you're the fraud. Or worse." With that, she pushed out of her chair and headed for the door.

He moved fast enough to stop her just beside the door. She still had free access to the exit, but she'd have to walk by him to get out. "You're right, of course," he said casually as she paused. "I'm not on duty right now, so technically I have no authority to bring you in here like this. But I am TSA and I am in charge of this little branch of O'Hare. And I am very interested in you."

She arched a brow at him, her expression cool. This close to her, he could see the rapid beat of the pulse in her throat. She wasn't as sanguine as she appeared. "Because you know I'm a tigress," she mocked. "Or maybe because you can't get a date any other way."

"How did you get the comb?" He held up the dragon half. "Did you steal it?" She could be a high-class thief. That would explain why things felt off with her.

"I didn't steal it! It was given to me!" Her hand shot out, faster than he thought possible. She almost grabbed it from him, but he was faster.

"Of course it was," he mocked. "Oh, wait, I thought ti-

gresses didn't give their tokens away. Certainly not this kind."
He tapped the cool jade against his lips. "It's too provocative."

"It's a comb!" she huffed.

"It's a signal," he answered. "You would know that if you
were a real tigress." He leaned in to her, letting her heat and
her scent wash over him. It burned in his blood and stiffened
his dick. Wouldn't it be great if she *was* a tigress? Wouldn't
it be wonderful to experience the ultimate in anonymous
sexual delight just once in his life? But that was lust talking,
not his logical, dispassionate brain, which told him he wasn't
that lucky.

"Please give me my comb. You have no right to keep it or
to interrogate me this way." Her voice remained strong, but
the timbre had dropped, becoming huskier. Could she be
getting turned on?

"You can leave at any time. The door's open, and I have
no legal way to hold you."

"Give me back my comb."

"According to tigress rules, I have staked my claim. You
have to give me something to get it back."

She arched a single brow. "Real tigresses do not come
that cheaply."

He doubted she meant the double entendre, but his lust certainly heard it. His imagination lost no time working out all
sorts of ideas about how to make her come. He shook his
head, his brain starting to fuzz out from lust. "Maybe I just
want information. How did you get the comb?"

"It was a gift from my aunt."

"Quite a gift."

"I'm her favorite niece," she returned, and when he arched
a brow at her, she simply shrugged. The movement was stiff,
but he didn't focus on her anxiety. He watched every shift and
wiggle of her beautiful breasts.

He forced his gaze back to her face. "Where did your aunt get the comb?"

She lifted her chin. "I didn't ask. She just told me to wear it today."

A signal, then, but not for sex. An exchange of some kind? It happened all the time, especially in O'Hare, the busiest airport in the world. "Who was supposed to meet you? What were you supposed to give them?"

She blushed: a rosy blush that turned her golden skin passionate red. And with that blush came the certain knowledge that he was right. He suppressed a sigh. She was nothing more than a common mule.

"Who?" he pressed. "Who were you supposed to meet?"

She swallowed, and her eyes grew heavy-lidded. "A man," she whispered.

Progress. He leaned in closer. She had backed up against the door, one hand clutching the doorknob, but her own body position prevented her from opening it. "Were you supposed to tell the man something?"

She shook her head, her eyes huge and her lips moist.

"Were you supposed to give him something?"

Again she shook her head.

"Then what?"

"I'm supposed to let him kiss me. On the wrist." She held up her left arm weakly.

He stared at her. She'd gone red from the tips of her ears all the way to the line of her collar and beyond. He took hold of her arm and inspected it, lifting her delicate wrist to the light. All he saw was creamy skin, the thin tracery of veins, and of course the rosy blush that seemed to heat every inch of her body.

"Is it laced with drugs?"

She stiffened. "I don't even wear perfume!"

He lifted her wrist, excruciatingly aware of his vulnerable position. As he leaned down to sniff, he exposed the back of his neck and his side to any number of body blows. But she didn't move, and her one hand was still trapped behind her on the doorknob. If she were going to fight him, she wasn't in the right position to do much more than whimper.

He inhaled. She was right about no perfume. He couldn't detect anything more than her own musky scent, but that was intoxicating enough. Damn, he was hard as a rock now. She smelled like a hot woman from an exotic tropical island. It didn't matter that it was way below freezing outside. Right here, next to her skin, she made a steamy Asian paradise.

He couldn't stop himself; he had to take the taste. He pressed his lips to the pulse point of her wrist. He heard her gasp and felt her tremble. It was too much for his self-control. Despite the risks, he had to taste her.

He extended his tongue and traced a long circle over her skin. She released a high keen of distress, and his gaze leaped to her face. Her eyes were closed. Her tongue slipped out to wet her plump lips. She wasn't frightened. She was aroused.

But just to make sure, he did it again. Instead of a simple stroke, he swirled lazy, erotic circles all over her flesh. Her breath hitched, her nipples tightened into hard points, and if he wasn't mistaken, her knees were going out from beneath her. All of her weight now rested against the door.

"You were supposed to let some man—a stranger—do this to you?" He couldn't prevent the hard, possessive edge to his voice. The idea that she would go weak in the knees for anyone else prodded the Neanderthal side of his nature.

The blouse of her *chong san* had short cap sleeves, which meant he had full access to the whole of her arm. He didn't waste time examining the questionable ethics of what he was doing. He simply stroked his lips across the creamy silk of her skin, riding ever higher on the inside of her arm.

She was still trembling, and her breath came in light pants. He wondered if he could make her come just from touching her arm. He decided to experiment. He nipped the skin just above her elbow, and she cried out. He soothed the spot with his tongue and she moaned. Lord, how he wanted to spread her right there and jam himself to the hilt.

"Why?" he asked her creamy flesh. "Why would you let someone do this to you?"

She shook her head. "A promise to my aunt." She gasped. "So I could be a tigress."

He lifted his head. So she did know about tigresses. "You're in training?" That would explain a lot. A neophyte tigress would feel off: not quite settled in her sexuality, not really sure of her intentions. Could it be true? Could she really be a tigress in training? "What's your name?"

"Ling Min," she said as she obviously tried to gain control of herself. "My aunt told me to be bold. To take what I want." She leaned forward and cupped his groin, using her thumb to stroke his length. It was obviously an untutored move, but his dick didn't care. It took all his willpower to remain still and not press into her hand. But if she kept it up…

He grabbed her wrist and twisted away. "I'm not that easy," he said, his voice coming out half words, half growl. He wanted it to be that easy. How he wanted it!

He stepped closer to her, leaning in to smell her hair, her neck. And when a smell wasn't enough, he began to taste. "Tigresses take from men. They steal male emissions and grow stronger."

"My aunt says that life eternal can be found in just one drop from a man."

He had no doubt about which "drop" she referred to, and his body nearly lurched from the thought. "But what about your drops?" he whispered. Then he quoted from the ancient text he'd studied in college. "If a tigress were to gift a man with her essence, then that man would taste paradise."

She looked down at him, her eyes stormy, but her expression fierce. "Is that what you want?" she whispered. "To taste paradise?"

"Oh, yeah," he murmured. Then he fitted words to action and skimmed straight down her body. His hands flowed over her breasts, pausing only briefly to flick her hard nipples. Then he outlined the flare of her hips, and slipped his fingers between the slits on the sides of her skirt. She was wearing panty hose, but that was hardly a challenge. He easily rucked up her skirt, hooked his thumbs around the waistband, and with one quick movement, pulled the nylon and her cotton thong straight down past her knees.

Her scent was strong here and the last of his restraint melted away. Any woman this responsive had to be a tigress. A real live tigress, here in O'Hare! And lucky him, he had the background to know just what to do.

He widened his hands and slid them between her naked thighs. She didn't fight him. He moved higher and higher until one thumb slid between her slick folds. Obviously her body wanted this; she was more than ready, in fact. He slid his thumb deep inside then drew it out slowly, keeping his knuckle high enough to roll over her clit.

She moaned softly, and her eyelids fluttered closed. He did it again and her hips began to move, her body undulating slightly against the wall. He dropped to his knees before her, pressing his lips to her hips, his tongue to her curls. But before he completely submerged himself in her, he had to know the truth. "You're a tigress, right?"

"Yes," she murmured.

"This is what you want?"

"Oh, yes."

It was all he needed to hear. Gripping her thighs, he spread her wider. How he wanted to drop his pants and dive in. But not yet, not this moment. Instead, he lifted her higher against the wall and let his tongue explore. Within moments he discovered that the ancient text was right: he was indeed tasting paradise.

CHAPTER TWO

ORGASM RIPPED through her. It was all Liz could do to keep herself from screaming. As it was, she moaned and thrashed against the interrogation room wall like the wanton she pretended to be. Oh heaven, the things he did with his tongue were beyond incredible! And still he kept going. She gasped and whimpered. She squirmed though he kept her hips pressed flat. She was going to scream! Oh my! Oh…oh…oh…

She grabbed hold of his hair and yanked him back. Her muscles were still pumping, her body still singing. And as he looked into her eyes, a cocky grin on his face, she had only one question: "Do you…condom?"

His grin faded. "No. You?"

She nearly cried. She wanted—she needed—the feel of him embedded deep within her. The glow was dimming, the waves fading to sweet ripples, and all she could do was look at her beautiful blond TSA agent and wish for more. Their eyes met and she saw an answering hunger in him. But it was more than that. She saw melancholy: a wish and an ache that she also felt deep inside. Then he blinked, and it was gone.

"Don't…" she began, but she didn't know what to say. *Don't hide from me?* They'd only just met.

"What?" he pressed.

She shook her head, then put some strength into her legs.

At the very least, she could reciprocate. She had barely enough control to steady herself, but she managed to keep from falling. She bent her knees, letting her hands slip down his torso toward his pants. "I can—"

"No," he said, stopping her downward motion by gripping one of her arms. He took a breath, then wiped his free hand over his face. He had the look of a man just realizing where he was and what he was doing. "I think I've compromised my ethics enough for one day."

"I don't mind—"

"No. Thank you, but, no."

They straightened together, both coming to their feet until they faced each other. And all the while, her mind was reeling. What had she just done? What had she let him do? She pressed her hand to his mouth, feeling the wetness there, smelling the scent of sex in the tiny room. "Don't cheapen this," she whispered. "We're two consenting adults. We're obligated to no one…" Her gaze sharpened. "You are free, right?"

He nodded. "For over a year now."

She glanced behind her. "And no one saw, right? No cameras or anything?"

He lifted his chin and looked toward the darkened window. Had he always been that tall? "We're alone. And the cameras are off, I swear."

She swallowed. She would have to take his word for it. "Then we're good." But what to do now? She couldn't just stand here with her panty hose about her ankles. With a quick grimace, she quickly shucked her panty hose, slipped her shoes back on and tidied her clothing. He stood back to give her room, saying nothing the whole time. She was extra careful not to look at the bulge in his pants. It took a lot of self-control, but she managed it. And when she was done, she felt a lot more composed. "No problem," she said to herself.

"None at all," he echoed. Then he shifted awkwardly, and she belatedly realized he was adjusting his dress pants. Given the size of the bulge there, he had to be seriously uncomfortable.

"Are you sure?" She gestured awkwardly to his problem.

He held up his hand. "Positive." Then his gaze sharpened on her. "And since when did tigresses worry about cameras and third-party witnesses?"

She shuddered. "Where exactly are you getting your information on tigresses?"

He frowned. "My dad was stationed in Hong Kong for a few years. We knew about them. *All* the boys knew—"

"Gossip, then. Boys creating stories—"

He shook his head. "I did research, too. Call it a college hobby. I've even read the ancient texts in their original language." His eyes narrowed. "Are you saying I'm wrong?"

She considered lying, but he didn't seem like a man who would stop at face value for anything. So she sighed. "No, not completely wrong, but not entirely right, either. We don't all go for group scenes." Her aunt had assured her that she could be a tigress with a very exclusive, very *private* practice.

He studied her face, and she had the uncomfortable feeling he was searching for lies. "You're a tigress in training, here in Illinois?"

"Until my plane leaves, I am," she said. It wasn't so far-fetched; there was even a temple in California. Then she lifted her hand. "My comb, please?"

He held up the dragon half of her comb, and his gaze shifted to study the delicate carving in the harsh lighting. "This is a true historical piece with real significance."

She took hold of the dragon and tried to pull it from his grasp, but he gripped tight. "Historical or not, Mr. TSA Agent, it is mine."

He reluctantly let go of the comb. "Tell me about your training. What do you do? *Why* do you do it?"

Those were questions too complicated to answer, especially since she was beginning to feel acutely embarrassed about her activities. She couldn't shake the feeling that the parents of her kindergarten kids would be horrified. But then, that had been the whole point of this anonymous encounter, hadn't it? To do something private and adult, and maybe ditch crayons and dinosaurs forever.

Either way, he didn't need to know the particulars. "Tigresses don't discuss their training practices. I'm sure you understand." Then she fiddled with the combs, linking them together before putting them back in her hair.

When she finally straightened, she noticed his gaze had gone cold as he stared at her hairpiece. "You're still on the prowl, then."

"What?"

"You linked the dragon and tigress together. You're still looking—"

"I didn't expect to meet someone who understood what they meant," she snapped. "Besides, it holds my hair better this way."

He caught her chin in his hand. His touch was unsettling. His gaze was even worse as he pinned her with his glare. "Not in my airport, Tigress Ling Min."

She yanked her chin out of his grip. "I hardly think you own O'Hare Airport."

He leaned forward, close enough that she could smell him—and her—on his skin. For a moment, she thought he might be coming in to kiss her, but then he flattened his hand hard on the door behind her left ear. There was no way she'd be able to leave until he moved.

"Am I under arrest?" she snapped, irrationally piqued because he hadn't been leaning in for a kiss.

"Until you change the combs, you are. Better yet, hide them. Put them in your purse or something."

She glared at him, but he was unwavering. Truthfully, she had no interest in finding another partner right now. She hadn't been on the lookout for him, much less another. But she didn't appreciate his domineering attitude. "You cannot dictate my actions—"

"TSA agent, remember?" he said. "Do I have to take out my badge again?"

"Bent ethics, remember?" she shot back. "You're hardly one to criticize me!"

She saw his jaw tighten and knew she'd struck home. Then he arched a single ragged male eyebrow. "Just how long until your flight? Do you really want me following you around until it takes off?"

"You'd stalk me? Just in case I might pick up another man?"

"In a heartbeat."

She believed him. There was no compromise in his attitude, no softening in his body. "But why? What do you care—"

"I care," he ground out. He didn't elaborate on why.

"And if I separate the combs, if I swear I won't so much as look at another man until long after my flight takes off—"

"Hide them. Then I'll let you go wherever the wind takes you."

"You'll stay in this room until I'm gone? Ten minutes at least."

She watched him think. It was a strange sight. She'd seen her students—especially the boys—scrunch up their faces and stare hard at something, their minds working furiously. There was nothing childish in this man's attitude or stance, and yet she still saw the marks of deep thought well below the surface. What was he thinking? What lay deep inside this man?

"Deal." His word came out hard and clipped, and she had no doubt he would stick to what he promised. As would she.

With a nod of agreement, she reached up and unlatched the two combs. It was really quite simple once you knew the trick. Later, she would inspect the mechanism thoroughly. Right then, she was more consumed with the sight of her TSA agent's gloriously broad chest as she scurried around him to grab her purse and drop the combs inside. All the while he stood there unmoving, watching her while his chest seemed to broaden with every breath.

"Thank you," he said, his voice thick and gruff.

She dared to raise her gaze off the floor, taking in as many details as possible. As embarrassed as she felt right now, she still wanted to memorize this encounter. She knew it would provide fantasy fodder for years to come.

She'd already noted his broad chest. She saw now that he wore a crisp, white cotton shirt: not so fine as to be luxurious and not so crisp after a long day. He'd said he was off duty, but he wore dress pants and a sports jacket. Even his shoes were nice: dressy cordovan loafers. It was the kind of outfit someone wore on a date, and she wondered where he'd been headed when he saw her in the bookstore. Did he have a girlfriend somewhere? Or did he make a habit of "interrogating" strangers? And did she really care since this whole experience had been just a brief experiment with casual sex? Fun, but by definition, finito. Done. Completely over.

She swallowed and straightened to her full height. She wanted to say something classy, some sort of goodbye that would linger in his thoughts. Nothing came to mind, and so she simply stood there staring at him. He pushed away from the door with a curt nod. Then when she didn't move, he turned the knob and pulled the door open.

"Down the hall and turn left. That will take you right back into the main area—"

"I remember." That was all she could manage. Two words, not in the least bit memorable. But it wasn't as if she could say, *Thanks for the fabulous orgasm. You're a great anonymous sex partner.*

So she hovered there, looking at him looking at her while neither of them spoke. There ought to be something to say between sex partners. But she couldn't think of a thing, so with a hollow nod, she inched her way past him and scurried down the narrow hall. In her mind, she kissed him goodbye; she maneuvered her fingers beneath his cotton shirt and stroked the glorious expanse of muscle beneath; she had a boxful of condoms, a huge bed with a down comforter and a zillion more fantasies to explore with him. She'd start with—

Liz gasped in shock. One fantasy fulfilled was apparently enough to get all her adult desires going full tilt. But that was excellent, she realized. That was exactly what being a tigress was all about. So as she slipped out of this dark area of O'Hare, she allowed her mind to play through whatever scenarios she wanted. Maybe, just maybe, this was the right new path for her life.

MATT WATCHED LING MIN from behind a pillar, suspicion burning in his gut. He'd believed her, believed that she was a tigress in training. He thought maybe his luck had turned. But then he found out she was boarding a flight to Telluride, Colorado. She was boarding *his* flight to Colorado. What were the odds of that? This couldn't be a coincidence. There *had* to be something crooked going on, but what?

He replayed every moment of their encounter despite the fact that it made his raging hard-on that much more painful. Moment by moment she had acted the innocent, and he had swallowed it hook, line and sinker. Could he have done it again? Could he have fallen for yet another bitch out to seduce a high-level TSA agent?

He closed his eyes for a moment, damning himself for a fool. He'd known something was off with her. Logic had told him that no tigress—trainee or not—would be on the prowl here. But one sniff of her glorious scent, one taste of her creamy skin and lust had overridden all logic. Why hadn't he listened to his brain instead of his dick?

He opened his eyes to study her again, seeing the sleek lines of her legs, the sensual way she held her head when all she was doing was staring out the window at the plane. Was she a terrorist? A criminal? That didn't feel right, either.

The problem was that she was either a gifted bad guy or exactly what she claimed, a tigress who gloried in anonymous sex. A criminal could discover his attraction to Asian culture and Chinese women; it wasn't exactly a secret. A criminal could learn that he was flying to Telluride to help out his parents. She'd dress to seduce, and then wander around until he noticed her. Ten minutes later he'd do things he'd never done before, loving every single moment of it.

But a career criminal would not make Ling Min's neophyte mistakes. She would disappear into O'Hare, let him obsess over their every second together and then reappear in a week or so with a line like, "I just couldn't stop thinking of you." That's what his last "girlfriend" had done. But Ling Min had slipped away while he waited the requisite ten minutes, only to pace the hallway in front of the gate. In front of *his* gate on *his* flight.

Even more telling, a criminal would not be so very bad about hiding her identity. The moment he'd seen her at his gate, he'd accessed the flight manifest. There was no Ling Min listed. There was, however, an Elizabeth Song, and why

did that name sound so freaking familiar? He couldn't remember, so he focused on the real question.

Was Ling Min a national security threat who'd made some
stupid mistakes? Doubtful. Or was she an innocent in a weird
series of coincidences? Ha! He didn't believe in coincidences.
Which left what?

He didn't know, but he was damned sure he was going to
find out. Unfortunately, she had the next move. She boarded the
flight, disappearing to the back of coach. He boarded well after
her then spent the entire flight in a state of heightened antici-
pation. Would she go to the bathroom only to be startled by his
presence on her flight? Would she wander up the aisle just to
see if he noticed her? What was she going to do? Only his
military training kept him quiet in his seat waiting for her move.

He waited.

And waited. She didn't do a thing. As far as he could tell,
she never left her seat. Maybe she intended to catch him in
baggage claim. So, after they landed he deplaned like everyone else, stepping off the jetway about five minutes ahead of
her. Then, at his first opportunity, he ducked into the shadows,
watching her every step. She came off the plane as expected
and headed down the hall with everybody else. Damn, she
looked good in that dress. It showed off her slim hips and
those legs. Not very long, but fit and well shaped. He couldn't
stop remembering the feel of them gripping his shoulders
while she came apart beneath his lips. Hell, he could still taste
her!

It wasn't until she boarded a limo to Weekend Pass—his
parents' brand-new ski resort—that he finally remembered
why Elizabeth Song's name sounded so freaking familiar.
She was one of their free weekend winners in the contest
from hell!

His parents' dream had been to run an intimate ski lodge

for couples, but the damn PR firm had brought in celebrity
Maddy Lov, Hollywood's latest swinging single. He'd had his
first intro to the starlet two months ago when he'd been out
helping with some of the construction. She was in town
looking at property, and the PR firm had brought her by. Then
bam, the starlet had formed some sort of attachment to him.
Suddenly he heard the two blond PR bimbos promising him
as security babysitter to a celebrity wild child.

And now Tigress Ling Min, aka Elizabeth Song, turned out
to be one of the contest winners? His mother had wanted a
contest for poets, for quiet romantics and book lovers. She'd
created the whole idea for a love sonnet contest. Looking at
Ling Min as she leaned over to retrieve her luggage, Matt sincerely doubted she was what his mother had in mind.

Something was wrong here. Something completely twisted
and so convoluted he couldn't begin to understand it. But he
would, he vowed. Quietly, though, because the last thing his
parents needed was to step into his nightmare life of terrorists and ruthless Mata Hari wannabes.

"That's quite a scowl."

Matt spun around, quickly smoothing out his expression.
"Dad!" Some defender of the country he was! He'd been so
intent on staring at a woman that he'd missed his own father
in baggage claim.

"Hello, son." His father wrapped him in a bear hug. Except,
of course, it didn't have quite the strength Matt remembered
from his childhood. He returned the grip gently, doing his best
not to notice that his father's blond hair was now completely
gray. Then he stepped back and scanned his dad from head
to toe. There were new lines on his father's lean face, and a
new stiffness to his once loose-limbed movements.

His father was aging, which made it all the more important that this ski lodge be a success. It was his parents' dream

and nothing was going to interfere with that. Most especially not a beautiful tigress spy.

"You didn't have to come pick me up," Matt said. "I could've taken a cab." He glanced out the door to where Liz Song was pulling away from the curb. "Or the limo."

"And miss my opportunity to grill you all the way home? Not a chance!"

"Dad, you know I can't talk about my work."

"Not about your job, you knucklehead, about your life. About girls and grandchildren. About the important things."

"My job is my life. You know that."

"I do," his father said as Matt collected his bag off the cart. "And it's a damn shame. Ten to one you were scowling about work just then and not a beautiful woman."

"You'd lose," Matt returned.

"There's a girl?" His father didn't even try to disguise the hope in his voice.

"And she's beautiful."

"So why the scowl?"

Matt shrugged, feigning casualness to the best of his ability. "You know. The usual."

"I do," his father snapped. "With you that means a beautiful bad guy, right?"

Matt squirmed, hating to admit that his father was right. "Technically, she's a bad girl."

"Takes on a whole new meaning when it comes from you." His father's voice turned softer. "Time was, back in the army, we were all looking for bad girls."

A lie if he'd ever heard one. His father had stopped looking at girls the minute he'd laid eyes on Alice, Matt's mother. According to family legend, the two had met, had one fabulous ski weekend and become engaged that Sunday night.

"How's the grand opening going?" he asked in an attempt to divert the conversation.

His father's sigh cut through the SUV. "We should never have hired that PR firm. When they promised a celebrity, they mentioned Alan Alda and Angela Lansbury, not this Maddie Lov! I tell you, we're stepping on paparazzi like they were cockroaches! Your mother's fit to be tied!"

"I thought you hired that other specialist. Some big-time PR fixer."

"Tony Rossi. He's handling that first couple—Tracy and Josh—with just the right touch, but there's something off about that other couple. At any rate, Felicia and Willard are taking up a lot of Tony's time, which means Maddie Lov is at loose ends and looking for you. Sorry about that," his father said with a grimace. "Seems she's anxious to hook up with her very own super G-man."

"I know. I got her e-mails." And her gifts. And her publicity photos.

"Now, I'm real sorry to make you do this. You've been taking a lot of vacation to help us out—"

"It's all right, Dad. I don't mind." How bad could one celebrity weekend be?

"But we wanted this lodge to be a place for the good people, you know? Where couples and families could get away and just be with each other for a while."

"It still can be, Dad. One bad PR event does not destroy an entire dream."

"Oh, we'll get that sorted out. That's not what I meant." He slowed the car at a stop light and turned to look at his son. "You spend so much time seeing the bad side of life—dealing with terrorists and drug smugglers and the like. It's making you a little paranoid. Your mother and I were hoping that your time at Weekend Pass would help you remember the good things."

"I know, Dad. You're thinking about your passes away from the military when you and Mom got your moments together." He sighed. "But that's your dream—"

"It's yours, too. You just don't remember."

"Not true. I do," Matt said. He remembered what he wanted: a girl and a family, just like his dad said. He just couldn't find the right one. Not when he was busy being stalked by terrorists and tigresses.

"Well, don't give up hope yet. But don't go for any paparazzi, either. They're cockroaches for damn sure. Do you know that one of them climbed through…."

The rest of the ride passed with his father regaling him with the incompetence of the lodge's security. It wasn't what his father meant his stories to be about. His dad meant them to be light funny stories about insane people, but all Matt heard were stories about bad security. His parents' measures were woefully inadequate to deal with a potential terrorist. Not that he really thought that Ling Min—or Liz Song—was a national threat. She was frankly too inconsistent for him to call in Homeland Security just yet. But from what his father was telling him, none of the lodge's security personnel would be remotely helpful in keeping track of the woman. Which meant, of course, that he would have to do it all himself.

That thought alone made him smile. And made his hard-on rage even harder.

CHAPTER THREE

LIZ WOKE LATE to the sound of her cell phone. She frowned at the display, then immediately popped it open. "Auntie Ting! How are you feeling?"

"Fine, fine, dear. And how was your special day? Did you wear the clothes I sent?" Her aunt's tone slipped through the lines like a good-morning caress. Her voice was mellow and sweet, and never failed to make Liz feel like the most special person the world.

"Yes, I wore the clothes. Is your stomach flu all better? That's incredibly fast—"

"And the comb, dear. Did you wear the comb?"

Liz straightened in her bed, her suspicions growing by the second. "Yes, I wore the comb. Did you know that it is some ancient signal for anonymous sex?"

A giggle of delight teased through the phone. "Did it work?"

Liz closed her eyes and groaned. "Auntie Ting, you didn't really have the stomach flu, did you?"

"Tell me what happened, little one," her aunt coaxed. "Is he with you now? I can hang up."

"No, he is not with me now!" Liz snapped, not that she hadn't spent the night dreaming about him. But that wasn't relevant. "You told me you were sick! That you couldn't come with me!"

"To the newest singles' hot spot? Don't you think your old auntie would be a rather strange companion?"

"Not if she's a tigress," Liz said with absolute truth. Her fifty-year-old aunt was why Liz was considering this whole career change in the first place. The woman was youthful, beautiful and so completely at ease with her sexuality that men and women both felt awed to be in her presence. It was amazing and had mesmerized Liz since her first family reunion twenty-five years ago.

"Tell me everything that happened, from the very beginning."

Liz opened her mouth to answer, but no sound came out. How could she put the most amazing sexual encounter into words? In the end, she switched tactics. "Are they all that amazing? I mean I never thought anonymous sex—"

"Why, Lizzy? Why was he amazing?"

"Because…" Liz fell backward with a sigh of delight. "Because it was different, it was exciting, and he did everything just right. Is it always like that?"

"Yes and no. It's always different. It's always special, but only if you make it so."

"I didn't do it," she said. "*He* did."

"How? Why?" her aunt pressed.

Liz shook her head. "I don't know. I just know I liked it. A lot."

Auntie Ting laughed, and the sound was melodic and filled with joy. "Well, it sounds like you better find that man and figure out a few things."

"I can't," Liz shot back. "Anonymous sex, remember? I don't even remember his name," she lied. She remembered his name, his face, his touch, his…everything!

"You have the combs. Go find someone else."

Liz looked over at the schedule of events for this weekend. As a contest winner, she had her choice of events, all of which would include scores of available men. But the thought of picking up someone else so soon after Matt Walker, blond TSA hottie, just left her cold. "I don't know if I'm cut out for this. If any of the kindergarten parents found out—"

"Don't think so much about ifs. Walk today's path, not tomorrow's."

"I'm not even sure what that means."

Her aunt's laugh flowed through the cell phone. "Of course you do, all women do. Just wear the combs, and don't forget the condoms. Bye-bye, little cub!"

Liz stared at her cell phone, her thoughts spinning. She wondered what Matt thought of their encounter. If she met him here today, would he laugh at the silliness of magic sex combs? She doubted it. They hadn't spent a lot of time together, but she didn't think he was the laughing type. Too bad, really. She'd bet anything a smile would look really, really good on him.

She pushed out of bed on a wistful sigh and went to dress. She had packed only adult clothing for this trip—not a large-pocketed jumper in sight—and so she felt gloriously sinful by the time she'd slipped into her miracle bra. No *chong san* today. Just a loose blouse and tight jeans.

Her hands hesitated over the combs. Did she dare? Could she invoke their special "magic"? Of course she could! If yesterday was anything to judge by, she could handle just about anything.

She pressed the two combs together, her confidence boosted because, frankly, what were the odds that anyone here would know anything about her combs? It was easy being daring when no one was likely to call her on it. But just the possibility that there could be another Matt out there somewhere gave her a secret thrill. She slipped the comb into her hair and exited her suite with an extra sway to her hips. Watch out, world: Tigress Ling Min was on her way!

She kept her saucy attitude long enough for the elevator doors to open on the main floor. The brunch buffet was through the lobby area and out poolside. Thankfully, it was a heated, enclosed poolside. She was still reminiscing about the last man her magic combs had brought her when her thoughts slammed to an abrupt halt.

Every person on the planet was crammed into the tiny buffet area. Cameras were flashing, beautiful people were strolling, and a stunningly gorgeous woman was holding court in the center. Liz felt her eyes widen in shock. Maddy Lov? So much for her dream of more "interesting" encounters with eligible bachelors. No one would look at her twice when Maddy Lov was in the room. My God, that woman was beautiful!

Liz stepped into the buffet area, drawn forward because everyone and everything seemed to be pulled to the mesmerizing woman. Liz had never thought much of celebrities, and certainly not about the newest media wild child Maddy Lov. And yet this close, she could feel the woman's charisma. Long blond hair flowed over her shoulders, her lush mouth pursed in a sweet pout, and her tragic eyes gazed over the crowd in a perfect match to her air of vulnerable innocence. Liz couldn't help but stare.

"Hey! Out of the way!" snapped a guy lounging at a table behind a plate of half-eaten ham and sausages. She stumbled as he pushed her aside. She recovered quickly enough to see him fiddle with his tie tack, carefully aiming it at Ms. Lov. A camera presumably. Wow, people really did use those things. Apparently, no one noticed, even though he was practically holding his tie tack to his eye.

"Wow," she said. "Nice, um, tie."

He glanced sharply at her, scanned her from head to toe, then apparently dismissed her. "Yeah. Thanks," he said, his gaze already going back to Ms. Lov. "Hey, do you know who the hunk is?"

She frowned. "Which hunk?" Truth be told, in this room there was a great deal of eye candy of both sexes.

The man rolled his eyes while gesturing with his chin. "With Maddy. The one with the scowl."

"I haven't a clue—" she began as she looked over her shoulder. Then Maddy leaned to the side to speak to someone and a familiar blond physique came into view. Liz felt her chest abruptly tighten in shock. It couldn't possibly be true. She was too far away to see for sure, but those piercing blue eyes, that beautiful blond hair and most especially that mouth pressed into a flat scowling line couldn't possibly belong to anyone else. Especially since the hunk in question was glaring straight at her. "Oh, no!"

"You know him?" the man with the camera tie demanded.

"No!" she squeaked as she started backing away. "Haven't a clue." So much for her bold tigress attitude. Liz was already turning tail to run like the fraidy-cat she was.

Except there was nowhere for her to go. With tie-camera guy on one side already reaching for her and a solid wall of buffet on the other, she had no choice but to grab a plate and start loading it up. Maybe he wouldn't notice her if she hunched. She could look like just anybody, right? Especially since she really was a nobody.

But two minutes of heavy panic later, the very voice she dreaded whispered into her ear. "Feeling hungry?"

She glanced down at her plate. She'd layered grapefruit slices on top of a waffle on top of sausage and eggs all in one sloshing mess. "Hmm?" she asked.

A very large, very familiar hand gripped her upper arm and turned her around. She avoided his eyes because, frankly, she knew if she looked into them, she'd lose it completely. Instead she resolutely stared over his shoulder to where security was making a commotion.

"Oh, look," she quipped in a way-too-high voice. "They caught the camera-tie man."

Matt didn't so much as turn his head. What he did do was reach up and grab her comb, which made her hair tumble down in front of her eyes. "On the prowl again, Tigress Ling Min? Or should I call you Liz Song?"

"This is getting kinda old," she retorted as she jerked her head to flip her hair out of her face. "Don't you know of a better way to pick up girls?"

"Why don't you come with me? You can give me dating tips." He tugged slightly on her arm, but she dug in her heels.

"I'm not falling for it again, Mr. TSA Agent," she drawled. "You have no authority here, whereas I am a guest of honor." Not that anyone had done anything special for her. Except for the limo—which was lovely—she'd missed all the opening hoopla. She thought there was a basket or something in her room, but she'd been too tired last night to check. And there had definitely been a picture of her and the other winners in the front lobby, but again, she'd been too tired last night to really look. "In fact, I think there's a special dance tonight—"

"Yeah, I know all about your guest-of-honor status. You claimed on your entry form to be a kindergarten teacher." He arched a brow as he quite obviously and leisurely scanned her body head to toe. "School must have changed a great deal from when I was a kid."

Liz tried to jerk her arm out of his grip. No go; he held her fast. "Obviously, you had bad teachers. Your manners are severely lacking." She used her most prissy teacher tone, but that was equally useless. If anything, his eyes got even harder.

"We're just going to talk, Miss Song."

"No," she returned. "We're not." And with that, she abandoned her overloaded plate and turned her most brilliant smile on the celebrity queen bee. "Ooo," she squealed in a pitch that rivaled the worst of her female students. "Miss Lov, I just love, love, love you! When I heard I was a *winner* and would get to meet you...omigod, I was just so thrilled! I couldn't talk to you last night because—" She stopped dead and turned tragic eyes on Matt. "I'm sorry, sir. I won't hurt her, I swear. I just want to get her autograph. Oh, please, it's okay, isn't it, Ms. Lov?"

"Matt darling, she's harmless," the celebrity cooed. "Let her come over."

And just like that, Liz's arm was released. She went straight to the celebrity's side, gushing all the way as she knelt in pretend adoration.

"Oh, thank you! Oh my, I don't have anything to write on—"

"Aren't you cute!" Ms. Lov gushed. "Matt, no need to stand there and glower. She's just a fan. And, sweetie, you can get my autograph this afternoon at the book signing."

"Excellent idea," Matt interrupted as he gripped both her shoulders and lifted her to her feet. "In fact, I'll show you where to place preorders for this afternoon. Come along, Ms. Song." So much for her clever escape.

"But—" Liz began as she tried to tug away. She never got anywhere. Maddy was already waving her off, and Matt's grip wasn't releasing anytime soon. Within moments she found herself whipped through the main lobby and into another secluded room, this one tucked behind the front desk. At least this time she knew that a good scream would bring scores of people—probably most of them with cameras.

Hmm, not quite what she wanted, was it? The thought of her and Matt plastered across the Internet made her rethink her scream. Perhaps she would keep her lip buttoned for a bit. Just long enough to figure out exactly how she wanted to handle her disappearing/reappearing TSA agent. Right now, he was glaring at her, his arms folded, muscular chest and biceps beautifully outlined by his white dress shirt.

She stared back. After all, two could play the staring game, but Liz had never been long on patience. That's why she worked with six-year-olds: they were the only ones she could outstare. "So talk, TSA Agent Matt," she snapped. "What are you doing so far from O'Hare?"

"What happened to Liz Song? Where is she? Is she dead?"

Liz blinked, wondering if she'd heard him right. "What? I'm right here." She waved vaguely in the direction of the lobby. "Isn't my photo out there?"

"Yours is, but maybe you assumed Ms. Song's identity long before this contest. So Tigress Ling Min, what's your real name?"

She echoed his stance—folding her arms across her chest—all the while wondering if he'd been hit on the head recently. "I'm Liz Song. My aunt gave me the tigress name Ling Min, not that that's any of your business. What the hell is wrong with you?"

"Recite the sonnet you used to win the contest."

She blinked, then started reciting. But the way he stared at her messed with her memory. In the end she stumbled to a halt right in the middle of line six. "Look, I don't know who you're looking for, but it isn't me. I'm Liz Song. I've got ID. Take my fingerprints or something."

"That's already in process, off your breakfast plate. Why did you pick me in the airport?"

"You picked me!" she snapped. "And now it seems like you're stalking me. Geez, you're running my fingerprints? How psycho is that? What's the name of your superior? Never mind. You won't tell me the truth anyway, but rest assured, Agent Matt—if that is your real name—I will report you and this harassment."

"Go ahead. My full name is Matt Walker, and my boss is Vicki Barr." Then he shifted forward to tower over her. It was an extremely intimidating pose, even if it did give her a rather sweet view of rippling muscles beneath white cotton. "I'm just doing my job," he said.

"No, you're not," she snapped as she tried to sidle backward. He looked great and all, but there wasn't enough space in this tiny room. She could hardly breathe. "If you were doing your job, you'd be in uniform, flashing a badge, and we'd be in an airport." She gestured at the tiny room. "I don't see any airplanes here."

"My job as security consultant for this lodge. Or didn't you figure out in your research that this is my parents' dream? I'll be damned if I let any Mata Hari wannabe mess that up for them!"

She stared at him, unbelievably shocked that anyone would mistake her for a terrorist. She didn't know whether to be insulted or really, really frightened for national security. "I'm just a kindergarten teacher."

"I thought you were a tigress."

"In training. I'm in training."

He snorted his disbelief, and at that moment she finally caught a clue. She looked at the dead seriousness in his eyes, the tight way he held his body and the implacable fury that radiated out of his every pore. "Oh my," she murmured. "You really are a TSA agent, aren't you? And you've gone completely off the deep end. You're seeing spies in every corner!" She shook her head, sympathy at war with fury inside her. "You need help, Mr. Walker. You may not realize it at this moment, but you need some serious professional help."

She watched him closely, hoping that sincerity would work where outrage hadn't. His eyes narrowed, but not at her. He seemed to be looking through her, and she caught a flash of uncertainty in his expression.

"It's okay, Mr. Walker," she said gently. "Just give me back my comb and I'll forget all of this." It was the wrong thing to say. One mention of her comb brought back memories of yesterday, which brought him right back to thinking she was a spy, for some God-only-knew-why reason.

"You were on my flight," he rasped out. "First you get me into that interrogation room, and we…"

"It was a step in my training—"

"And then you're on my flight." His gaze hardened. "I don't have the patience for games. Tell me what happened to the real Liz Song, and I'll put in a good word for you—"

"So I can avoid the electric chair? Do people really say stuff like that? Or are you just a psycho getting his lines off TV? I *am* Liz Song. And you—"

"I'm not letting you out of my sight until I get the truth. But you're running out of time. I've got police checking Ms. Song's apartment right now."

She blinked. This could not be happening! "You're going to traumatize my cat!" Not to mention her mother, who was stopping in to feed Fatboy.

"Do you feel the net closing in? It's only going to get worse. Just tell me what I want to know—"

"I am not a terrorist spy!" she almost screamed. "My mom is going to have a heart attack."

"Where is Liz Song?"

"Right here!" She tightened her hold on her arms, her mind whirling. Some fantasy weekend this was turning out to be. The one time she needed to prove that she was nobody special was the one weekend she decided to become exciting and daring.

"What's your real name?" His voice had gentled and was

almost sympathetic, but Liz wasn't fooled. It was just another TSA tactic.

She sighed, mentally giving in to the inevitable. "Tell you what. In the interest of helping out a—" she almost said friend, but they were not even remotely friends "—a government agent, I'll let you take my fingerprints, rifle my belongings, even blast my face over the Internet. Whatever it takes to make you believe that I'm just me—a kindergarten teacher from a Chicago suburb."

He narrowed his eyes, suspicion growing in his gaze. "And why would you do that?"

"On the condition that when this is done, you seek counseling from a professional. Someone who deals with agents gone überparanoid."

He frowned at her, suspicion rolling off him in waves. "You'll let me pry into your life? Ask any question I want?"

She shrugged. "I'd like to get some skiing in, but I get the feeling you'll be hounding my every step if I don't."

"I'll be hounding you anyway," he said. "All that questioning and probing will keep us in close quarters, probably for the entire weekend."

Had he actually made that sound sexual? And had she really gotten a shiver of delight at the thought? Liz swallowed. "This isn't some elaborate come-on, is it?"

He shook his head. "I don't sleep with terrorists."

She laughed. It was so bizarre that he thought boring old her was a national threat. Welcome to the world outside of crayons and construction paper. "All righty, then," she quipped, her sense of the ridiculous kicking in. "Do we go for the thousand-watt interrogation lamps now? Or can I get breakfast first?"

His lips twitched as if he actually thought about smiling. No such luck. His expression quickly flattened out and his tone remained cold as he opened the door. "By all means, get some breakfast."

She smiled sweetly at him and sailed out the door…right into a kissing contest.

CHAPTER FOUR

MATT STRUGGLED NOT to grin. He had her now! Her plan was fairly obvious. Under the guise of helping him, she was giving him full rein to ask questions, probe into her life, to find out everything about her. This gave her time to become friends with him, insinuate herself into his psyche. Then, the moment he let his guard down, she would strike with whatever plot she had in mind.

What she didn't know was that he was onto her, and that he never, ever let his guard down. Not since Lily. And intimacy went both ways. At some point, she would make a mistake and he would be right there, ready to nail her to the wall.

He followed her through the main lobby then on to the buffet area, watching the elegant sway of her hips. It wasn't until she stopped dead at a rowdy cheer that he thought to look into the room. A couple in full clinch was on the front dais by Ms. Lov. Raucous comments came from all around until the couple separated with bright-red faces. Matt couldn't hear what the man said as he murmured something to the red-faced woman, but within moments, the two rushed away.

"I thought you were hungry—" Matt began, only to be interrupted by the celebrity-nightmare woman he was supposed to be babysitting.

"There you are, darling!" Maddy Lov cried to him. "Come on up here. We're playing a game that I think you'll adore."

He sincerely doubted it, given what he'd just seen. "Sorry, ma'am," he said. "I'm on duty."

"No, you're not!" Maddy trilled. "You're with me!" And just like that, every eye in the room was riveted to him, everyone wondering who Maddy's latest boy toy was. Even worse, Liz gave him a tight smile.

"Go ahead. I swear I won't skip away on you."

He gripped her arm. "Not a chance," he murmured. In fact, now might be the perfect moment to start pushing that intimacy between them. He turned to Ms. Lov. "What's the game?"

"A kissing contest," Maddy answered. "Is it really possible to make someone's toes curl during a kiss? Both people have to have their shoes off." She wiggled her bare and expertly manicured feet.

He arched his brow. Had the other couple been shoeless? He hadn't even noticed.

"So come on over," Maddy cooed. "And pucker up!"

"Oh, no," he said with pretend shyness. "You're too much for me, Ms. Lov. I'd much rather try this with someone a little—"

"A little easier?" Liz snapped from his side, already stiffening in outrage.

"I was going to say closer at hand."

Liz arched a mocking brow. "I'm pretty sure Ms. Lov will move as close as—"

"I don't want Ms. Lov," he said softly—and as seductively as possible—right in Liz's ear. He felt her mouth open to object, so he kept going just to forestall her. "Her boobs are plastic, her feet look weird, and her hair has knots in it. I don't want her."

Liz twisted to look at him more closely, her forehead furrowed in thought. "They're called extensions."

"What?" Had he realized before how beautiful her eyes were? Up close, her brown irises took on a luminescent light. Like fine mahogany in sunlight, only lit from within.

"The knots in her hair. They're extensions."

"Hmm," he answered. "Take off your shoes."

"No," she retorted. But this close he could see the uncertainty in her eyes.

"Then I'll have to arrest you for starting a riot."

She blinked in surprise and he gestured to the room. Apparently, she hadn't noticed how people were chanting, "Take it off!" He took that as a good sign and toed off his shoes.

Flushing a beautiful rose, she bent down and unhooked the straps on her low pumps. It was likely a cheap ploy to distract him with her nicely curved rump, but he was human enough to enjoy the sight. He noticed, too, the way that Maddy Lov was glaring daggers at him, but he simply shrugged and threw her a wink. He was supposed to be controlling the starlet, not throwing her into a hissy fit. She pursed her lip in a moue of distaste and then looked away, but she didn't seem as if she was about to have a meltdown. Which left him free to focus on the delectable Ms. Song.

Liz straightened, now a few inches shorter, while someone in the crowd started yelling questions.

"Have you two ever kissed before?"

"Never," Matt responded.

"Are you prone to toe curling?" someone else called.

There were other questions, all of them rather raunchy. Matt tuned them out in favor of watching Liz's growing blush. He had to touch it, to feel the heat building beneath her skin. He stroked her cheek, knowing that it would deepen the red. It did. And her eyes widened.

The crowd was beginning to scream, "Do it!" Matt smiled. If they only knew what he and Liz had already done. He knew, as a gentleman, he ought to ask her if she was okay with this public kissing thing. Then he remembered that he still had her comb in his pocket.

On impulse, he drew it out of his pocket and showed it to her. "Consider this kiss payment for returning your comb."

She nodded without comment, her eyes still huge. But then he saw her change. Where one moment she was nervous and shy, the next her gaze jumped from his to the coiling dragon, then back to him. When she returned to meet his gaze, he saw a spark of daring. More than a spark because she arched her brow at him.

"I'm a tigress, right?" she said. "And tigresses have no problem with kisses—public or otherwise." And then, to his total shock, she arched her head forward to wrap her luscious lips around the jade dragon. He'd been so involved with watching the change in her expression that he'd almost forgotten it hung there between them. Not so now.

He watched with growing excitement as her lips wrapped around the jade carving. Then she slowly, carefully, drew it out of his hand using only her mouth. When he had fully released it, she smiled at him and finally took the comb from her mouth. Without shifting her gaze from his, she neatly repinned her hair, the crowd hooting and hollering the whole time.

Then she lifted her chin and looked at him. "Are your toes curling yet?"

With a start of surprise he realized that, yes, damn it, his toes were gripping the carpet. Just as another part of his anatomy had sprung to hardened attention.

She glanced to the crowd. "I believe I won this round—"

Her words were cut off as he pulled her chin back to his. "Not so fast, tigress."

Then he kissed her.

He meant to go slow. After all, seduction was a game played by inches. And yet, everything about her pushed him to extremes. This kiss was no different. He took her mouth with his. He claimed her boldly and possessively. He pressed his mouth to hers and stroked his tongue across the seam. And when she softened for him, he pushed inside. He touched her everywhere he could. He teased her, he toyed with her and he branded her. Then he felt her hands gripping his shoulders, her fingers pulling him closer, and he could not stop himself.

His free hand slipped around her waist and he drew her tighter against him. She arched her neck; he arched her back so that he had deeper access. And when her left hand went from his shoulder to burrow in his hair, he barely restrained himself from ripping her clothes off right then and there.

In the end he had to break away just to breathe. But he didn't go far. He buried his face in her neck and inhaled her sweet scent. No perfume, just sweet Liz. He shuddered as he tried to regain control over himself.

It helped that all around them the crowd had erupted into raucous cheering comments. Within a second Liz was going to come out of her daze and stiffen up in embarrassment. Sure enough, she jolted backward in his arms, though he still held her tight. They stood nearly nose to nose as her eyes darted around like a panicked animal, and her breath shortened to quick pants. He had to say something fast or she'd bolt.

"Tigresses don't care about public sex, remember?"

It was just what she needed. Her eyes skipped back to his and held. As he watched, her spine straightened and her expression shifted. She didn't quite exude assurance, but there was a definite shift toward confidence. By the time she gave him a trembling nod, he knew that she was in control again.

"No curled toes," Maddy crowed from the sidelines. "Guess you don't have what it takes, Mr. Walker."

Matt didn't even bother responding to the jibe, though his masculinity did force him to glance down. The truth was Liz was on her toes and he was holding her pressed tightly against him. His toes, of course, were curled all the way up to his heel.

His gaze transferred to Liz's face, lingering on the rosy flush to her skin, the dark passion in her eyes and the full sweet plump to her lips. How he wanted to ravish her. No sweetness, no hesitation, just drag her back to his cave and possess her in every way possible. He swallowed, stunned by the force of his emotions. No doubt about it: he was falling fast.

He couldn't let that happen. Not until he knew exactly who and what she was. Which meant that he had to get her alone— to study her—but in some place where his lust couldn't override his good sense.

"So…" he began, his voice coming out as a croak. Then he cleared his throat. "Um, do tigresses ski?"

Her brows contracted a moment in thought. "I don't think so. Not as a rule," she said in an equally throaty purr. Then her eyes flashed in delight. "But I'm just in training, and I love the snow." With that, she pushed herself out his arms. His pride allowed him to believe that she went slowly, almost reluctantly, but the end was just the same. She stepped away from him, toed on her shoes without buckling them, then smiled saucily at him. "See you on the slopes! Double black diamond." With that, she slipped away.

"SO HAVE YOU ALWAYS lived in the Chicago area?"

Liz slanted a pointed look at her personal snoop. He'd been relatively quiet all the way from the lodge to the slopes. But now that it was just the two of them on the ski lift together, apparently her reprieve was over.

"It's just a question," he said casually.

"Liar!" she shot back. Just because she'd agreed to let him accompany her didn't mean she had to talk. Naturally, he gave no response to her accusation. They both knew that everything about him had a double agenda. But she'd also promised to let him snoop into her life. Ergo, she was honor bound to answer.

"Okay," she said with a sigh. "I was born at…um…some hospital. I don't really know where but it was in Indianapolis. Then we moved to Lisle, Illinois. Went to school there, then the University of Illinois. Engineering, and, God, what a waste that was." She slanted a glance at him. "Great program, wrong choice. I hated it. Barely graduated, then spent fourteen months traveling."

"Over a year?"

She nodded. "Yeah. I backpacked all over. Asia, U.S., Europe. Mom and Dad worried themselves sick, but…" She shrugged.

"You didn't care?"

"I did care. But they kept sending money, so they couldn't have been too worried."

He frowned. "Or the thought of you alone and penniless in someplace like…" His voice trailed away on a croak. He was clearly imagining some of the worst places on this earth.

"Someplace like Turkey?"

His eyes shot wide. "You backpacked through Turkey?"

She shook her head. "Bus."

"I feel for your parents," he said with a shudder.

"Yeah. So do I…now. Back then I think I was just too full of myself to understand the risks." She closed her eyes, remembering the wild, wandering girl she'd once been.

"You look like you had a good time," he said. Was there an edge to his voice?

She opened her eyes. "I did, but it got lonely, you know. I made friends easily, but that's not the same thing as putting down roots." She laughed. "I know I sound corny, but it's true. I needed a home to come back to. Problem was, all I had was my parents' house. I needed my own place, my own space."

"So you came back when you were what—twenty-two?"

"Twenty-three. Arrived on Mom's birthday. God, she was so happy she cried for days. Every time she looked at me, the tears would just start flowing. Then she'd kiss me and say, 'I'm so glad you're back.' Made me feel guilty as hell."

He leaned back, his gaze disturbingly clear on her face. "You ran out of money, didn't you?"

She felt her face heat. "Yeah. Even my parents had limits. My plan had been to get home, get a waitressing job for a bit, then leave again. Mexico, I believe."

"But you didn't."

"I started babysitting for my neighbor. She had two boys, Ted and Will. Ted was a nightmare child. Will was game for anything that Ted could come up with. And Ted came up with a lot."

"Sounds awful." He was watching her closely, and his lips were tightening. What was he thinking? What she wouldn't give for a secret decoder ring to his thoughts.

"You'd think so, and it was. But I loved it." She laughed. "Go figure. I'd gone all the way around the globe to find myself. Turns out I figured it out by babysitting the kids next door."

"You just—wham—discovered that you loved kids and wanted to set down roots?" His voice was harder than she'd heard in a long time, and she frowned at him.

"You don't believe me," she finally realized. "You think I made up all of it just to paint myself as some wholesome girl." Fury lanced through her, but then what did she expect? He'd stated from the beginning that he didn't believe a word she said. "Fine. Don't believe me!"

They rode in silence a moment. She stared at the stunning scenery with a sour taste in her mouth. How did you prove honesty to someone who was bound and determined to see you as a liar? Then his voice broke in to her thoughts.

"You must have seen a lot on your travels. Tell me about those."

She snapped her head back. His voice was soft and somewhat apologetic, but she wasn't ready to forgive him. "I saw people, Matt. Good ones, bad ones and twisted, hurting, mentally deranged ones." She glared at him, making it clear exactly which type he was. "But they were all just people trying to get by however they could."

"Is that when you met the tigresses?"

She frowned, trying to remember the exact moment she started thinking about the carnal art as a life choice. "I told you. My aunt is a tigress. Mom and Dad both have family back in Hong Kong, so I've been seeing her on and off all my life." She frowned, picturing her aunt. "It's not that she's so beautiful. I mean, she is, but not in the usual way. She just gives you her entire attention, like you're the most important person in the world."

"I thought it was a sexual practice."

"It is, but it's more. It's kind of like geishas. They're sexual creatures, but they're so much more. Sure they explore sexuality—or at least the tigresses do—in every way, shape and form. But that's only a means to an end, a single step on the fuller path to a more realized you. Or me."

"You don't sound like you know what you're talking about."

She grimaced as she turned back to him. "I'm learning. To tell you the truth, half of what my aunt says is shrouded in mystical words that make no sense to me. I've already made plans to spend the summer with her at the temple, but in the meantime…"

He leaned forward. "What? In the meantime what?"

She shrugged. "In the meantime, she sent me the comb, dress and explicit instructions." Their eyes met, and she could tell they were both thinking about exactly what those explicit instructions entailed. Liz couldn't help but wonder about what might have happened if their encounter had gone on a little—or a lot—longer.

Thankfully, she had a distraction right at hand. They'd made it to the top of the first lift. They'd have to take a second to get to the black runs. She hesitated, wondering if she dared live up to her double-black-diamond taunt. She'd skied double black a couple times, long ago. When she'd been a hell of a lot more in shape.

"Want to start with something slower?" he asked, pointing to the blue run.

Yes. "No, I'm good. Unless you want to?"

"Nope. I'm good."

"Great," she returned, annoyed with herself for letting pride overrun her good sense. But she was committed now unless she wanted to confess that she wasn't nearly as daring as she pretended. Not! So with a determined push, she headed for the next lift. After all, black diamonds were a girl's best friend.

SHE SKIED AS IF SHE was born to it, Matt thought as he eyed a ten-year-old brunette flying down the run. Liz, on the other hand, moved like a broad-bottomed barge. She had all the earmarks of a self-taught skier who hadn't touched a pole in a decade.

"I'm a little out of practice," he lied as he steered her to the easiest of the black runs.

She didn't object. In fact, she looked relieved. Thankfully, he'd spent a lot of his teens on skis. He'd be able to keep up with her no matter where she went. Unfortunately, there wasn't much any one skier could do for another during that split second when fun turned into disaster. If she flew straight into a tree, all he'd be able to do was scream.

He frowned as he looked at the way she fidgeted on her skis. "You sure you want—"

"Oh, come on…slowpoke." She was already puffing, but

he couldn't tell if it was from exertion or anxiety. Neither one was good.

"Really, Liz—"

"Bye!" She was off, and he had to scramble to be a breath behind her. Sure enough, she moved like a barge... with a lot of momentum behind her. Aw, hell. She was going to crash!

"Liz!"

She turned. Snow went flying. She went flying. Her poles and skis went flying. And all of it went in different directions.

"Liz!"

He made it to her side as fast as possible, which wasn't nearly quickly enough. In his head he was already calculating times and distances for an airlift to the hospital while simultaneously trying to remember all his first-aid training.

"Liz! Can you hear me?"

She groaned as she rolled over in the snow. She was pink and flushed and probably freezing from the cold, but she managed a sheepish groan. "Okay, I confess. I haven't skied since Switzerland."

"Does anything hurt?" he asked. He'd already begun touching and squeezing every part of her.

"My pride has been obliterated."

His breath was easing as she showed no signs of going into shock. "On your body, Liz. What's hurting on your body?"

She giggled. "I know what you meant, stupid. I'm not that out of practice." She heaved a big sigh as she started to push herself up. "It was a controlled fall, Matt. I'm fine. Where'd my skis go?"

He helped her sit, his heart still racing, his gaze scanning for signs of injury. What he saw instead was her flushed cheeks, bright eyes and ruby-red lips. He could not be thinking what he was thinking. Not when he still suspected her of lying about…well, something. But apparently lust didn't care about its target. It simply lusted. *He* lusted.

Their gazes caught. He couldn't see her breasts through her heavy parka, but he'd swear every part of her abruptly tightened. Her eyes widened, and her mouth slipped open. She was thinking about their time in O'Hare. She had to be. He certainly was. He vividly remembered what she tasted like, what it had been like to stroke her sweet flesh, to feel her shatter beneath his lips.

He leaned forward. She'd licked her lips to a bright red sheen that just begged him to—

"Are you all right, ma'am? Do you need any help?"

Matt started. Some sharp government agent he was. He hadn't even heard the safety patrol come over. The kid was carrying Liz's skis and hauling out his cell phone at the same time.

"Do I need to call for assistance?"

"We're fine," Matt said with barely restrained irritation. He hadn't a clue why he was annoyed. It couldn't possibly be that he'd been thinking of acting on any of his thoughts. Not out here in the *snow*.

"Yeah, fine," Liz said. She reached out and grabbed her skis, then started maneuvering them beneath her. "Just overconfident. Not an epic disaster." The way she said it made Matt look at her sharply. Her tone suggested that something else—something like their almost-kiss—*would* have been an epic disaster. Which it would have been, of course. No way was he kissing her again until he understood who she was.

With that thought firmly in place, Matt and the kid helped her stand back up. She looked fine as she settled back down on her skis. She shifted back and forth, looking stable and unhurt.

"Thanks," she said to the kid. The boy nodded and zipped

away. Then Liz turned disgusted eyes back to Matt. "He called me 'ma'am.' Do I look like a ma'am to you?"

Matt frowned. "Just how long has it been since you skied?"

"Long enough, apparently, to have aged into my grand-mother." Then with a determined jut to her chin, Liz pushed off. This time she moved less like a barge and more like a luxury cruise liner—smooth, slow and all class.

Grinning, Matt rushed to keep up.

CHAPTER FIVE

"WHAT'S YOUR FAVORITE thing about teaching?"

Liz grimaced at her companion. After her inglorious be-ginning, she'd done great on the black run. They were now on the way back up, and the inquisition had started again.

"Here's how my day goes," she said, her temper obvious in her clipped tone. "I get up at six-thirty, shower and dress. There's time for a latte and a muffin on the corner and then…" For the whole ride up the mountain—and the ride after that—she detailed her typical day. She had meant it to be coldly clinical, but he kept interrupting her with good questions. Then she'd get sidelined into one memory or another and soon they were laughing about Play-Doh mishaps or really, really bad potty accidents followed by the worst timing ever in a fire drill.

By the time they'd made it back to the top for their third run of the day, she'd forgotten that he was spying on her. What she hadn't forgotten—in fact, had spent a lot of mental time remembering—was the way he'd seemed as if he was going to kiss her earlier. How odd that the one moment that stuck in her mind was of the time she'd been butt flat on the cold wet snow. It almost made her wonder if she should wipe out again.

But then he'd ask her another one of his really insightful questions, and she'd be lost in memory or academic debate—

he had some rather archaic ideas about education—or simple laughter. He had the most wicked sense of humor when he let it free. In fact, it'd be a perfect afternoon if only she could stop thinking about kissing him.

MATT NARROWED HIS EYES, watching Liz's hips swivel in near perfect timing as she slid to a stop at the end of the run. She was getting better, and Matt was getting hornier by the second. It wasn't just her shapely tush in those tight ski pants; it was everything about her. She had a laugh that lit up all the dark places in his heart. Her whole body seemed to glow when she talked about her kindergarten kids—even the most difficult ones. Especially the difficult ones. And when she smiled at him, he felt as if he had just won the lottery.

But it couldn't be real. Nothing this good was ever real. So he kept poking at her, using all the charm he could muster. But if she was slipping up, he didn't see it. And he would never see it if he didn't stop gazing at her like a lovesick teen.

Buck up, wussy, he silently ordered himself. *Do your job.*

He grimaced and launched into his next set of questions. "So what do you do when you're not chasing around six-year-olds? I know it's not skiing."

"Ha!" she said, as she flipped her hair out of her face. "I'll have you know I've been on a Ski-master at least, um, three whole times in the past, uh, year or so."

He laughed. "I stand corrected. Other than your vast amount of Ski-master time, what do you do? You must have a hobby of some sort."

She wrinkled her nose at him and started moving away from him toward the lift. "You know my hobbies," she said with obviously forced calm. "I'm a tigress in training."

The reminder that after this weekend she'd be spending

nights picking up men for the purpose of sexual energy absorption made him violently ill. Or perhaps just violent.

"You know I don't believe you, right?" he lied. He didn't want to believe her, but the fact was that she had been extremely open to him in O'Hare. For all he knew, she did that sort of thing all the time.

She shrugged, but the movement was tight. "Believe what you want. But if you prefer, I do have one other hobby. It's kind of girly."

His eyebrows shot up, rather intrigued. Plus, this new topic had the added benefit of steering him away from too-charged thoughts of Liz as a tigress. "I'm all ears."

"Have you ever heard of note-carding?"

He hadn't, but the concept enthralled him for the rest of the ride. Who spent hours making something you could buy at your local Hallmark store? Except it sounded absolutely perfect. And she was absolutely perfect for loving such a mundane, creative hobby.

How he so wanted to believe it was real. Except it couldn't be, because no one was this perfect.

SHE HAD NEVER BEEN so hungry in her life, but she didn't want to stop skiing. She'd forgotten how much fun it was, especially with Mr. Sexy Inquisitor by her side. But the sun was going down and her stomach was growling. And truthfully, her legs felt like Jell-O, so the prudent woman would go inside.

"One more run," she said. "You up for it?"

"Around you? Always," he said in a completely deadpan voice. But there was a rueful twist to his lips that made her think he was speaking about something else entirely. Could he...? His parka covered too much for her to see, then her stomach rumbled loudly, distracting her.

"Then I've got to get some dinner."

"That's what you said last run," he returned with a grin. Then he started the long, laborious strokes to the lift. Liz tried to follow him. Truly, she did. But Jell-O legs did not go very far. She made it about two feet, then crumpled with a gasp.

He was at her side in a moment, his powerful legs moving him around quickly despite the skis. "Problem?"

She leaned over and braced her arms on her wobbly legs. "Yeah. I'm not sixteen anymore."

He laughed. "I bet you were a holy terror in your teens."

She frowned. Did she confess the truth? "Yeah, I was a wild child. Excitement at every turn." Against her will, her voice had turned dry and the truth did indeed slip out. "No, actually, I was very boring. I got home late for curfew… twice, I think. Never got caught driving home drunk. Actually, I never really got drunk. Cheerleading was too important."

"I can see you as a cheerleader. Did you make homecoming queen, too?"

"No, but our squad had more pictures in the yearbook than the queen did anyway." She grinned. "Not that I counted or anything."

He frowned. "What about all that traveling you did? That sounds pretty wild to me."

She straightened with a shrug. "That was wanderlust, and not knowing what I wanted to do with my life." He looked at her, his gaze heavy and…deep. What was he thinking when he searched her face like that? She didn't know, and she didn't really have the energy to figure it out right then. "So…dinner?" Taking a deep breath, she forced her body to make it to the ski return area.

Naturally, he was perfectly smooth as he paced her. "Do you remember a cheer?"

"From that long ago?"

"Come on. Let me hear one."

She slanted him a sidelong glance. Was he testing her? Did he want to see how deep her "cover story" went? She shrugged. "Fine, but don't expect me to do a cartwheel or anything." She took a deep breath. "Sine, sine, cosine, sine, pi is 3.14159. Go Tigers!"

He stared at her. "You're kidding, right? That was a high-school cheer?"

She shrugged. "What can I say? I went to a geek school." She looked at him and sighed. "Benson Academy in Lisle. You'll have to guess at the year because I'm not telling."

He flushed a dull red. "I wasn't spying—"

"Yes, you were. But that was our deal. You pry, I answer, then you go to therapy." She couldn't keep the edge out of her voice. How she wished he was interested in her as a person and not as a potential spy.

She plopped down on a bench and started working off her ski boots. He settled down beside her, his body so still that she ended up looking at him. His gaze was on her, dark and unfathomable, but when her eyes traveled to his mouth, she saw it twist in self-mockery.

"I want to know about you, Liz. Who you are, what you want out of life. What makes you laugh and cry. Everything."

"You sound so sad when you say that. As if you don't really want to *want* to know."

His lips curved in a smile. "Well, no man likes to lose his reason to lust." Her eyebrows shot up at that and he abruptly grimaced. "Don't tell me that surprises you."

"No," she admitted, her face heating in a blush. "I knew that in O'Hare." She swallowed and looked at her feet rather than at him. "I just don't think you've lost your reason. Not the way you think, at least." She sighed and pushed off the bench. "Matt Walker, you confuse the hell out of me, and not in a good way at all."

He walked by her in silence as they turned in their skis and boots. But then as they waited for the shuttle that would take them back to the lodge, he touched her cheek. It was a gentle caress, but the heat in his fingertips burned straight through to her soul.

"Don't leave me hanging, Liz. How do I confuse you?"

She couldn't look at him as she answered, so she filled her gaze with the gorgeous view. But her awareness fixated on him. "Chemistry, we got in spades." She smiled ruefully. "You don't know how awesome that is for me."

He laughed. "It's not so bad on my end, either."

"I've told you about me, Matt," she continued. "I'm just a kindergarten teacher. I wear jumpers with big pockets, and I smell like markers."

"Not when I first saw you," he returned. "That dress did not have pockets—"

"That's my other side, and a recent experiment," she interrupted.

"But it doesn't fit, Liz. You sound happy with your kindergarten kids, markers and note-carding. So why train to be a tigress?"

"It doesn't fit *your* black-and-white view of the world! What, a kindergarten teacher can't ache for sex? A modern Tantric can't like kids?"

He shook his head. "I'm not the one who's black-and-white here, Liz. Don't you think you hop between extremes just a bit? You can't do engineering so you hobo it for a year? You're tired of teaching so you head off to a remote island in China?"

"For a summer! To try it out!"

He shook his head. "I don't believe it. Something's different around you. I just don't understand what."

Stalemate. She huffed as she glared at him. "I don't know how else to prove what I'm saying Mr. Paranoid TSA Agent. So I'm done." She twisted and started to walk away.

"What?" he said to her retreating back. "We had a deal!"

She spun back to him. "I've kept my part of the deal. For the past six hours on the slopes. I blew off all my 'winner events' just to do this with you. And in that time, I've talked about everything. You know more about my daily job than my principal. I gave you the names of my boyfriends up through college, and I've told you about my favorite food and favorite pizza." She turned and looked him in the eye. "Now tell me something about you."

"That wasn't our deal—"

"I'm changing the deal. Talk or I'm going to eat dinner alone."

He sighed. She thought for a moment that he was going to answer, but then the shuttle pulled up. He was extraordinarily solicitous as he helped her inside to the first passenger bench. Then he slipped up to the front seat—away from her.

Disappointment ate at Liz. Obviously, that was Matt's answer. He wasn't going to talk, so he'd left her to sit up front. She dropped back in her seat and turned to stare mulishly out the window.

"Liz, I would like you to meet my dad. He's the owner of Weekend Pass. He and my mom, Alice."

She blinked, her head whipping back to look first at Matt then his dad. "Um, hi. Nice to meet you. You have a lovely lodge."

"Naw. The lodge is just a place," his father answered. "What I got is a great son."

"Dad—"

"Even if he is afraid of snow."

Liz frowned. She couldn't possibly have heard that right. "I beg your pardon?"

Mr. Walker pushed the shuttle into gear. "Yeah, sure," he said as he eased into traffic. "Matt skis like a regular jackrabbit now, thanks to me, but let me tell you I had quite a time of it getting him outside in the winter."

Matt turned to look at her. "Don't believe a word of this."

"Ha! His sister, Carrie, got him in the face with a snowball, and after that snow was the biggest terror in his life."

"I was three!"

"Seven," his father shot back. "It was after my bit in Korea and before I was stationed in Hong Kong. My boy was seven before he saw any snow. Completely freaked him out."

"Yeah, well, it was a really big snowball. Filled with grit and stuff. And it wasn't the snow I was afraid of, it was Carrie."

"Yeah, she does have a mean throwing arm, that girl."

Matt folded his arms across his chest. "She could pitch for Major League Baseball."

Liz laughed. It was so funny to see her big, bad TSA agent with his chin tucked in, grumbling about his big sister. "Sounds like someone I'd like to meet."

"Don't worry, you will," his father answered. "She's on the warpath. Apparently, Matt ducked out of some big book signing. You turn off your cell or something?"

Matt's face turned all innocent. "Oh, was it off? I must not have noticed."

His father shrugged. "That's between you and Carrie." Then he glanced back at her. "But we'd really like some pictures of you, if you don't mind, since you missed the opening ceremonies and the book signing. Maybe at the dance tonight?"

"Sure," Liz answered, while inside she couldn't suppress a glow. Had Matt ditched his responsibilities just to ski with her? It warmed her heart even if it was because he thought she was a terrorist. Meanwhile, Matt was working to change the topic.

"You'll like Carrie," he said to her. "She's a willowy blonde—small-boned, like you—but a firecracker inside. Really athletic. She thought about pro tennis for a while."

"My kids think about a lot of things," said Mr. Walker with a laugh. "Did Matt tell you he was in the police academy?"

Liz leaned forward. "No, he didn't. Was it in Chicago?"

"No," Matt answered. "Down in Texas."

"Yeah, my boy thought he was going to be a big, bad Texas Ranger. Problem was, he'd never seen a snake outside of a zoo."

"Not true! Joey had a pet something or other. Don't you remember? He fed it mice."

"And did seeing Joey's caged corn snake help you out in South Texas?"

Matt shrugged. "Not so much."

"What happened?" Liz asked.

And so it began. With the help of Mr. Walker, she heard about Matt's childhood, a lot of which was spent in foreign countries. Not a word about his job or anything remotely sensitive—which was fine by her—but about Matt the nervous-Nelly kid who did not like eating soup but was a whiz with chopsticks, who spoke five languages but wouldn't climb a rope for fear of spiders. By the time they made it in to dinner an hour later, she was still laughing about it.

"I can't believe a kid who was afraid of snow went into the air force," she said during the dinner buffet.

He shook his head. "Well, Dad was career army, so the military was always a serious option."

"But…snow? And snakes?"

"And spiders and—"

"Soup. How can you be afraid of soup?"

"The Chinese like *cloudy* soups. You can't see what's in there until it's too late." Then he shrugged. "After that disas-

trous snake thing in Texas, I knew I had to find a way to face
my fears. A big burly drill sergeant seemed the most likely
person to force me into it. Plus the military got me to Asia in
a way I could never afford on my own."

"Don't do anything halfway, do you?"

He shook his head. "I thought I would be flying jet planes.
Not a muddy ditch or a snake to be found. Cockroaches,
however, do seem to survive everywhere. We even had races
with them."

She wrinkled her nose. "Gross!"

He laughed, the most carefree sound she'd heard out of
him all day. "You could say that the military helped bring
out my inner little boy, complete with a fondness for dis-
gusting bugs."

"Another recruitment slogan—not!" She pulled open her
crusty bread roll and spared a moment to appreciate the hot
yeasty smell. "So how did you end up with the TSA?" she asked.

She knew the question was a mistake the minute she said
it. One mention of his current job, and he closed up like a
clam. His eyes canted away and, wham, they were back in
suspicion territory. He answered casually, of course. "Oh, it
just seemed to fit," he drawled. "I had skills from the air
force, was no way, no how going back into the police academy, and with my fondness for all things Asian—" He winked
at her. "I ended up as a specialist in the TSA."

She frowned at him. "Just how much of a fascination is
there with all things Asian?"

"Asian history major in college, only average with the languages—Mandarin, Cantonese, Korean—but I'm an ace re-
searcher, and I do love finding obscure stuff in old scrolls."

"Like the history of Chinese tigresses?"

He grinned. "My sex cult fascination began in my ado-
lescence." Then before she could ask more, he shifted topics.

"So what did you think of being a kindergarten teacher your first year?"

They were back to the inquisition. She looked at him, her gaze steady as she fit the pieces together. "So you just slid your nervous-Nelly fears into more adult terrors."

His eyes widened in surprise, but he didn't deny it. "Terrorists are real, Liz. Liars, frauds and people who stalk TSA agents actually exist."

From his tone she guessed he had firsthand experience. "Matt," she began, but he shook his head. He wasn't going to open up more.

"Talk to me about something mundane, Liz," he said softly. "No inquisition, I swear. I just want to learn about you and your life. Maybe I'll remember what regular people do in their day-to-day lives."

There was no way she could refuse, especially when she heard the desperation in his voice. Some part of him obviously knew he'd gone off the deep end. Unfortunately, she had no idea when überparanoid Matt would return. It didn't matter. While he was being nice, she would do what she could to support him. So she started talking again. But as she launched into the story of her first parent-teacher conference, she noticed that he really hadn't set aside his suspicions. He might have stopped thinking of her as a terrorist, but he was now watching everyone else in the room. Just a casual perusal, but he saw everyone and everything.

"Something wrong with that guy over there? The one in the smoky-gray jacket?" she asked. It was the third time he'd stared at him.

Matt shook his head. "Nope. I was just studying the tattoo he has on his neck. I get flashes of it when he turns his head. But the woman at the table behind me is another journalist." He motioned to one of the lodge's security guards. A whispered conversation later and the woman was being firmly escorted out.

"I guess you're still working, huh?" she said.

He shook his head. "I'm here to help out my parents with their opening weekend. But I can't help it if their security sucks and there's no one else to step in."

She was about to say that a journalist was not a national threat, but a beleaguered-looking blond woman rushed up to the table. She was wearing the lodge uniform and looked ready to spit nails. "Thank God I've found you," she gasped. "You were supposed to be at the signing with Maddy. She threw a royal tantrum when you couldn't be found!"

Matt frowned and leaned back in his chair. "All I promised that woman is that I would be here this weekend." He spread his hands. "I'm here. I didn't say I'd babysit—"

"You did, too!"

"Nope."

The woman glared. She leaned in and drilled him with an icy stare. Nothing. Then she abruptly rolled back on her heels with a huff of disgust. "You were a hell of a lot easier to intimidate when you were four."

Matt released a bark of laughter. "Liz, meet my sister Carrie."

Liz smiled. "The snowball queen."

The woman grinned. "You betcha!" Then she turned back to her brother. "You got a pass this afternoon, little brother." She glanced curiously at Liz, but then seemed to pull herself back from asking. "But as of this moment, you're back on duty. I need you soothing ruffled feathers on that Lov woman. No, ax that. Our parents need you." She glanced significantly at Liz. "He wouldn't do squat for me."

Liz could see the denial forming on Matt's lips. She wasn't sure if he was going to refuse to help his parents or claim that he would die for his sister. Either way, it didn't matter. Liz needed a break, so she reached out and touched his hand. "It's okay, Matt, go do your thing. I'm tired anyway." It was a lie of sorts. She wasn't physically spent at all. She was weary of Matt's constant suspicion. So she pushed up from the table with false regret.

He stood up, as well. "There's a dance later. We could—"

Carrie interrupted. "The dance is now, brother dear, and Maddy wants to do it with you."

Liz smiled. That was a double entendre if she'd ever heard one. "Go do your duty as a good son," she said. "I'm going to take a hot bath." Then she paused just before leaving. It was time to make things clear to him—for both their sakes. "This has been a very fun day, Mr. Walker. I trust you got everything you needed from me."

"Liz—" he began, a flash of panic in his eyes.

She ignored it. "Enough, Matt. I'm tired. If you don't believe me now, you never will. Now I trust you will leave me alone to enjoy what's left of my holiday weekend."

She waited, her brows arched in a pointed look. In the end he finally gave her a curt nod of agreement. "Enjoy your stay, Ms. Song."

It was what she wanted, or so she told herself. Fighting the sadness, she stood and walked away. It was almost worth the pain just to hear his sister's comment.

"Good Lord, you are one big screwup, aren't you?"

"I'm defending the country!" he snapped back, and that was the last she heard as she made it to the elevator doors.

CHAPTER SIX

"I'M DEFENDING the country!"

Liz collapsed on her bed, Matt's last words echoing in her head. Lord, he thought he was being noble. Too bad he was both right and wrong. He was protecting the country, and his job had completely consumed him, leaving nothing left of Matt, the man.

And how she missed Matt, the man! She'd seen glimpses of him all day. She relived every moment of their time together, focusing on when he let a piece of his soul free. When he laughed or—best of all—when he bantered with his family. If only she could get him to stay in that place, the human place free of suspicion and doubt. Then they might really have something. Then she could see hanging out with him for more than just a gloriously anonymous moment in O'Hare.

But how? What exactly lurked beneath his surface? Was there a clue for her in something he'd said? And what caused those moments when his expression turned excruciatingly sad? What did they mean?

A dozen times, she started up from the bed to go find him at the dance. She'd even promised his father that she would make an appearance as guest of honor. But at the last moment she would stop herself. Despite everything, she was sure that a part of Matt still suspected her of something nefarious.

Why in the world would she want to spend *more* time with a paranoid jerk? But he wasn't really a jerk. Which meant…

Which meant her thoughts were going in circles, and she had to escape them. Since every muscle in her body was beginning to ache, she decided to search for the hot tub. Her swimsuit was a very tasteful black one-piece that nevertheless showed off what curves she possessed. She put her hair in a bun and, for the first time in two days, left the dragon/tigress comb behind. She wasn't looking for sex, just hot, steamy water. Unfortunately, one look into the Jacuzzi area told her that *her* goals and everyone else's didn't quite meet up.

The tub was a large round bubbling pool filled with Maddy Lov hangers-on, most of them men. They greeted Liz's entrance with cheers and offers of whatever mixed drink had made them completely out of control. She thought about turning tail and running, but she was a modern woman, right? And with all the distraction from Matt this afternoon, she'd completely abandoned her tigress-in-training goals. What she had here was not a tub full of leering men, it was a hot tub of potential men to explore.

Lifting her chin, she slipped into the least overstuffed side of the pool. It rapidly filled. Two men pressed up against her from either side. One of them was the camera-tie guy from earlier. She tried to squirm away, but there was nowhere to go. Even her pointy elbows earned her little more than room to breathe.

"Guys," she said. "I'm sore and tired and just want the heat."

"I'll heat you—"

"Don't say it!" she snapped. "God, please do not say a corny line here."

The camera-tie man blinked bloodshot eyes at her. "But I can make you hot," he whined.

"No, no, you can't," she answered in her best stern-teacher voice. Then she grabbed the other man's wandering hand as tightly as she could. "And neither can you."

They both backed away with sullen looks. Unfortunately, after a few more slurps from their drinks, they were back for more. With reinforcements. Liz tried to glare them away, but drunk, horny men were much less easy to control than hyper-active six-year-olds. Go figure. She was about to give up and go back to her room when she noticed a dark figure hiding in the hallway shadows. A dark and well-proportioned male leaned against the wall right behind the towel stand. Truthfully, he could have been anyone with broad shoulders and a trim waist, but this person stood absolutely still.

Matt. She knew it in her bones. He was watching her, waiting for her next move in some devious terrorist plot. She grimaced, abruptly disgusted with the man for being so stupid. So he wanted to see her as some lying criminal? So be it. She could play down to expectations. She thrust her breasts as forward as she dared and grabbed the arm of camera-tie guy.

"Hey!" she squealed. "Aren't you the guy who got kicked out this morning? That's so awesome that you got back in! How'd you do it?"

The guy immediately puffed himself up. "Well, I'm like a supersecret agent guy, you know. You have to be, in my line of work."

She smiled playfully at him, though her attention remained on the shadow outline of Matt. "Oh, I never thought of it like that. So, you're…um…good at getting into places where you're not supposed to be, huh? I'd bet you're really, really good with a camera, too."

"I've been compared to Ansel Adams," he answered. Then he laughed with a fairly honest show of false modesty. "Not favorably, mind you, but compared!"

She tilted her head. "Well, the comparison is enough, right? I mean, like any good ad exec knows, it's all in the way you slant it."

"Right!" He leaned forward, his gaze wavering between her eyes and her cleavage. "Have you seen my work? I mean, I've made it into *People.*"

"Oooh!" she cooed. His arm slithered around her waist, and she was pulled way too tightly into the cloud of his very bad breath. On the upside, though, Matt's silhouette had just taken a half step forward. Time to go in for the kill—quickly, preferably before she had to inhale again. "You are exactly who I need to talk to! I need some pictures of an airport. You know, inside an airport."

"Inside? Like inside where?"

She patted his rather underwhelming chest. "Those details will come later."

"But airport security is a whole different—"

"I can pay," she said. "And I've got this TSA agent completely under my control. He'll do whatever I ask."

"Really?" he said, his eyes narrowing. "Then why do you need me? I mean, if he's under your control and all."

Good question. Apparently, camera-tie guy wasn't as stupid as he appeared. "Well…" she wheedled. "I need some really, really good pictures."

"Oh?" he asked as his other arm slipped around her thigh. "I don't believe you," he said. "You see, I've been watching you."

"You have?" she squeaked. She had thought that with her arms between him and her, she could push off his chest and break free. But this guy spent his career being strong-armed by security guards. He wasn't nearly as weak as she'd thought. Meanwhile, his breath was not getting any better. "I mean, you don't?" she gasped.

"Nope," he said as he started to stand, leaning over her with his larger weight.

Well, wasn't this great? Even the paparazzi knew that she was just a kindergarten teacher, but big TSA agent all but had her up on charges. Now what was she going to do? Especially since she couldn't legitimately pray for Matt to step in and save her. She had, after all, just set this little charade in motion.

"You know," she said, her voice too high to sound stern. "I think I've had enough heat, for the moment. I want to go back to my room now." She pushed against him, and—like magic—he released her. Or so she thought. What he really did was shift to stand up from the pool, one hand still wrapped tightly about her upper arm. Though she was able to take a single deep breath, she was still locked tightly in his grip.

"Good idea," he said. "I'll escort you." He gave her a wink. "Don't want any evil TSA agents mucking up the works."

Actually, that was exactly what she wanted. Unfortunately, one desperate glance over her shoulder told her that her stalker TSA agent had just disappeared on her. A moment of crushing disappointment gripped her, but then more immediate problems reasserted themselves. She had to get free of this guy now. All by herself. "No problem at all," she said to both herself and Mr. Grip-Of-Steel. "He's under my control, remember? And, um—" she tried to lift her arm free "—you're giving me bruises."

"I know." He grinned as they both stepped free of the pool. "I work out."

"Great," she drawled, not in the least bit pleased. "Course, so do I," she said as she twisted her arm around his, managing to break his hold. Unfortunately, in the time it took her to break his hold there, his other arm had snaked around her waist. Octopus, much? She winced as his hold around her belly tightened. Oh, this was not going well. "Look, just stop it. I don't want— Umph!"

She'd thought his breath was terrible. His kiss was even worse.

OKAY, SO MAYBE LIZ wasn't a spy. No one could be that bad at lying without being legitimate. Unless she was faking being bad at it....

Matt closed his eyes and tried to get a grip. He knew she wasn't a terrorist spy. He'd known possibly from the very beginning, but there was something about her that just drew him. And something about her that was off. Liz, the kindergarten teacher, and Liz, the tigress, just didn't fit together, and he couldn't seem to rest until he found out why. Unfortunately, that meant that he was standing out in the hallway stalking her like a dweeb of the first order. And worse, she'd spotted him.

He'd seen the very moment when she'd noticed him lurking behind the towel rack. Yeah, sure, he was on the other side of the glass wall trying to look like a nobody waiting in the hall for somebody unimportant, but she had seen him anyway. Her eyes had narrowed, and her body had gone stiff. Then she got an angry thrust to her chin and turned to the nearest sleaze-bucket. It wasn't easy to hear through the glass wall, but he'd made out every "I have a TSA agent under my complete control" word. Which meant, of course, that she had not only seen him but was now baiting him.

He knew he should just give up and go to bed. He obviously sucked at being incognito. If Liz had wanted to be with him, then she would have hung around after dinner instead of coming here to hot-tub around with the nearest jerk. And now his presence was pushing her to take terrible, stupid chances with drunk paparazzi. He should leave. If she was a tigress novice like she claimed, she would be able to handle one drunk photojournalist. He even made himself step down the hallway out of sight.

But then he rounded the corner, stomped in through the double glass doors, and was on the bastard like a bad dream. There was no collar to grab, but there was a roll of fat just above his Speedos. Matt took a great deal of pleasure in pinching it and pulling backward as hard as he could. The guy squeaked and whipped around with a drunken punch. Matt blocked it easily, then cocked the bastard's arm high enough to elicit a keening wail. Then Matt looked at Liz. He wanted to say something—anything—but he couldn't find the words. So he turned his attention to the easier problem.

"Didn't I throw you out earlier?"

"I got a reserv— Aieee!"

"It's been canceled," he said. Then he firmly and rapidly walked the man out of the pool area, out the front door and down to the parking lot. He paused long enough to let the SOB grab his shoes and haul on some clothes, but that was it. It was dangerously cold—especially for a wet, nearly naked man—but the walk wasn't far and Matt let him put on his coat and shoes before they hit the elements.

Not so for Matt himself. He didn't even have on his sports coat, but he liked the cold. It put certain things into excruciating clarity. Things like: Liz looked fabulous, all wet and flushed from the hot tub. Just as she'd looked fabulous as she attempted moguls that were too much for her. She'd gone tumbling into the snow and come up laughing. All investigations into Liz's past had come up with exactly what she'd claimed: a kindergarten teacher enjoying a fantasy ski weekend. But most important, the cold made him realize that just thinking about Liz made him harder than a rock despite the plummeting temperature, and that his sister was right: he was an asshole of the first order because his suspicions had royally screwed up what might have been good.

He stood in the parking lot even longer after that realization. He watched the hot-tub jerk start his car and drive off while Matt's ears went numb. But even then, he couldn't move. This is what he'd come to: standing in the freezing cold, protecting his parents' investment and fantasizing about a woman he still couldn't trust. Except, of course, that he could because she was nearly exactly what she seemed. Except, he couldn't because he still wouldn't let down his guard.

In short, this was *his* problem, not hers. What the hell was wrong with him?

Then he felt a scarf wrap around his head. A heavy coat descended across his shoulders a second later. He hadn't even heard the person approach, but he knew—he hoped he knew—who it was. A moment later, Liz spoke, her voice low and husky and a little bit trembly from the cold.

"He's gone, you know. And you're going to die of cold."

He glanced back at her. "You were wet. And where's your hat? Do you know—"

She pressed a finger to his lips. "Shut up, macho man."

He did.

"Thank you for rescuing me. You're still in desperate need of therapy, you know. You were stalking me, and I'll bet my last dime that some part of you still thinks I'm a terrorist spy. But you're awful sweet and I like your parents, so it'd be bad for you to freeze to death."

She fell silent, obviously waiting for him to speak. But she still had her two fingers on his lips and no way was he going to do anything to dislodge them. Except maybe to kiss them. So he did. He pursed his lips first, but then he opened his mouth and stroked her with his tongue. She gasped, and he felt her tremble against his lips. Within seconds he was licking

her palm, caressing with his tongue while her breath shortened into pants. By the time he started working his way up
to her wrist, though, he realized that not all her quivering had
been from him.

She was freezing. "Let's go to the hot tub," he said.

She groaned. "God, no. I'm never going back there."

Matt shook his head. "Not that tub. I've got one all my own.
Back in my private cabin." He looked up at her and wondered
if she understood his unspoken thoughts. If she went back
with him now, they would end up in bed together. There would
be no stopping him from having her. She had to know—

"Okay."

He blinked. "Are you sure? Do you understand—"

She abruptly flattened herself against him and wrapped her
arm around his neck. He bent forward easily, leaning down
to kiss her, but she stopped him just short of his goal.

"Swear to me."

"What—"

"Swear to me that you'll go into therapy. Damn it, Matt, I
think your job is eating you alive."

He dropped his forehead against hers. "I swear," he said.
She was right. He needed to seek some sort of counseling.
"Now come to bed with me."

"I thought you said hot tub."

"That, too." Then he closed the distance between their
mouths. He couldn't hold off any longer. He kissed her as if
she was his one lifeline to sanity. Maybe she was. It didn't
matter, so long as he got her into his bed right away.

He didn't even break the kiss as he scooped her up in his
arms. She didn't weigh more than most of the luggage he inspected. And she obliged him by wrapping her other arm around
him and keeping the kiss going in spite of her new position.

They made it to his cabin and then his bedroom. Not fast

enough, but what in his life ever came on time? Or in the way that he expected?

"Quit thinking!" she ordered into his mouth.

Excellent advice…

IF EVER THERE WAS a fantasy come true, this was it. He was even carrying her! Liz couldn't help but surrender to the magic of the moment. There was a desperation in his touch, a need for her that surpassed anything she could have imagined. He wanted her. He thought she was sexy and dangerous and all those wonderful descriptors that could never be attached to Liz Song, kindergarten teacher. That alone sent her libido into overdrive. Add to the mix that he was one helluva sexy man and every touch became like fire.

Her mouth was already tingling from the way he nipped at her lips. But when she opened for him, he swooped inside and the flames ignited. Burning heat followed his every touch, and she was soon gasping from the searing hunger of it all. She arched her head back, trying to catch her breath, but that only gave him room to kiss and stroke her jaw, her neck, and—oh, yes—that wonderfully sensitive spot right behind and below her left ear. She shivered in his arms.

"Are you cold?" he asked.

"Heavens, no."

"Me, neither."

He had to jostle her a bit as he fumbled for his keys. She helped as best she could, but he wasn't going to let her stand, and she didn't truly want to leave his arms. He was just fitting key to lock when she grabbed his face. "Please, please tell me you have condoms."

A slow smile spread across his face. "A whole box, if you want."

She grinned. "I want. Oh, yes—" Her words ended on a

gasp as he finally got his door open. She had a brief view of a sterile little cabin. Warm, masculine colors surrounded her, as if someone had spent time trying to make the place homey. But there was little feel of him here. "Don't come here much, do you?"

"Hmm?" One-handed, he pushed her sweatshirt up over her head. She'd had little time to get dressed after he walked camera-tie guy out the door. She'd thrown on a sweatshirt and jeans over her bathing suit. Sneakers had completed the outfit until she'd met Matt's mother at the front door. Alice had been the one to push his coat into her hands. Then Liz had walked out into the cold to bring Matt in.

"This suit makes me crazy," he murmured once the sweat-shirt was tossed on the floor. "It made me insane to watch you in that tub wearing this. I wanted to break every bone in those guy's eyes."

"I don't think there are bones in the eyes," Liz answered, ridiculously pleased by his compliment.

Matt didn't answer. He was kissing his way down her shoulder, taking the suit strap with him. He had finally stopped walking when they made it to his bedroom. She didn't even see the decor except for the large bed in the center. Then he let her stand unsteadily on her feet as he peeled the top of her suit down to her waist. But he didn't take it past her hands. So she stood there, her arms pinned to her sides while he kissed his way down to her breasts.

Her skin was chilled here from the damp swimsuit, so his tongue felt especially wonderful as he warmed a long, mean-dering path to her right nipple. Then he took it into his mouth, swirling it around and sucking it in a way that made her knees give out.

"I'm going to fall," she murmured. But what a way to tumble…

"I've got you," he said, and he did. He gently guided her down to his bed. And while he spent his time with her other breast, his hands worked at the fastening of her jeans. Within moments she had slipped out of the confining shoulder straps, and he had begun to shove both suit and jeans down past her hips. He did all this while teasing her nipple in an unrelenting current of pleasure.

"Matt," she gasped. "Matt, get naked, already. I can't take much more of this."

He lifted up enough to grin at her. "Your wish is my command."

She grabbed his head and pulled it to her mouth. Then she thrust her tongue inside him with a boldness she'd never before dared. His hands spasmed where he clenched her hips, which only pushed her to further fierceness. Only when he groaned deep in his throat did she release him. "Consider yourself commanded," she said. Then she leaned back and got to watch him strip naked.

His hands were shaking, but no more than hers. His movements were jerky and rushed, but there was still time to see gloriously sculpted muscle, a sweet dusting of chest hair and his full, proud sex. What she liked most, however, was the way his butt muscles shifted in a truly delicious pattern as he shoved down his pants.

"You have the most perfect ass," she blurted.

He canted her a startled look. "Really? I never thought about it." Then he twisted as if to look at his behind, simultaneously giving her a full view.

"Liar!" she shot back. "You have thought about it. Or more likely, dozens of women have already told you."

He turned back to her. "Dozens. Hundreds, even." Then he leaned in, bending his knees as he began to crawl up on the bed. "Which makes my ass completely and totally boring.

Whereas yours…" He suddenly swooped down and flipped her over. She squealed in surprise, but that didn't stop him. She was facedown and he was stroking her butt with two large, firm hands. "Yours is absolutely fascinating."

She'd never been massaged there before, certainly not with the deep strokes he was giving her. And certainly not with his thumbs sliding deeper and deeper between her thighs. She couldn't help herself. With his every stroke, she lifted her butt higher. He shifted until he stepped between her feet. His knees widened hers open, and soon she was on display before him.

She wanted to say something, but no words came out. Only a deep groan and a hum through her whole body. He wrapped one of his hands around and slid it deep between her legs. He stroked her—once—and she sobbed. Her thighs were quivering, and she pushed up on her hands just to get closer to him. It didn't work.

He suddenly disappeared. She twisted around in shock just as she heard the foil packet rip. He was putting on a condom. Lord, she'd completely forgotten about that, and even so it was killing her to wait while he put it on. He fumbled once and cursed. She released a weak laugh and their eyes met. It was a long full moment of shared need.

"I want to go slowly, Liz. I do—"

"Get it on and get going. That's a command!" she responded.

He grinned and, thankfully, finished with the condom. Then he climbed up on the bed, pushing her forward on all fours, angling her slightly as he got behind her. Then she felt him wrap himself around her, his hands on her breasts as he lifted and caressed her. She trembled at the sensations, but it wasn't enough and it wasn't where…

He was pulling her backward. She maneuvered upward as his hands slid to her hips and—oh, yes—between her legs.

He stroked her expertly then. Up and down, up and down with one hand while the other guided her backward. With an easy, incredible, amazing slide, she settled right onto him. He filled her utterly and she arched at the wonder of it all.

His lips were on her shoulder, kissing and laving around her neck. "Look," he said. "You're so beautiful."

She opened her eyes, startled to see that she was looking at the large, full mirror of his dresser. There she was in lustful display, her back arched and his hands on her breasts. Her legs were spread and his cock was embedded deep within her, glistening wet as he slid out and back in. Was that her, so open and bold? And was that him, his eyes dark and passionate as he watched her move on him?

Then he groaned as she lifted and lowered again. His hand slipped between her legs, but she hardly needed the help. She leaned forward to give him better room to move and then she reveled in his powerful thrusts.

"Grab hold," she murmured.

He did. His gripped her hips and slammed into her. One more… Oh, yes!

Her climax exploded through her. His breath shuddered across her shoulder as he slammed into her again and again. And then they were shaking together, rippling and soaring in ecstasy.

Bliss!

Eons later, she collapsed in his arms. Joy lapped at her senses, and she snuggled deeper into his embrace. He lazily kissed her neck, then nuzzled that spot behind her ear. She could not imagine a more perfect moment, and she murmured her delight. Then she felt him rise up just enough so that he could whisper into her ear.

"I believe I promised you a hot tub…."

CHAPTER SEVEN

THEY MADE LOVE in the hot tub, their movements slow, their pleasure leisurely. Though they started with the bubbles churning the water, he quickly turned it off. "I don't want anything distracting me from the feel of you," he said. And then he kissed her, stroked her and slowly filled her.

That's when it became beautiful. Not because of the steady thrust and withdraw, but because he spent the whole time looking straight at her. Their eyes met during the first thrust, and their gazes held long past the final ripple. At first it felt uncomfortable, but then she rapidly came to love it. It was as if he saw all of her and adored it. No matter what he did to her—or she to him—he wanted to see her face.

And now, hours later, she rolled over in bed to find him lying on his side looking at her with that same total attention.

"What do you see?" she whispered.

"You."

She looked back at him, held his gaze and felt his presence ripple through her consciousness. "No," she murmured to herself as much as to him. "You couldn't see me. Not so soon. No matter how much it feels like you do—you don't."

His expression wavered and he frowned. "Are you trying to make me suspicious of you again?"

"What? No!" She lifted up on her elbow to face him on the same level. "God, Matt, you are so confusing! Why can't a statement just be a statement? We've just met. You couldn't possibly know me as deeply as it feels."

He shrugged, his expression evening out. "Maybe. Doesn't matter. I go with my gut."

She grimaced. "Is that the same gut that had you thinking I was a terrorist spy?"

His skin flushed a dull red, but his eyes never wavered. "I thought you bore watching. And you did." He paused. "I'm sorry. I'm really, really sorry for thinking you were a criminal."

She swallowed, wondering if she dared risk pushing him to open up. Then she remembered she was her new bold, adult self and what the hell. He needed to face the answers much more than she needed to hear them. "Why are you so suspicious, Matt? Is it really just the job?"

"Nope." He abruptly flopped backward to stare up at the ceiling. She followed, sitting up to see him more clearly. But it was too dark to see anything, so she abruptly switched on his bedside light.

They both flinched at the sudden brilliance, but she'd come to a conclusion. "We don't have a lot of time here," she said as she glanced at the clock. "We're heading toward dawn on the Sunday of my fantasy weekend, so let's skip straight to confessions. I'm Liz Song, a boring kindergarten teacher." She took a deep breath and decided to plunge right in to the full story. "I went to a funeral a few days ago. A friend of my mother's, but I've known her all my life."

She glanced down and saw that she had his full attention. His eyes were calm and focused, and she didn't see any judgement in them. That gave her the strength to continue.

"She was a kindergarten teacher, just like me. A nice woman with friends, just like me. Her death was kinda sudden. She got sick and passed on as well as these things can go, but…" She shook her head, not knowing how to continue.

"What?"

"She was in her late fifties and really well liked. A nice, nice lady who will be missed. In fact, she could be me, thirty years from now."

He arched his brows. "You saw your future in her?"

She nodded. "Yeah. Just a boring old kindergarten teacher. She was even buried in a light-blue dress with big pockets. Not quite a jumper, but close." She looked down at her hands. "I started wondering what happened to the Liz Song who backpacked the world? The daring woman who explored Turkey by herself? And then I thought about my aunt."

"The tigress?"

She nodded. "She's sexy, exotic, and when you're with her you feel her presence. It's not that being a teacher is bad. Far from it. But my aunt is so much more. So very, very much more."

"So you decided to become her? Isn't that a bit extreme?"

She shrugged. "Maybe. But I've been thinking about it for a while, and I'm not quitting my job, just planning a summer."

"And picking up men in O'Hare." He grimaced. "Isn't there some space between teacher and anonymous sex—"

"It's not always about that!" she snapped. "But I had to do something extreme, something to really snap me out of where I was. And picking up a guy in O'Hare was just one possibility."

He abruptly surged up. It was like a roll that came up and over her until she was suddenly flat on her back beneath him. She felt the power in his body, the press of his groin, and the white-hot heat that was all him. Part of her responded immediately. Part of her went wet and gooey, and she nearly wrapped her legs around him right then and there. But they'd already gone well beyond anonymous sex, and this time she wanted more.

"Matt—" she began.

"Don't do it," he rasped against her neck. "It's too dangerous. You don't know who you'll end up with. You don't know—"

She pressed against his shoulders even as she shivered beneath his lips. "Matt. Matt!"

He lifted up, his eyes dark and haunted.

"I've given you my story. Now it's your turn." His expression darkened, but she didn't give him any time to object. "My choices are for tomorrow. Today—right now—I want to hear about you. How did you end up suspecting a kindergarten teacher of international terrorism?"

He stared at her, his body immobile, his expression unfathomable. And then with a sigh that came from deep inside him, he nodded. "Okay," he finally said. "You deserve that much." So with a groan and a last lingering push against her, he slid to the side. He kept his legs entwined with hers, and one of his hands idly stroked her shoulder, but she wasn't going to get distracted.

"Matt?"

"Paranoia pays," he said. "That's the crux of it. Every one of my promotions has been because I noticed things, I saw plots where everyone else just saw unusual. I asked a question where someone else didn't bother."

She nodded. "But that's on the job—"

He shook his head. "Only once. All the other times I was off duty but still paying attention." He sighed. "That's what I do. I look for bad things everywhere."

"And you usually find them." She twisted to look him directly in the eye. It took him a moment, but eventually he met her gaze. "But lots of people are conscientious. There has to have been a trigger point."

"Like the funeral for you?"

"Yes." Then she poked him in the shoulder when he didn't answer. "So what happened?"

His gaze slid from her face down her neck to her chest. "You're not getting me to confess with that view," he said dryly. It took her a moment to realize that the sheet had slipped down and she was lying beside him naked to her waist. And wasn't that a measure of how comfortable she'd become with him? He reached out to stroke her, but that way held no answers at all. So she reluctantly batted his hand away and pulled the sheet up to her chin.

Then his cell phone buzzed. It was on the nightstand by the bed, and she waited as he thumbed it off. He didn't even look at the display, but he wasn't spilling his guts, either.

"Talk," she ordered. "And that's a command."

He smiled, but the expression was more wry than happy. "It's actually a rather boring tale. I met a woman."

She waited, but he didn't say anything. "Not enough, Matt. Spill the whole truth."

"And nothing but the truth?" When she wasn't drawn into his banter, he sighed. "Yeah, okay. Well, she was perfect. She was daring, beautiful and loved all the things I did. And she was Korean. We went to dinner together, then to great violent movies, then snowboarding. I should have suspected something from the start. No woman wants to see *First Blood* twice in the same week."

Rambo twice? Yeah, he should have guessed. "So she was perfect, huh?"

He flashed a look at her dry tone, and she smiled with false innocence. Then he looked back over her shoulder at the wall. "I thought I'd died and gone to heaven."

"No," she said softly. "You thought you'd found what your parents have."

He swallowed. "Yeah. I guess I did."

"She was playing you? For what?"

"I can't tell you the details. I'd just gotten my last promotion, was head of security for an entire wing of O'Hare." He fell backward then and threw his arm up over his eyes. "Yes, she was a criminal. Yes, I was her chump mark. And, yes, I nearly lost my career over it, mostly because I still believed her. My boss and his boss had to lay out all the evidence piece by piece in front of me. It took them two hours and still I didn't want to believe it. Not until I saw her in custody. I looked her in the eyes and saw the real her. The conniving, manipulating, heartless bitch deep inside her, and I knew I'd been a fool. A total and complete fool."

Liz didn't speak. Her throat was closed up. How awful to have your heart and your country betrayed in one hideous swoop. No wonder he was torn up. No wonder he didn't trust any woman—tigress or not. She wanted to curl into his side and hold him tight, but that wouldn't help him. He didn't need her tears on his shoulder just then. He needed to lay his fears out in the open. "Did you...did you help her? I mean before you knew?"

Beneath his covering arm, he nodded. Then he took a deep, shuddering breath. "She played me good. I never overtly gave her anything. Never talked about anything I thought was sensitive or classified, but we were together for months. Things slip out. And she was a master at getting me to talk."

Months! The ache just got worse and worse. "You never suspected?"

His arm slipped down and he stared sightlessly at the ceiling. "Not a bit."

"I'll bet the sex was good, too, huh?"

"Yeah, it was great." He lay there in silence, a slight frown on his face. Then he abruptly turned to look directly at her. "But it wasn't really good. I didn't realize it at the time. I mean I'd never...I mean I was younger then." He grimaced. "I thought I was in love, and so I worshipped her body, you know."

Liz flinched. She knew. She'd just felt worshipped head to toe—multiple times—and it hurt a bit to have him talk about this terrorist bitch in the same way.

"But it wasn't real," he said. "I didn't realize it then, but now…looking back…there was always this condescension in her reaction. I mean she enjoyed it. We both did, but I always wondered afterward if she really liked it. I think I felt that she was holding something back, which of course made me more desperate to open her up, so I was more desperate to please…" He sighed. "You get the picture."

She did and it broke her heart. "So you've learned. You made a mistake—you're human—and you won't be fooled again."

He laughed in a tight, dry way. "Yeah, I learned. But not until this moment." He reached up to stroke a finger along her cheek. "Not until you."

She blinked, shuddering at the fire he ignited in her from just a single stroke. "What?"

"Don't you see? That's what I was thinking when I was looking at you. I felt the difference. I *know* the difference now. You are so open in sex. Everything is out there without hesitation or restraint."

She shifted, feeling uncomfortable and a bit ashamed. "Yeah, well, I guess you release my inner slut."

He touched her shoulder. "No, no, you don't understand. It's wonderful. It's honest. I think I'm in love with you."

She stared at him. Truthfully, he looked as startled to say it as she was to hear it. But then she kept staring at him, and his gaze didn't waver. He obviously thought it was the truth. The problem was she so desperately wanted to believe him. Except she knew it couldn't be true. He'd created an image of her that couldn't possibly be real—first as a tigress, then as a terrorist spy, and now as Miss Wholesomely Open. None of them were the real her.

Eventually he'd realize that she was not daring, not exciting, not any of the things that she'd been during this fantasy weekend—or at least not yet. And until she made the decision to become a tigress completely, no way could she hold his attention, much less stay on either of his pedestals—the sensual tigress one or the wholesome teacher one.

But when she tried to say all those things, they wouldn't come out. She wanted to be his perfect woman forever, but she simply wasn't. And the realization hurt. It hurt so badly that she lost all control of her tongue.

"Rebound, much?" she drawled. Then she winced at the coldness of her own voice. "I mean, Matt, I really like you, but you're a real mess right now." That wasn't what she meant at all! "I mean you think I'm this tigress woman and the sex is amazing and so you think…you believe…"

"I don't believe," he said in a tone almost as cold as hers. "I feel. I feel good with you, and I haven't in so long."

"You've been hurt badly. I can't imagine how badly. I mean, it's so raw." She was babbling and she couldn't stop herself, but the truth was that she was the one who was feeling raw. "It's not like I really know you, either. I mean this was my experimentation into the world of Tigress Tantrism and you've done everything perfect including saying you… saying…"

"That I love you."

She closed her eyes, fighting the tears. "It's not real. None of this is real."

He didn't respond for a long moment. And once again, the room was filled with the buzz of his cell phone. She heard him silence it with a curse.

"Liz, look at me, please."

She did. His face was open and vulnerable, and it scared the hell out of her.

"What if it is real?" he asked. "What if what we feel for each other—"

"But it's not," she interrupted. "I'm not even remotely who you think I am."

He straightened up to face her eye to eye. "Of course you are!"

She touched his lips, pressing her fingers against him for one last caress. This was killing her, but she knew that she had to get out now before she lost herself in pretending to be someone she wasn't. "What did all your research say about tigresses? Are they the hang-around-and-marry type?" she asked.

She felt him go very still against her hand. She saw his eyes widen as the life died out inside them. Then he slowly, resolutely pulled her hand away from his mouth. "Are you saying you're going to do it? You're going to commit to the temple in Hong Kong, to having sex with countless men, to knowing every erotic secret available to womankind?"

She nodded. She wasn't even sure why except that it was a convenient lie to give him. It gave her a legitimate reason to escape without completely crushing him. Or her. Except he did look devastated. And she felt as if she was about to shatter.

"Liz—" he began, but she shook her head.

"I…I need to go. It's all been too much." With that she grabbed her clothes and fled. Her hands were trembling as she pulled them on. He was right beside her, yanking on his own clothes and talking the whole time.

"We need to talk about this, Liz. You can't just run away."

"I'm not running," she lied.

"Looks that way to me," he snapped as he yanked a T-shirt over his head. The fabric hugged his muscled torso and she started to cry. The tears just flowed down her cheeks. God, he was a beautiful man. "Liz," he groaned.

She shook her head. "It wasn't real," she repeated. "I'm not who you think I am." That was a lie. She was the one who didn't know who she really was. She was the one who needed to find herself first before she started talking about love with anyone.

He reached for her, but she flinched away. She headed for the door, but he got there first, holding it shut with one hand. "Look," he said. "I know this went too fast. Hell, I'm still reeling. You've got to be, too."

"It's not that. I mean, I am, but—"

"Just listen a moment, okay?"

She nodded, unable to manage anything else. At least the tears had stopped for this second.

"It's been too fast. Neither of us knows what we're saying anymore. Just promise me you'll think about it."

She released a pathetic whimper. She'd probably be thinking about this for the rest of her life. He pulled her into his arms, wrapping her tight. She couldn't stop her body from melting into him as her tears started up again.

"I don't know who you are!" she said against his shoulder. She really meant she didn't know who she was, but she couldn't get anything else out. When she managed a shuddering breath, when she was able to pull herself together enough to stop sobbing like a toddler, she pushed herself out of his arms. It was hard, and she didn't want to go, but she was an adult, she reminded herself. And adults knew that ripping off a Band-Aid was easier than doing it inch by horrible inch.

"This might be real," he said. He stroked his thumb across her cheek, his touch excruciatingly tender. Then his cell phone went off again and he cursed.

"That's real," she whispered as she pointed at his phone. Then she fled.

A HALF HOUR LATER Liz was packed and ready to go. She'd spent the entire time both dreading and hoping that Matt would come banging on her door. But he didn't, and so she was packed. And now…now it was dawn, and she had way too many hours before her flight. What to do? What to do?

She could always sob into her pillow for a while. Or call Sarah and moan. Or stare at the wall and remember. Not!

She needed to get up and out. She needed to stop thinking and do something. Surely she could avoid Matt in a resort this size. After all, she was the guest of honor! There had to be all sorts of fun things she could do.

There weren't. She ended up wandering the hall and thinking way too much about the meaning of life. It didn't help that she felt too sore to ski, too anxious to sleep and too nervous about running into Matt to do much but feel at loose ends. At least she discovered what the urgent summons on his cell had been about. Turns out a drunken photographer had broken into the storeroom of unsold Maddy Lov books, drawn kissy hearts all over the copies, then passed out. Matt was embroiled in sobering up the man, making him pay for the damage and soothing the horrified starlet.

Liz watched a whole hour of the drama from a dark corner between the towel stand and a large fern. Terrorists, drunken photographers and starlets—even aside from the spy plots, Matt had an exciting life. Liz slunk away about the time Maddy and the photographer were angling to set up a private photo shoot with Matt. What did Liz have that could compete with lounging about naked with Maddy Lov?

"Snow sculptures!"

Liz blinked as an apple-cheeked woman wearing an apron came rushing forward. Mrs. Alice Walker from last night, the woman who'd given Liz a coat to put on Matt.

"Snow sculptures!" the woman cried again as she grabbed Liz's hand and started tugging her to the back.

"I beg your pardon?"

The woman turned around with a huff of disgust. "Look, we got pictures of the opening ceremony, but you weren't there. We got photos of Felicia and that Lov woman. We were going to do something at last night's dance, but you didn't go. And then you and Matt…outside…well, anyway."

Liz felt her cheeks heat. "Please say there aren't pictures of that."

"Well, not official ones. And we need them!" Matt's mother grimaced as she gestured out the window. "You're awake now, we've got photographers coming out of our ears, and we've got snow. Lots of snow. So please, sweetie, do an old woman a huge favor and participate in our last official event—sculpt something for the cameras, and then I'll drive you to the airport myself!"

Liz laughed. What else was she going to do? She allowed Mrs. Walker to bundle her into a lodge jacket and fuzzy gloves, then shove her out the doors. Fortunately, a sparkling extra foot of snow had fallen during the night, so there was plenty of material to work with. But what to sculpt? And how?

She never thought she'd be grateful for years of clay art. She had intended to push together a simple snowman, but within a few moments of beginning the basic shape, her artistic side began to push through. No simple snowman would do for her. She was intent on snow woman extraordinaire!

It didn't turn out that great. She wasn't going to win any sculpture awards, but two hours later, she had a plump snow woman complete with Mrs. Walker's apron and a pink fuzzy hat. Then beside her snow woman lounged a sleek, feral tigress. The cat had decidedly humanlike features, sticks for whiskers, and a little bit of cleavage that somehow did not look odd. When Liz finally stepped back, she realized she was looking straight at the two pieces of her own personality right there for everyone to see. On the one hand, aproned kinder-garten teacher. On the other, a wild, sensual beast of a snow kitty.

"No subtlety there," she murmured to herself.

"I like it," returned a low voice. Matt, of course.

She spun around to see him lounging in the doorway with two mugs of coffee in his hands. He extended one to her, and she took it gratefully, heating her face with the steaming brew, but she didn't drink. Instead, she looked into the depths of the black liquid and realized what she wanted to say to him, though it took her another long moment before she had the courage to face him.

"You can't be in love with me," she said softly, "because I don't know who I am yet."

His gaze flickered from the snow sculptures back to her face. "I can't hang around and watch? See where you end up?"

She shook her head. "Don't you think you've got a little self-discovery of your own to work on, too?"

He didn't answer in words. He simply held her gaze for a long, long time. But in the end, his head dipped in ac-knowledgment. A second later he turned around and walked inside.

CHAPTER EIGHT

THE NEXT THREE MONTHS of self-discovery taught Liz two very important things. First, self-awareness took a really long time. And second, talking sex-cult philosophy with her aunt could be extremely fascinating but ultimately rather frustrating. Liz did not want to go out patrolling for men, either with or without her magic sex combs. In fact, she really had no interest in sex with anyone except for her missing blond TSA agent.

Well, he wasn't exactly missing. They'd been corresponding every day via e-mail since she'd left his parents' lodge. She'd heard all about the Sunday-morning wrap-up with Maddy Lov. Apparently, sometime after brunch the celebrity hooked up with the drunken photographer and the two rode off in her limo, much to the delight of Mr. and Mrs. Walker. More important, she'd heard about how Matt chose to take a leave of absence from the TSA to help his parents at Weekend Pass.

And here it was nearly three months later. The winter storms were freezing rain instead of snow, but the wind was just as cold. She had started living for her e-mail weeks ago, and now the man she'd been fantasizing about suddenly appeared in her classroom door. Yes, she'd just finished putting away the kid scissors when she turned around and saw Matt standing right there. Naturally, she was dressed in a shapeless blue jumper and had clay in her hair.

"You look good," she said as her pulse kicked into high

gear. He wore soft jeans that hugged his rear and a turtleneck that made him look a little like Bruce Wayne. But what really made her smile was the way his eyes didn't hop around checking out the environment. His mouth looked soft and sexy, not pinched as it had been a few months ago. "You look relaxed," she realized.

He smiled, a slow seductive movement that set her lips tingling. "You look like the hottest teacher on the planet. God, what I wouldn't give to be one of your students," he drawled.

She flushed. "I think you're a little old for color-changing markers."

He shook his head, strolling into her room and instantly removing all the oxygen from the air. She wasn't able to do anything—not even put down the cardboard cutouts of the alphabet she had in her hands. How she had dreamed of this moment, and yet, here she was—shapeless jumper and all.

"Liz—" he began.

She held up her hand and the letters *M* through *Q*. "Before you say more…" She took a deep breath. "Before you *do* more, I have something to show you."

He straightened, a wary look in his eye, but she was determined. She put down her cutouts and crossed to her desk.

"I've been carrying this in my purse for the past few months, just in case."

"In case of what?" His voice stayed in the mellow place that she'd only heard their last night together. It was deep and sexy, and it stole her breath away.

She held back her fears by a force of will. "In case of this. In case you showed up out of the blue and wanted to—"

"To take up where we left off?"

She nodded. "You have to understand." She pulled open the drawer that held her purse, then fished inside for the photo wallet. She turned and held it out to him. "It's my aunt,

Tigress Ting Wu. She sent me the combs because of some tigress calendar. If you want full-on exotic, she's the one. Or there are younger women at the temple." She straightened, flipping her clay-matted hair out of her eyes. "I am still exploring it, but I don't think I can ever fully give up teaching. I, um, I really like being a kindergarten teacher."

He flipped the photo book closed after hardly a glance. "I know."

"No, Matt. Really look." She opened it up for him, forcing him to see her aunt. The woman was the epitome of sexuality in every man's exotic fantasy. Lush lips, rich black hair, a waist that was as supple as a willow reed, and eyes—God, her eyes were her best feature—they could look right into your soul and draw out your deepest, darkest fantasy…and then fulfill it. She was everything that Matt was looking for when he talked about a tigress.

Liz took a deep breath. "I've been talking a lot to her about you." Then she flushed. "Well, more about why that encounter with you in O'Hare was so special. Why did I like it so very, very much?"

His eyebrows rose, but he didn't speak. She didn't blame him. It had taken her months before she figured out her own answer.

"We weren't pretending then, we weren't even thinking. We were just ourselves having a glorious physical moment. It was only later—when we started thinking—that things got confused."

He shook his head. "You mean when I got suspicious. When I screwed up." He rubbed a hand over his face. "I started out thinking you were unusual, but then you were on my flight to Colorado and I just went off the deep end. I thought you were stalking me."

She nodded, but her words contradicted him. "I did my share of baiting, too, of feeding into your suspicions."

He stepped forward, his eyes serious but calm. "Don't try to excuse me, Liz. I was insane." He took a deep breath. "My therapist says that often happens when a man falls in love. Add in job burnout, and I should have been locked up."

She arched a brow. "You're in therapy?" Despite his almost daily e-mails, he'd been noticeably silent on that issue. He'd written about his parents and the lodge and how much he loved the work there. Nothing about seeing a professional counselor.

He glanced away. "Yeah, well, I didn't want to say unless it took. I'm talking to someone who specializes in my kind of case." He looked back at her as if searching for some affirmation in her. "It's basically job burnout, but in a rather, um, paranoid way."

"You don't say," she drawled.

"You *did* say," he returned. "And I needed to hear it." Then he shifted his stance, but his eyes held hers. "I'm sorry. I'm so sorry about how I treated you. I didn't know how to be anything but suspicious. I'd forgotten how to believe."

"And now?"

His lips curved at the corners. "I believe in you, however exotic or girl-next-door or whatever you want to be. I believe in you. In me. Maybe—" his eyebrow quirked hopefully "—maybe in us?"

She smiled, warmth and excitement making her heart beat triple time. "Maybe…" she said.

"So can a burned-out agent kiss the sexiest woman on the planet?"

"You're okay that I'm not really exotic?"

He grinned. "My therapist thinks I've got an unhealthy obsession with teachers."

She blinked. "Really?"

He laughed. "No, just you." Then he stared at her. "Aw, hell," he groaned.

He kissed her. He grabbed her arms and pulled her flush up against him. His mouth was hot, his tongue was aggressive, and his hands…oh, my, his hands were slipping from her shoulders to her waist to settle low on her back as he gripped her. She almost squeaked in alarm as his hands shaped her bottom, drawing her tight against his full groin. But somewhere along the way, her squeak became a throaty purr. As he plundered her mouth, she raised a leg and began stroking the inside of her thigh against his soft jeans.

Then he broke away with a gasp. "You kill me, Liz."

She swallowed, wondering if that was a good thing or bad. But one look at the hunger in his eyes made her so hot she couldn't breathe.

"But I have to ask…" he continued.

Her heart lurched at his tone. He sounded afraid.

"Are you going to train to be a tigress? Are you going to Hong Kong? I mean, I want you to explore whatever you need to explore, but I don't think I can handle you stalking other men. I don't know—"

"Tantrism isn't just about anonymous sex. In fact, in some ways it's not about sex at all. There's a ton of meditations that can be done all by yourself. And even more with a single partner. In fact, there are a lot of married Tantrics."

His eyes lit up at that, and in it she saw hope. "Are you still going to spend the summer in Hong Kong?"

She nodded. "But I thought…you know…maybe with a partner. He'd have to be blond, though. Because my first partner was blond and I just can't get him of my head. Or my heart."

He grinned. "I'm blond. And I love Hong Kong." Then he sobered. "I was messed up and an ass in Colorado," he said. "But I'm getting better. I know what I want, and damn it, Liz, I want to spend a whole lot more time with you wherever you are. Whatever you're doing."

"I was an idiot, too. I ran." She straightened enough to face him eye to eye, but he didn't let go of her, and she didn't relax her hold on him. "So, yes, Matt. Yes to now, to tomorrow, to however long you want." Then his mouth was on hers, and the world fell away for a time. A wonderfully long time.

"Can you leave school?" he asked when they separated for a moment.

She smiled and slowly disentangled herself from him. "Done for the day." She grabbed her coat and purse, loving the way he watched her every move as if she were a dream that was about to disappear. "And, um, Matt…"

"Yeah?"

"I've still got the comb…somewhere on my body. Maybe right next to my tiger-print thong."

His expression shifted, and his eyes seemed to light with blue fire. "Is that a challenge?"

She smiled and began to saunter to the door. "You'll have to catch me to find out." Then she laughed and ran. He followed a split second behind her.

Within moments she was well and truly caught.

* * * * *

WEEKEND MELTDOWN

Anna DeStefano

* * *

To Vicki and Jade, my fabulous partners in crime.

And to our editor, Stacy Boyd—a Southern girl at heart, who will always find a glass of fresh lemonade awaiting her at my home.

You ladies are tops in my book!

Dear Reader,

My stories almost always come to me as characters first. And they are almost always set in the South. So, naturally, I seemed like the perfect fit to write a wild, winter read about the grand opening of a chic, romantic Colorado ski resort! Who knew?

Well, Stacy Boyd did, when she called asking if I'd like to join the fun. And, of course, she was exactly right. What a blast!

Such a lush, new setting was an exciting change— for both me and my career-obsessed heroine Felicia, who was more in need of a "Weekend Meltdown" than anyone I've ever met. Felicia simply *had* to get over losing the scumbag love of her life. With a little pushing, and one irresistible, irritating hunk of a hero to spar with, she's soon on her way to leaving her ultraconservative comfort zone far, far behind.

And speaking of heroes. Tony Rossi... He's all business. He's got no time for meltdowns or fashion-obsessed, hard-partying women like Felicia. Even if she has a poet's soul and her kiss is hotter than anything he's ever known...

From their first searing kiss, about five seconds after Felicia arrives at the lodge, to their final passionate embrace, this unlikely couple-in-the-making will enchant and bewitch you. You'll find yourself rooting for them every step of the way. Enjoy!

Anna

P.S. I love to hear from readers and fans. Please visit me at www.annawrites.com, and win prizes during my regular contests and book-release parties on my blog, www.annadestefano.blogspot.com!

CHAPTER ONE

"YOU'LL HAVE THE romantic-getaway reputation you're paying me for." Tony Rossi flashed Tom Walker a confident smile. "I guarantee it."

A whoop heckled him from the lobby's oak bar, where rock star Maddy Lov was holding court. Lov was A-List Productions' problem for the weekend. Not Tony's, thank God. But the lodge's floundering PR firm had figured what better way for Weekend Pass to grab Internet tabloid attention than to leverage the latest pop princess *du jour* for all the viral press they could get.

The ensuing chaos was dangerously close to pushing away the romantic couples the Walkers wanted drawn to their lovely jewel in the mountains.

"A 'Weekend of Poetry and Romance,' huh?" Walker asked.

The theme had been his and his wife's brainchild. So was the online sonnet contest, the winners of which were the weekend's guests of honor. Now Tony's job was to promote his ass off at the eleventh hour, to counter A-List's missteps. He was a one-man show, an insanely expensive PR gun for hire, and he never let a client down.

Walker's attention shifted to a buxom ski bunny prancing by. The party girl's snowsuit was unzipped so close to nirvana, Lov's contingent of paparazzi had her under round-the-clock surveillance.

"Well." Tom clapped Tony on the shoulder. "You're our closer. Get it done!"

With a glad-I'm-not-you glance, he headed behind the Tucson-inspired registration desk and disappeared into the lodge's offices.

"No luck to it," Tony reminded himself.

Luck had revealed its mercurial ways to him at a tender age. He'd made his own success ever since—screw the odds against him. Weekend Pass might be a mess, but it was his highest-profile account yet. His professional future was riding on delivering on the promise he'd just made.

Maddy Lov had been watching Tony's exchange with his anxious client. She smiled from the epicenter of her sea of admirers, as if she'd heard every word and relished the trouble her girls-gone-wild approach to ski resort chic was causing Tony.

The day kept getting better and better.

Liz Song, the author of one of the contest's winning poems, was snowed in somewhere *not* Colorado. The second contest couple, whom Tony had wanted settled in before that afternoon's welcome festivities began, was MIA. At least Felicia Gallo and her guest were on their way in from the airport.

She and her amazing poem were the real deal the Walkers needed to show off the lodge. And Tony, and the schedule of events he'd created and subsequently leaked to the press, was determined to make sure that's exactly what happened.

He'd gladly left classic literature behind after high school. But poetry was the language of lovers. And twenty couples were arriving at Weekend Pass, expecting the luxury poetry weekend the Walkers had dreamed up. A romantic vibe he wasn't letting Lov's full-tilt-boogie mania tarnish.

The Walkers would have their dream, despite A-List's bungling. He'd organized a flurry of expensive, last-minute publicity on every available travel magazine Web site. Couples bookings had quickly surpassed the singles coming to "Party with Lov." The sonnet contest winners were going to romance the socks off the guests. That's just the way it was going to be.

He jerked at his lapels, resettling his black wool sport coat on his shoulders. Or as settled as the jacket could look, considering the distressed finish of the shirt he'd thrown on beneath it—without a tie. Appearance was an essential part of the PR game. He did his job and kept the wrinkles at bay. But dawning a conservative shirt and tie every day wasn't going to happen. Neither was getting excited about the arrival of a hard-core romantic like Gallo.

But as he headed for the carved wood and stained glass doors that opened onto the lodge's portico, he caught himself smoothing the front of his tailored slacks.

Damn, man!

Felicia Gallo's coming with the date the Walkers urged her to bring. Get her settled, give her the weekend itinerary, then get back to Maddy Lov before one of her groupies torches the lobby!

Except, all day, while Tony had been keeping an eye on Maddy's boom-baby curves, it was Felicia Gallo's soft features he couldn't get out of his mind. He'd studied her head shot as he'd designed and distributed a flurry of press releases. Soft waves of dark-blond hair. Sparkling, princess-blue eyes. Her smile was sugar sweet.

So why did it make him think of wicked sex and satin sheets? Why did he keep imagining the warmth radiating from her expression smoldering into nuclear waves that could melt even a frigid Colorado January?

She made him think of sex and drama, and he never let his sex life get anywhere close to dramatic.

Standing at the curb, Tony checked the time on his Tag Heur Manaco. Then he checked himself. Gazed at the snow-covered landscape he'd spent the past three weeks hyping to anyone who'd listen.

Felicia Gallo, and the warm intelligence dripping from every word of her poetry, was arriving any minute. He would work her pedigreed business success and romantic heart to the resort's advantage. If a part of him wanted to sample any of her *warmth* for himself, he'd deal with it. The same way he dealt with the few things that ever managed to surprise him. He'd ignore the impulse to indulge in weak feelings that would only bring him trouble, then he'd get back to work.

A speck on the frozen horizon crept closer—one of the Town Cars Tony had reserved for the weekend's VIPs. The corporate lawyer with a lover's soul would be inside, along with the man she'd invited to share her romantic prize package.

But the poet from Ms. Gallo's poignant biography picture didn't emerge from the luxury car. Out teetered a high-maintenance fashionista instead, wearing four-inch heels and the kind of severe style he'd seen firsthand on Madison Avenue.

Nothing turned Tony off more than the brittle kind of bombshell striding toward him.

Her hips swayed as if she was on a mission to captivate every man in sight—because she knew she could. Gallo's smile zeroed in on Tony, as if she were playing a role, and his part in her production was to do her bidding. She wrapped a hand around the back of his neck, meeting him eye to eye—a woman who had no intention of being ignored.

Then she leaned in to whisper, "Hello," with both her wicked perfume and a husky, sensual voice.

Turned off or not, Tony's body instantly *hello*ed back.

He found himself sipping the taste of champagne from her

lips, groaning while she licked, then sucked, at his tongue. Her bottom wiggled beneath the vibrant purple of the catsuit-cum-snowsuit she'd worn with her skyscraper stilettos.

Actually, a firm cheek had found its way beneath each of his palms.

His hands skimmed across the softest female flesh he'd ever touched, and kept right on skimming, encountering not the barest trace of panties.

Damn!

His fingers clenched, and her breath hitched. A rough sound that brimmed with wicked promise. Then she jerked away, shock vibrating through her body, her pupils expanding, her head slowly shaking.

Tony's body screamed for more. A spark of reason argued that his hands were better off in his pockets. His palms settled the matter by pulling the enticing globes of her ass closer. She squirmed, but in the next second her body brushed his hardness, and her resistance evaporated. She burrowed her head against his neck, her teeth nipping. Lost in the rush, he settled her tighter against his straining flesh and lost what was left of his mind.

Wrapping a fist in her wildly curling hair, he pulled until he had her lips again. Her taste.

"Good Lord, Fe," a masculine voice chided. "Get a room before you devour the beautiful man for dinner."

Tony opened one eye, then the other. The woman in his arms panted, her legs sliding down his thighs and calves until the toes of her outlandish shoes touched the sidewalk, then the heels. A wave of uncharacteristic protectiveness had him pulling her head to his shoulder, shielding her face, while she pulled together whatever wits she still possessed.

It took him longer than it should have to do the same. Then he took stock of the man the wanton in his arms had arrived with. A man dressed as expensively, and as vividly, as Felicia Gallo herself.

Tony made his hands drop to his side.

"I suppose," he rasped, "that this is the muse for your words of enduring love. The *date* you were encouraged to invite to share your romantic getaway?"

"Wh-what?" Afternoon sun shone fire red in the deep blond of Gallo's hair. Her features softened in confusion. Something of the woman in the picture Tony had studied emerged.

"Your new boy toy wants to know if he has competition for the weekend." Gallo's flamboyant friend winked, his gaze skimming from Tony's laced-up dress shoes to his untamable hair. "And I want to know if you plan to share the wealth."

A strobing flash of light momentarily blinded them.

"Kiss her again, Rossi," demanded one of the photographers constantly cruising the lodge. "That was hot!"

More flashes followed, attracting the attention of passersby who otherwise might not have noticed Tony's insane reaction to the kind of female he wanted nothing to do with. The nexus of his *wholesome* PR plans for the Walkers.

"Rossi?" The hard-core sex goddess who'd been mauling him blushed from the diamonds winking in her earlobes, to the tantalizing cleavage spilling from her top's plunging neckline. "Omigod!"

CHAPTER TWO

"YOU'RE DRUNK, Ms. Gallo."

Felicia was drunk all right, swimming in a golden, sensual haze. But *not* from the few glasses of expensive wine she'd imbibed between the airport and the lodge. Blinking, she tried to clear the dazzling glare from her vision. Glare that had nothing to do with camera flashes.

"Ms. Gallo?" prodded the sinfully sexy man holding her.

His mouth was near her ear, so no one but her would hear. The wash of his breath over her sensitive skin wrecked her balance even more.

"I'm per-perfectly fine," she insisted.

And just to prove it, she didn't shamelessly throw herself at Tony Rossi again. No matter how badly she wanted to.

This was all Willard's fault. All of it.

"Of course you're fine, darling," insisted the mastermind behind her humiliation. Willard hitched a supportive arm under her elbow, then batted his lashes at Rossi's Steve McQueen glare. "I'm sure this fine specimen has a valet at his disposal, to fetch our bags away while we get you checked in."

"Everything's exactly as described in your prize package." Rossi stared down the photographer who was still snapping away, until the poor guy gave up and got lost. "If you think you can manage, Ms. Gallo, I'll help you register, then take you to your suite so you can…rest. I'm sure you'll want to be at your best for tonight's activities."

And Felicia's best clearly wasn't good enough at the moment.

"Steve McQueen" seemed to have forgotten his enthusiastic participation in her Willard-inspired naughtiness.

"No fear this weekend," Willard had insisted ever since they'd jetted away from Manhattan. Willard and her, and the brand-new wardrobe she'd purchased to ramp up her battered sexual confidence. "No holding back."

She was a goddess, she reminded herself. Not a woman so wrapped up in her high-powered career that her fiancé had dumped her for the coat-check girl at Willard's East Village trattoria, Viva!

Too kiss-wobbly on her platform sandals to make another scene by stomping away—but determined to remind Rossi that it had been *his* tongue inspecting every inch of her orthodontist's handiwork—Felicia sidled closer. She ran an acrylic nail down the yummy fabric of his expensively distressed shirt. Batted her own heavily massacred lashes.

"I think you'll find that I'm always at my best, Mr. Rossi."

Willard's wicked chuckle was a dear thing, no matter how pissed she was at him. She let him lead her into the lodge. He'd pay later, when they were alone and she'd reclaimed enough brain cells to punish him for baiting her into embarrassing herself. But for now, she needed his sass to feed her own.

Head high, adding extra sway to the undulation of her hips, she tossed her hair over her shoulders and left a frowning Rossi at the curb.

"Well played, my dear." Willard led her into the luxurious lobby that wasn't exactly the tranquil, Gatsbyesque scene she'd expected. "How come you never put that weenie, Phillip, in his place like that?"

"You promised never to say that name to me again." She fake-smiled through her teeth at a passing couple.

"Well, your Big Mistake of 2007 didn't deserve you. And you haven't deserved beating yourself up over the asshole for two years. How did it feel, propositioning the first hunk of a man you saw, then leaving him in your dust?"

"Mortifying." And unsatisfying.

It had to be the sparkling wine they'd found waiting for them in the Town Car, making her crave more.

Two glasses?

Right!

That's why she felt so woozy.

Rossi, the real culprit behind the buzzing in her brain, had a backside as amazing as his front. And of course, she couldn't keep her eyes off him. He flanked the bellman and their cart of bags as far as the elevators. Then he headed Felicia and Willard's way, oozing such intoxicating intensity, she realized she was panting for air.

"Why did I let you talk me into this?" she whined.

"Because it's a freaking dream weekend, girlfriend. And you're going to take advantage of every second. You're more in need of a winter meltdown than any woman I know—including myself."

"You just want to swap lip gloss secrets with Maddy Lov." She ignored her friend's wounded moue. Out of the corner of her eye, she tracked Rossi's approach, and every amazing thing his body did to the tailored slacks he wore. "This farce is about *you* storing up tidbits to share with your divas in Manhattan."

"You're the only diva I care about this weekend, love." Willard caught her tugging at the fur-trimmed neckline of her top. His eye roll destroyed the last of her champagne's golden glow. "You're wearing Cloe played with Blahnik. Very shut-your-mouth-I'm-not-an-uptight-lawyer-freaked-out-about-being-the-main-draw-at-the-party-of-the-season! Now own it. Take some chances. Let me see you slinking back into your lawyer's shell, and mama's going to slap your hand—or some other part of your anatomy."

The threat came with another affectionate wink.

Felicia laughed.

Even being annoyed with Willard called to creative, exuberant parts of her. The parts she usually draped with classic Chanel suits and St. John dresses, when what she secretly lusted after was Prada and Cavalli.

"How are we doing?" Tony Rossi asked at her side.

Speaking of lusting…

"Never better." She focused on her surroundings, rather than the impulse to run her hands through the guy's caramel-brown hair again.

Romantic couples cuddling by firelight would have been a bit much, she supposed. But Weekend Pass's aura was more like Manhattan's high-energy dating scene than a quaint venue for the poetry readings, elegant dinners and the wine and cheese cocktail hours described on the lodge's Web site. Willard was right. It *was* going to be the party of the season.

He drew her to the registration desk, an arm draped supportively about her waist. A cheer went up from the lobby's wood-paneled bar. Gales of laughter followed. Felicia glanced toward the mayhem, the skin on the back of her neck tingling at Rossi's nearness.

Maddy Lov was one of her father's law firm's top celebrity clients. At one firm VIP function, Felicia had watched Maddy drink men twice her size under the table, daring her besotted admirers to keep up. And Rossi thought *Felicia* needed a nap so she could rein in her inner wild child? The kind of alluring wild child she'd let her ex-fiancé's rejection convince her she'd never be.

Suddenly fed up with years of weak second-guessing, she left Willard to handle things with the registration attendant and turned on Rossi. She thrust out the plunging neckline of her halter top and smiled her best siren's smile.

"This place isn't *exactly* how things were described in the prize package," she challenged. "I must say, I'm a little disappointed."

"I know exactly how you feel." Rossi stopped checking out her cleavage and consulted what looked like a vintage watch. Then he took in her over-the-top ensemble again, making her even more determined not to let him know how unsettled she felt in her risqué fashion. "Why don't I show you to your suite, while your *friend* finishes taking care of the particulars. I'm already late to help set up for the welcome reception, and—"

"No need." Willard took her hand and kissed her fingers. "But once I help this lovely creature freshen up, maybe you and I can get better acquainted."

Rossi's answering annoyance went no further than the chill in his gaze.

"I'll look forward to it." He sounded as if eating dirt would be more appealing, but his congenial smile was rugged perfection. "Especially since Ms. Gallo's due to recite her grand-prize-winning poem after dinner."

"I'll try extrahard to make it a memorable moment." She pushed past Rossi, annoyed by this all-business side of him. Where was the passion and lust from before? "And I'll look forward to your critique afterward."

Critique? Willard's raised eyebrow asked as they neared the elevator.

Eat shit! she smiled back, feeling Rossi track their progress toward their third-floor suite. Once inside the elevator, she turned and met his gaze, shivering.

What kind of man made even blatant disapproval look sizzling hot?

The doors whooshed shut. Willard watched her rub at the chill bumps skittering up and down her arms.

"The first man you saw wasn't the old guy at the concierge desk," he quipped. "That's a plus."

She punched him as a reward. He'd dared her to seduce the first unsuspecting guy she saw. And, like a fool, she'd played along, just for fun. What could it hurt?

The elevator slowed, then stopped.

"I just sexed up the most obnoxious man in the place," she reminded her friend as they exited. "The guy's acting like he's ready to toss us both out, when *he* was crawling all over *me* outside. I'm an asshole magnet."

"You need to relax and enjoy the ride. Stop worrying. I wouldn't mind finding someone that 'obnoxious' of my own to spar with this weekend."

"He's all yours." Felicia needed someone less…*everything*.

"Ah, good." Willard ushered her toward their suite. The cart with their things on it was positioned outside the open door, the bellman still unloading. "See, darling. We get to stay the night, despite you shamelessly making the most fantastic man I've ever seen your love slave."

"I did not make Tony Rossi my love slave!" Felicia turned into the suite in time to catch the shocked expression on the bellman's face as he screeched to a halt in front of her.

"I'VE LOST MY MIND," Felicia insisted several hours later, at the welcome dinner's cocktail reception.

"It's the altitude." Willard smiled up a passing waiter, then shamelessly checked out the guy's butt.

"It's your bad influence." Felicia straightened and re-straightened her fuchsia Versace minidress.

"Enjoy." He eyed the nonexistent back of her outfit. "You fit in perfectly here. Forget about Rossi. It's just dinner, Fe."

"Yeah, and it was *just* a few sips of wine in the car. Just a dare to loosen me up. *Just* a kiss."

"No, honey. *That* was straight-up sex with your clothes on. Whatever crawled up Tony Rossi's ass after you lifted your spell on him, that man's the hottest thing in pants I've seen in a long time—and you had him melting all over you."

Yeah, except who had been melting whom?

Willard had egged her into entering her sonnet in the contest in the first place, after he'd shown up at her door late one night on his way home from clubbing. She'd been in her rattiest guy pajamas—a pair of her ex's, actually—and that's when she'd finally gotten it. Her best guy friend had a sexier wardrobe and dated hotter men than she had in years. It had been time to stop wallowing in the efficient, business side of her personality that Phillip had found so boring. Time to mine for passion, before the well dried up.

But a secret part of Felicia wondered even now if it wasn't already too late.

"Don't throw in the towel!" Willard insisted. "I won't hear of it. Men will be crawling all over you and your couture tonight, gay or straight. If you're not going to work this fabulous makeover for *you,* the least you can do is be my arm candy until I land myself a live one."

It *was* a beautiful dress. One of her favorite purchases for the trip. When she'd tried it on at Bergdorf's, she'd felt a forgotten piece of herself coming back to life. The same passionate piece that had kicked into high gear downstairs, in the arms of a man who'd left her feeling giddy, then completely dismissed once he'd decided she didn't suit his PR plans.

The judgmental bastard!

She was a guest for the weekend. She could quit this scene

anytime she wanted. But that would mean walking away with her designer tail between her legs.

Was she really going to prove her ex and her own subconscious right, by conceding that leave-them-panting sexy had never been her talent and never would be?

Hell, no!

She snatched a glass of champagne from a passing waiter's tray and raised the flute to salute Willard.

"Let the games begin!"

TONY HAD HEARD OF men buzzing around a woman like bees near a honeypot. And he'd spent the past twenty-four hours running interference between Maddy Lov and the hard-partying crowd that trailed after her. But he'd never seen anything like Felicia Gallo, wearing Versace's finest as if it were a second skin. Or the effect she was having on the rising testosterone level in the banquet room.

She'd wrapped herself up in his mother's favorite designer. She was wearing matching heels so high, every step she took without mishap was a triumph of fluidity and grace.

Versace was on the wilder end of the designer spectrum. But it was a must-have wardrobe staple for the adventurous socialite. Or so Tony's mother insisted every time she spent a fortune on the label's newest line. Too bad Gabriella Rossi had never showered the same attention on her husband and only child. Not that Tony's father had minded.

The two still lived the same jet-set lives as when they'd relegated Tony to boarding school at too young an age—alternating their time between Aspen and Milan, Florence and Madrid. New York and Paris during fashion season. L.A. for the awards shows, which were the few months out of the year during which Tony sporadically saw them.

Their empty relationship was the envy of everyone they

met, and his mother's glamorous, sophisticated facade was their crowning, glittering glory. A facade the "romantic" Ms. Gallo had obviously honed to her own advantage. Gone was Felicia's skintight purple snowsuit, which he doubted had seen the first flake of winter ice. In its place were swirls of severely cut color and silk that invited a man to smooth his hands over every restless curve and valley.

She'd collected quite a bevy of admirers throughout the cocktail hour. A roomful. And her friend, Willard, dressed to kill in what looked like Armani, was scoping things out for himself. Actually, he was headed Tony's way!

"She's really something, our little poet, isn't she?" The man held up a copy of the program Tony had carefully designed, complete with a border of hearts and flowers that reeked of romance.

Tony had spotlighted Felicia's sonnet on the cover page. He glanced at the poem again, trying to match it to the woman sipping a cocktail and flirting with the besotted men standing on either side of her.

"She's…unexpected," was the best reply he could manage.

Wickedly complex and appealing in a primal way that he couldn't take his eyes off. But, unexpected or not, she was nothing more than a principal player in his business plans for the opening. A means to an end, that it was his job to control.

"She's not the only unexpected distraction tonight." Willard sighed in response to Tony's scowl. "You're gorgeous. A young Paul Newman, but rough around the edges. You clearly have a sense of style most heterosexual men refuse to own. But you're straight as an arrow, aren't you? Pity."

Willard was a straight-shooter. Right up Tony's alley. And he seemed to have a precarious hold on Tony's star poet's leash.

"It doesn't matter what I am." Or what he wanted outside

the job. Tony's gaze tracked the way the curve of Felicia's bottom rounded against the hint of a skirt that finished off her dress. "I'm working. When I'm working, focusing on anything or *anyone* else is out of the question."

"Uh-huh." Willard was watching Tony watch Felicia, his knowing smile almost as wicked as his friend's ass.

"Listen—" Tony turned his head to make it clear that he didn't have time for whatever games Willard wanted to play.

But out of the corner of his eye, he saw Felicia stumble—right into the waiting arms of one of the bachelors panting after her.

"Shit!"

CHAPTER THREE

TONY HUSTLED ACROSS the dining room, Willard at his heels.

Felicia tried to disentangle herself from the overly helpful guy whose hands were sliding all over her curvy figure. A figure that Tony had no business feeling proprietary about.

"I think you'd better find someplace else to be," Tony said to the man.

"I'm just helping the lady," the guy blustered, a few drinks past sober.

"Very noble of you—" Willard glanced at the man's name tag while Felicia struggled for freedom, her complexion blanching to paper white "—Stewart, is it? Let me introduce you to Kaitlin, Stewart. She's just the kind of woman to appreciate such a gallant gentleman…."

Felicia drooped as her savior was led away. Willard's backward glance made it clear what Tony's job was. As if Tony needed an excuse to put his own hands on the woman wilting of embarrassment before him.

"Let's sit you down before you—"

"Fall down?" She reached for him.

Reluctantly.

The flirty fashionista's spunk became a surprised blink as their gazes locked. Their fingers touched. Laced together. Hers shaking. His own not exactly steady.

Watching at a distance, witnessing her revel in wrapping

every man there around her finger, Tony had been more jealous than worried about the evening's success, distracted by the other eyes tracking Felicia's every move.

He'd wanted her out of that damn dress, he realized. He'd wanted *his* hands on her.

And now they were.

He made himself help her to a table, then let go. He took the chair beside her.

"You can get back to your job." She self-consciously plucked a roll from the bread basket and began to butter it. "I'm fine."

"How long has it been since you've put anything into your body besides booze?" he bit out, blaming her for the surprising feelings she kept igniting in him.

"Long enough to be feeling no pain." Her expression cut through both him and his criticism. "But I'm far from drunk, so don't waste your energy taking more shots at my character. My jaded heart is immune to disapproving men."

But not as unaffected as she'd like him to believe.

Her hand shook as she lifted the roll to her mouth, shamelessly licking at the butter and crumbs oozing from it. He snatched the bread away. He wanted to snatch the simple expression off her face, too, because it wasn't ringing true.

There were shadows in Felicia's eyes he hadn't taken the time to see before. A hint of the deeper emotion that flowed through her poetry. Emotion Tony had no time for.

She trailed a fire-red nail up the loosely knotted tie he'd donned for dinner. Up his spine, into his brain. His gaze zeroed in on the matching lipstick he wanted to kiss off her mouth. A waiter dropped off a refill for Felicia's cocktail. Something fruity served in a martini glass, with flavored sugar coating the rim. She plucked it from the table, and her tongue flicked out for a taste.

"Want some?" she challenged, playing it so far over the top, it was obvious she was intentionally baiting him. And if he didn't miss his guess, she was hurting herself with each spiteful jab.

He took the glass, his mouth settling on the same spot her tongue had brushed. Holding her gaze, he drained every last drop.

"What's say you skip the poetry reading portion of tonight's program?" He clunked the glass back to the table. "Whatever retaliation you have planned because of my behavior earlier isn't advisable, I assure you."

"Worried I'll ruin your elegant evening?" She snatched the glass so she could lick at the sugar he'd left untouched. "Or are you afraid you'll like the show a little too much?"

"Afraid?" he heard himself growl.

Aroused to distraction was more like it. Maybe even a little scared—for her.

He craved business challenges. Searched them out. Conquered them.

But this woman...

Was she out of her element in her designer duds and seductive glamour? Or was she a sexual player on a level that even he'd never seen? The kind of challenge a competitive man like him couldn't back down from.

"I think you're afraid that you want me," she purred. "Even though you completely disapprove of me."

"Stop torturing the man, Fe." Willard bent to give her a quick kiss. "Look who I latched on to, on my way back from de-Stewarting you."

By Willard's side was none other than Maddy Lov. The pair sat, then joined Felicia in smiling at Tony like a trio of Cheshire cats.

"Did I miss something?" Maddy asked. The woman hadn't

missed a second of fun since she and her entourage arrived earlier that day. "I sensed palace intrigue, watching you three when Ms. Gallo checked in. I must say, *Fe,* is it? Your poem was so romantic and dreamy, I cried when I read it. I was gob-smacked when someone told me who you were. That dress is to die for. And those shoes! That knockout figure. Are you really a high-powered lawyer? No wonder you've drawn even our Mr. Rossi under your spell."

"Oh, I think Mr. Rossi might just be immune." Felicia didn't seem particularly pleased by the reality.

"I should see what's keeping the Walkers from getting things started," Tony said, not as immune as he needed to be.

"Rest easy, lover." Willard nodded toward the front of the room. "Looks like someone's got you covered."

Tom Walker, holding a portable mike, welcomed everyone to dinner. Tony stood anyway, intending to distance himself from the table of people driving him over the edge.

A husky laugh stopped him.

"Chicken, Mr. Rossi?" Felicia challenged.

There was that vulnerability in her eyes again, shifting so subtly beneath her sarcasm, he still couldn't get a clear read on her. And he usually had people pegged with a single glance.

"I'd figured you as more of the tough guy who could handle anything," she teased.

"So did I," Willard and Maddy agreed in unison.

The two gave each other an animated high five that turned heads all over the room. Tony resettled in his chair as the salad course was served, resigned to not making even more of a scene.

Business.

Tonight was about business.

He could ignore the rest for a few hours more.

Another couple arrived and sat, completing their six-top.

"May I have your autograph?" the twentysomething woman gushed at Maddy, in a soft, Southern drawl. "I can't believe I'm having dinner with Maddy Lov! Jackson, take our picture. You don't mind, do you?" she asked everyone else.

She put her arm around Maddy and cheesed a grin for her date's digital camera. Maddy draped a tattoo-festooned hand on Felicia's shoulder and pulled her into the frame.

"Don't leave this sexy woman out of the shot," she insisted. "Her poetry touched even my jaded heart."

Felicia stalled, startled, but she smiled on cue. Then she shied away, the vampy vixen visibly shrinking into her daring ensemble.

"Don't tell me you're doubting your talent." Maddy nudged her with an elbow. "I've already spoken with my producer. I want to use your poem on my next album."

Felicia choked on the new drink a helpful waiter had brought to replace the one Tony chugged. Then she took an enormous swallow that made him wince.

"You?" She cleared her throat. "I mean, I'm flattered, but... A rock song?"

"I've been looking for the right project for a ballad, and your words really hit home. So sad. Yearning." Maddy glanced to Tony, then back at Felicia. "It's about someone searching for the perfect soul mate we all dream about. How long did it take you to write it?"

Tony realized he was holding his breath as he waited for the answer.

"Actually, I don't remember." Felicia stared into her glass. "I was twenty-one. It was a long time ago... I'm not even sure I can read it to everyone tonight, because..."

"Because someone broke your heart?" Maddy was watching Tony's reaction again. "But you have to recite your sonnet.

I want a video of the moment to podcast on my blog. And I'll sing it one day, mark my words. It'll be magic. Everyone identifies with the beauty of a broken heart, don't you agree, Mr. Rossi?"

Tony unclenched his fingers and dived into his salad, tuning out the scene at the table. He scanned the room. The romantic candles and flowers and golden light were just what he'd ordered. Couples were quietly dining—even the A-List team was reveling in the moment, when they'd been frantically manufacturing tabloid-worthy gossip all day. Paparazzi was everywhere, including the photographers recording images and video for the running Internet blog Maddy would update throughout the weekend.

Tonight's update would be classy. Sophisticated. Romantic. Exactly the mood Tony had promised the Walkers. Tom and Alice raised their wineglasses in a silent toast when he looked their way. His first triumph of the weekend.

But the taste of it was bitter, because the sparkle was gone from Felicia Gallo's vampy defiance. There was a sadness in her eyes that made him want to call off the poetry readings once and for all. Not because he was worried Felicia would use the moment to intentionally cause him more headaches. But because the poem seemed as personal to her as he'd sensed weeks ago.

Reading it would hurt her. He was certain of it. And he suddenly didn't want any part of that, no matter how much the emotional moment would help the Walkers' business.

FELICIA NODDED AT THE waiter who took away her barely touched lamb and replaced it with a decadent chocolate soufflé.

"Remember, no holding back," Willard chanted in her ear.

Her queasy stomach rumbled a warning. She picked up her spoon anyway, and dived into the two thousand calories sitting before her.

"The *man,* Fe," her friend insisted. "Go after the man with gusto, not the dessert."

"What man?" Felicia caught herself licking every trace of chocolate from her spoon.

So did Tony Rossi.

"That's the spirit!" applauded the rock star sitting to Willard's left.

Rossi ripped his gaze away from Felicia's mouth and attacked his own pastry.

"More wine?" Willard offered the bottle of excellent Merlot that had been paired with their meal.

"I don't think so." Felicia pushed her plate away, her stomach churning onward. "Not when I have to recite my poem in a minute."

"Please. You'll be brilliant." Willard handed over one of the elegantly designed dinner programs. "You can read it off the cover if you need to."

"But you won't need to, will you, Ms. Gallo?" Tony's tone should have been nasty, after the way she'd baited him. But instead, the huskiness in that deep, deep voice and the smoldering interest in his green, crystalline eyes challenged her.

Beguiled.

Tempted her to want the passion that had sparked between them to mean more than a misguided dare gone horribly awry.

"Anyone who can create emotion that compelling," he continued, "by stringing together a few words and phrases, can handle speaking from the heart without a cheat sheet."

"Look out," Maddy observed in a stage whisper, talking behind her hand. "He's got it bad for you, honey."

Tony threw down his fork, but the clatter was muted by enthusiastic clapping. Tom Walker stood at the other end of the room, asking over the mike how everyone was enjoying their evening. He introduced another contest winner first. The man rose to read his sonnet.

It was sweet, romantic and obviously written for his companion. When he was through, Tom's attention, along with the rest of the room, shifted to Felicia. She balled her napkin in her fist and braced to flee as he introduced her and told the guests they could use their programs to read along with her recitation.

"No holding back," Willard repeated.

Rossi's bad-boy eyebrows rose in a concerned arc, when she would have expected another challenge to put up or shut up. Her stomach did more backflips, and not because a roomful of eyes was now trained on her.

Tony seemed almost drawn to her, whether he wanted to be or not. Just like Phillip had been, until he'd gotten her out of his system in as humiliating a way conceivable.

So learn your lesson! Put this player in his place, then walk away before he does.

She stood, needing to prove to him and herself that she could do this. But when she began speaking, the words didn't come out sexy and sultry and cynical enough to shut Rossi down for good. Her eyes filled with moisture instead, and her heart began beating with the rhythm of her poem. Willard's hand rested supportively at her waist, as she explored the mysteries of the heart, each phrase stroking her body like a lover's caress. A silent song that would haunt her forever.

Love and loss.

Hope and desperation.

A young woman's heart.

Every woman's heart.

Every human being's need for someone to belong to. Someone to cherish her or him for exactly who they were. Forever.

Each word existed only for the next. At least, that's how it had felt when Felicia had first written them. And how it felt now, as she watched through unshed tears as Tony Rossi's stony features softened more with each passing second.

And then it was over, and Tony was just sitting there, still and stunned. And she was rushing across a room of clapping guests, many of them openly weeping through their smiles.

CHAPTER FOUR

"INTERESTING EVENING," Maddy said while Tony stared after Felicia.

Willard chuckled. "Wait till the sun comes out tomorrow."

Maddy laughed. Said something more that Tony missed. Frustration, and something softer, sent him hustling after a soft-hearted chameleon wearing a hard-core diva's dress. All around him, diners happily returned to their desserts. The grand opening's first official event had been a resounding success.

Tony left it all behind.

He caught up with Felicia in the deserted hallway outside. Grabbed her arm. Spun her to face him. Wiped a tender thumb through the tears trailing down her cheek. Kissed her more gently than he knew how.

"What the hell are you playing at, lady?" he whispered against her lips. "What's going on in that beautiful head of yours?"

Her laugh was as unsteady as his galloping heartbeat. He had no business needing to hear Felicia laugh again. But he did. Just once, for real. For him.

He tortured them both with another kiss. When she was the one to pull away, he gave her the shake he wanted to give himself.

"What are you up to?" he demanded.

God help him if he understood why he needed to know.

Except that hearing her recite her soulful poem had drawn him under the same spell that her sultry kiss had that morning.

Felicia licked his taste from her lips. A saucy glint sprang to her eyes—a reflection of her insecurities, he was starting to realize, rather than an innate talent for mischief.

"Why, I'm having an honest-to-God weekend meltdown, Mr. Rossi." Her next laugh was more of a hiccup, tugging at both his curiosity and the heart he'd have sworn no longer knew how to feel.

"I'll be damned if I understand who you really are," he mused, completely off balance and almost hating her for it.

"Well, that makes two of us." She nodded. "When I figure it out, I'll be sure to keep you in the loop."

"And how do you plan to figure it out?" A new feeling took root…deep.

Jealousy.

"Trial and error, I suppose." Her finger was doing that sliding thing again, up and down his chest. Over the fabric of his shirt, his tie, until her palm covered his heart. "Like everyone else who's here looking for a good time, I'm going to let loose and enjoy myself."

"No limits? No regrets, come Monday?"

"Why not?" Felicia's expression shifted from naughty to pensive. Then defiant. "Playing it safe can wait, until I get back to the real world."

"Some stupid bastard must have hurt you badly, if playing it safe is reality for a woman like you."

"You have *no* idea."

Tony couldn't resist kissing away the brittle smile that followed.

"So," he summed up, aware that his touch was responsible for the goose flesh shivering up and down her bare arms. "That poem you wrote when you were a kid isn't about *your* heart anymore? You just used the naiveté of your youth to get a free ride this weekend?"

"Just like you're using romance to earn a big, fat commission—even though you don't buy a word you're selling."

"I guess that makes us both nonbelievers, when it comes to love," he conceded.

He pulled her closer, knowing he had to stop needing the feel of her body under his hands.

Instead he controlled the next kiss. Felt Felicia's confusion and let it go to his head. She'd been running him in circles from the moment she'd arrived. It was a powerful thing, knowing he affected her the same way. But it was also humbling, and the power wasn't his to keep.

It was take and be taken. Being swamped in sensation and then giving back more, and still more, until they were both spinning out of control. Into each other. Beyond the frustration and anger.

Tony already knew how the satin feel of her lips would fire through his blood, and he welcomed the rush. He took the kiss deeper, harder, until her trembling sigh told him she felt it, too—the need he didn't want, and neither did she.

But neither of them could deny it.

She was pulling his head closer. Both of them struggling. Demanding. Giving in, just like her tender poem promised true lovers always would.

"Darling," intruded a pesky voice of reason. "Don't think I don't appreciate a VIP view of this scrumptious scene. But you might want to let Maddy fly solo at being the resort's wild child for the rest of the evening. You'll exhaust yourself at this rate."

Tony steadied Felicia as they inched apart. He glared at Willard.

"What, not working the room with Ms. Lov?" Tony asked. "What's a party animal like you doing cruising the hallway?"

"What's a shark of a PR professional like you—" Willard brushed nonexistent lint from Tony's lapel "—doing cornering a woman who's had too much to drink to know better than to throw down with the biggest cynic in the place?"

"I'm…" Felicia licked her lips, then licked them again, as if she couldn't get enough of the flavor Tony had left behind.

She rubbed her forehead with a shaking hand and stepped toward her friend. Guests began milling around them, on their way to whatever postdinner destination promised the best time.

"I…I'm not feeling very well…" Felicia stuttered.

"You've had a very big first day, Fe," Willard reasoned. "Let's away, before you turn into a pumpkin. There are many more worthy men to seduce tomorrow."

Felicia didn't look back as they disappeared into the growing crowd. And Tony forced himself to turn away—just in time to greet Tom Walker with a handshake.

"Where did you disappear to?" the other man asked. "The A-Bombs are in there stirring up a poolside mix and mingle for tomorrow morning. Knowing them, it'll probably turn into a wet T-shirt contest. And Maddy's invited everyone to the bar—first round of drinks on her."

"I was just getting some fresh air." Tony plastered on his best I'm-on-it expression, as the A-List duo headed their way, the think tank's intangible assets spilling out of their dresses. "I'm ready for whatever postdinner recon is need."

What *Tony* needed was to get his act together, before the Weekend Pass opening and his professional rep went down for the count.

Felicia might be the most intriguing female contradiction he'd ever come across. But, vulnerable poet's soul or not, her intention to enjoy a few days of mindless debauchery might wreak havoc on his and the Walkers' plans. She was one more whacked-out woman to add to his growing list of things to keep his eye on—and his hands *off*—while he manufactured a romantic mirage out of the mess people kept creating.

No worries.

Toni Rossi was on it.

"Darlings, what a quaint dinner," said one of the A-Bombs—he couldn't remember which at the moment, and he couldn't have cared less. "Timeless ambience. Tearful ending. Now everyone's warmed up and has a rosy glow in their hearts. Time to rock the night way! Oh, Maddy! Wait up!"

The duo rushed after Lov, like puppies after their gravy train.

Yeah.

No worries.

"KILL ME," FELICIA BEGGED, hiding in bed the next morning. "Just kill me now."

How could she face anyone downstairs today after running, crying, from the ballroom after reading her poem. And she'd kissed Tony Rossi—again! Craved not just his touch, but every drop of confused admiration in his voice.

She'd wanted a night full of sultry and sexy, with someone easy. Someone fun. Why couldn't she keep her hands off the last man in the place capable of showing her a harmless good time?

Why!

No answers floated down from on high.

"You dragged me out here, princess." Willard pulled back the blackout curtains that were shielding her headache from the morning sun.

"*I* dragged *you?*" Felicia winced into the light and burrowed under the down duvet. Swaddled in luxurious darkness, she felt the scorch marks she imagined the sun had left on her retinas begin to heal. "This was your idea from the start."

"I merely suggested that you get out of Manhattan and let that lovely hair of yours down. *You* searched the Internet for ski resorts, when you can't even walk on snow without falling on your face. You drudged up a heartbreaking poem from your past that even a perpetually disgruntled man like Rossi couldn't stay immune to."

"But *you* got me drunk the night I entered the contest. You dared me to do it, just like you—"

"—like I *forced* you to make out with that gorgeous, uptight crank yesterday? Twice! And I *forced* you to buy out half of Fifth Avenue, so you could give your fabulous alter ego some fresh air? No one pushes you anywhere you don't want to be, Ms. Thing. You dived into the deep end yesterday. Now tread water or drown!"

"I must be having a midlife crisis," she mumbled through snowy-white, Egyptian cotton.

"You're twenty-eight."

"This morning I'm ninety."

"Have a bubble bath. A taste of the tea and dry toast I ordered for breakfast, and you'll be ready to conquer hills that are alive with the sound of music."

"No hills." Felicia's stomach churned. "No more daring do. I'm boring. I'm risk averse. I'm a contracts lawyer, for heaven's sake."

"You're just feeling testy," her friend countered. "I'll check the minibar for something to set things aright."

"No more alcohol. No—"

A knock on the door to the den that separated their bedrooms pounded spikes through her head.

"Make it go away," she begged.

"Oh, no." Willard smacked her bottom, his aim dead-on, even through the covers. "That's your breakfast. Get some clothes on, sunshine. I have a date with Lov, and it won't do for me to arrive stag. Makes a man look too desperate. Maddy was smitten with you last night, and I mean to use that to my best advantage. Hair of the dog, eye of newt, whatever it takes." He breezed away. "Time to get you back on your fabulous feet and out that door."

"I'm not leaving this suite until our ride's ready to whisk us back to the airport Sunday." She poked her head out slowly. "Worship your rock idol solo from now on."

Meanwhile, she'd be hiding from Tony Rossi like the coward she was. And from the fantasies about him—them—that had taunted her throughout the night.

Wicked dreams.

Wet and wild and decadent, each of them ending with a nightmarish flash of the disapproving scowl Rossi had thrown at her after their first kiss. She hadn't dared look back when she'd run from him last night. But in her dreams she hadn't had a choice. She'd needed to believe he'd been just as affected as she was. But time after time she hadn't been enough.

Each time he'd shaken his head and walked away.

"Come eat your breakfast," Willard called from the other room. The man could make even turning dead bolts sound classy. "I ordered your favorite jam. Strong coffee, and— Well! Hello, there, handsome."

Felicia slithered to her feet and righted the straps of the teal silk nightgown she'd dragged on before falling into her restless sleep. Then she gingerly charted a path toward the living room. The glare from the floor-to-ceiling windows was morning soft, but it sliced through her aching head anyway.

Stumbling to a standstill, she clenched her eyes shut, rubbing her palms down her bare arms.

"I'm not up to eating anything, Willard. And I—"

"Looks like you're not up at all," chided the voice from her

wet and wild and decadent dreams. "I have breakfast scheduled for the two of us and one of the lodge's owners. Did you
get the copy of your agenda the staff slipped under your door
this morning?"

A squint in the general direction of the suite's door confirmed that the star player in her nocturnal fantasies was
standing beside her friend, looking yummy and controlled and
too damn hot. Right down to the impeccable loafers Tony
wore with creased khakis, a crisply ironed royal-blue dress
shirt and a thin leather tie, knotted but left loose around his
unbuttoned collar.

"I dropped by to discuss the day's events." His smile was
as dangerous as ever.

She opened her mouth to beg off any commitment that
required her to spend another confusing second with the man.
But Tony's raised hand stopped her.

"And I wanted to apologize," he offered. "We got off on
the wrong foot yesterday, and—"

"I doubt feet had anything to do with you two swallowing each other in public." Willard plucked a piece of paper
from the floor.

"*And,*" Tony continued, "to take full responsibility for
letting things get out of control the way they did."

The distaste in his tone stung, even though Tony was
giving Felicia the clean break she needed. Did he have to
sound as if facing her again made him want his second
shower of the morning?

"We were both…not at our best." She let her lawyer's
voice lead, flashbacks of the ecstasy of his touch testing her
resolve.

"Precisely," he agreed. "And while I can appreciate your
need to let go this weekend and enjoy yourself—the owners and
I would take it as a personal favor, if you'd *enjoy* your morning

with a bit less abandon than you did your afternoon and evening. As an all-expense-paid guest of lodge, please remember that your behavior reflects on Weekend Pass's image."

Felicia's brain reengaged so quickly, her ears did that ringing thing that usually only happened when she'd decided she was going to win a "winless" case, no matter the cost in sleepless nights and twenty-hour workdays. She realized her mouth was hanging open and shut it.

"The Walkers look forward to seeing you at the events they've arranged specifically for you." While Tony continued his little speech, he took the paper from Willard and handed it over.

Her agenda.

"Oh, the weekend's just beginning, Mr. Rossi." She straightened her spine as she relaxed her lips into her version of Maddy Lov's impish smile. "I couldn't possibly make any *specific* commitments. Following some fussy old schedule seems so terribly boring, don't you think?"

"But you have an obligation to—"

"She's a VIP guest." Willard inspected his perfectly manicured nails. "You're not suggesting that Felicia perform for her room and board, are you?"

"Of course he isn't." In the boardroom Felicia never let a client or an opponent see her sweat. Rossi had not only stolen a night of her sleep, but he'd just thrown down an offensive challenge she wasn't letting slide, emotional hangover or not.

She stepped closer, until the tips of her aroused breasts brushed his shirt.

"Mr. Rossi wouldn't insult a high-profile guest who's supposed to blog on the lodge's Web site at—" she glanced at the itinerary "—two o'clock. You didn't mean to suggest I'm an embarrassment to your clients, did you?"

She pouted, her face tipped up to his, while she folded the printout twice and inserted it into the pocket of his khakis.

She curled her hand in its warm nest. Brushed his skin through the fabric. Lingered as long as she dared. Then she slid her fingers up his side, not stopping until she'd smoothed them over the mesmerizing dimple in Rossi's chin.

She'd lost her mind.

Again.

Tony slowly exhaled.

"Of course that wasn't what I meant to say." He grabbed her wrist and moved her hand away. The muscles in his arm quivered as he let her go.

From anger or from her touch?

A weak part of Felicia needed it to be from her touch.

"I was simply remarking," he bit out, "on how your behavior last night might have been perceived by others."

"*My* behavior?" she simpered.

At least she tried to simper. But her voice's raw edge was more "kiss me again" than "kiss my ass." She fiddled with the satin bow at the center of her nightgown's daring neckline.

"I wasn't the only one spicing up the welcome dinner," she said. "And as I read them, there was nothing in the contest guidelines stipulating that a winner attend any event once she arrived. Or was I mistaken?"

Rossi's brows drew together.

Those bottomless eyes stared into her soul.

"The contest prize package is yours to take advantage of as you please," he conceded. "Designed to delight a poet's soul. You're booked for a complimentary couple's ski lesson at ten o'clock. Perhaps it would be best if you…rested instead." His cool glance from her bare feet to her ratty morning curls said he was officially beyond caring. "If you can't make skiing, maybe we'll see you at the ballroom-dancing exhibition and lessons at eleven. A local news station will be televising the event, so don't feel you have to attend if you don't—"

"—think I can waltz without making a fool of myself?"

It shouldn't hurt, this well-dressed bad boy's snap judgments of her character, particularly since she *was* behaving like a party girl. There were worse things than being mistaken as a wild card and a daring flirt.

Willard's smirk said *he* was enjoying the show.

But there was an emptiness filling Felicia, piercing inward from where the heat of Rossi's body had brushed hers. A chill racing across her skin that rubbing her arms didn't soothe. All because her dreams had been right on. Another man she couldn't stop herself from craving was over her. While her heart—correction, her *hormones*—refused to wise up.

She was tempted to concede defeat. To get back to hiding under the covers and licking her wounds. But that had been her MO for too long. And this weekend was supposed to be about breaking that pattern.

"So the ski lessons?" Tony prodded. "Should I let the pro know he can work another couple into your slot?"

"I'm certain *I* can find somewhere cozier to be." Willard's stare asked if Felicia was really going to let this man toss her aside, with no retribution.

"The ski lesson's two hours from now?" She put every bit of seduction she could muster into her walk back to the bedroom. "Surely I can rustle up another warm body to *couple* with in the snow by then."

"I GUESS I EXPECTED Felicia Gallo to be a little more Laura Ingalls Wilder, and a lot less Rocky Mountain *Vogue* out on holiday," Alice Walker complained to Tony in the lodge's main restaurant.

She lifted her orange juice and tossed it back as if it were a shot of tequila.

It was D-Day. The grand opening was in full swing. It was

now or never time to make the world take notice of the blood, sweat and equity Alice and Tom had invested in this place. And one of Tony's employers looked as if she needed to be drinking her breakfast.

None of the three winners of the love-sonnet contest were showing signs of romance sweeping them away. The press was covering every move they made. And Maddy Lov and A-List were determined to turn the place into an international night club!

Of course, the Walkers were still skittish, even after last night's success.

"I think Ms. Gallo was more jet-lagged than anything yesterday." Tony forced down a forkful of eggs Benedict, while Alice toyed with her waffles. "She didn't mean to—"

"Crawl all over you when she arrived, in a getup that was better suited for Monte Carlo than the frozen wilds of the big Northwest?"

"That was…" The hottest three minutes of his entire life. At least until he'd cornered the woman after dinner and gotten himself into even more trouble. "…unfortunate."

"A picture of the two of you was the lead this morning, on several of the gossip Web sites. You trumped Maddy Lov." Alice raised her glass for a refill from a passing waiter. "We *did* ask you to do whatever you had to to counter Maddy's antics. I guess Tom and I should have been a little more specific."

"I controlled the situation as best I could, without drawing additional attention to Ms. Gallo's…enthusiasm." Tony didn't like the taste that Alice's *uh-huh* expression left in his mouth. "It won't happen again."

"So you're going to keep an eye on Felicia today, as well as Maddy?"

"All the contest winners are booked solid with romance-friendly events I've made sure the press is panting to cover."

"But is Ms. Gallo really here looking for romance? That's the question. Are any of them?" Alice sighed. "That's the PR dynamic you've set into motion, and the press is determined to have their answer. Maybe Tom and I are just kidding ourselves, thinking we could make a go at spinning love stories instead of killer parties."

"You'll have your couples' retreat in the mountains. The world will flock to the idyllic atmosphere you want to share." Tony was going to make his clients' vision happen, whether he believed a word of it or not. "Once people hear about your magical grand opening, you'll have couples booking suites two years out."

"Magical? Is that what Felicia Gallo is?"

"All the contest winners," Tony insisted again, maybe a touch too quickly. "They'll show Weekend Pass at its best, just wait and see."

"But Felicia seemed to be of particular interest to you at last night's dinner." Alice didn't exactly sound displeased by the observation.

"She and her 'date' and Maddy are well on their way to becoming fast friends. It was a volatile combination that required careful attention."

"But Maddy and that Willard fellow aren't the ones you followed after dinner. How is Felicia this morning? I assume you've checked with her personally, to see if she's squared away for the day."

Of course he'd seen Felicia. And of course he'd played it all wrong, while her sheer nightgown and her sassy attitude had driven him crazy.

"Ms. Gallo has her itinerary," Tony hedged over the rim of his coffee mug, remembering Felicia's veiled threat to misbehave—just to spite him. "She was particularly eager to hit the slopes in a few hours to take a ski lesson."

And to search out some other man besides Tony to frustrate to distraction.

"Isn't that her now—" Alice pointed to the hallway outside the restaurant "—heading for the indoor pool in a thong and a fur coat?"

CHAPTER FIVE

"YOU MIGHT BE putting it on a little thick." Willard actually sounded nervous.

"Doesn't this say I'm confident and looking for fun?" Felicia took the drink one of her new friends—Charles—offered. Something fabulous he'd promised would kick the morning off just right.

"Actually, it says Madonna. Before Guy Richie. Hell, before Sean Penn."

Felicia lifted her chin and let the full-length mink her father had given her for Christmas slither off her shoulders to pool at her elbows. She hitched her hip, to better display her Gucci one-piece bathing suit—and the body beneath the sweep of unlined, white Lycra.

A man she hadn't met stumbled at the edge of the pool, righted himself just in the nick of time and continued on his way to join the growing band of admirers she'd collected since arriving. Last night Willard had heard about a morning pool party while everyone waited for the powder on the slopes to peak. *He* was the one who'd decided pool attire would be perfect for scoping out today's man of his dreams.

For Felicia, it had sounded like just the ticket to make sure Tony's sexy frown was the furthest thing from her mind. She shook back the hair she'd made sure was glossy and flowing, propped her free hand on her hip and swallowed a giggle as the body temps of the men circling her rose several degrees.

Being a bad girl could become a dangerous addiction.

"Good Lord." Willard chuckled. "You're out-vogueing Maddy Lov herself!"

"You're telling me!" Maddy saucied up to the group and looped her arm through Willard's. "You missed this guy's salsa dancing last night. But if this is what beauty sleep does for you, girl, you made the right choice."

"Salsa dancing?" Felicia elbowed her friend's ribs. "You told me you turned in early, because there wasn't much going on."

"A man's got to do what a man's got to do." Willard nodded to a gorgeous guy who'd just walked up. Brad Pitt gorgeous, with *Legends of the Fall* hair and a *Thelma and Louise* six-pack above his well-endowed Speedo. "Roger, you made it!"

Willard moseyed off with Mr. Pitt.

"Fast worker," Maddy quipped. "I was a little surprised when he left that guy all *Lonesome Dove* on the dance floor last night. Then I realized Willard must have been heading up to look after you. Now that he's paired off, let's pick you a playmate for the day."

A perky blonde bopped over to them. Felicia caught the rock star's eyes inspecting the backs of their sockets in response.

"Maddy, I'm so sorry I'm late. Our alarms didn't work this morning. Neither of them. And then there was some snafu in the kitchen, and our breakfasts arrived late and cold and—"

"Yes, that can happen, when the catering staff has to wade through snowdrifts to get to your chalet." Lov's dazzling smile never faltered, but she reached for Felicia's drink. "Fe, let me introduce Samantha DeWitt, half of Weekend Pass's crack PR team."

Felicia swallowed her smile as Maddy slammed the drink back. "I thought Tony was responsible for the grand opening's PR."

"The Walkers brought *big dog* in at the last minute," the blonde answered with attitude. "Something about wanting to be sure they establish a solid rep as a couples' resort destination. But Evelyn and I have everything under control. There's no reason why singles can't have a blast here, too. Right, Maddy? Now, about getting you onto the slopes later, where—"

"Where everyone can see me fall on my ass in the three feet of ice that came down overnight?" Maddy snarked. "No, thank you."

"Amen." A waiter had already replaced Felicia's drink. She sipped with gusto. "Who's Evelyn?" she asked.

"Manic blond PR rep number two," Maddy provided under her breath. "Why don't we make a morning of it right here?" she added, loudly enough to have heads turning all the way to the poolside bar and back.

Shouts of agreement went up. Glasses raised.

"How about a contest?" Maddy took Felicia's glass and handed it to Samantha, then dragged Felicia's mink the rest of the way off. "Boys versus girls."

She threw off her own cover-up, and tossed both wraps to the stunned PR rep. Then Maddy Lov struck a droolworthy, hands-on-hips pose that belonged on her next CD cover. That is, if the CD required a picture of her wearing a silver replica of the exact same bathing suit Felicia had donned.

The men around them cheered even louder, all but beating their chests as they picked up Maddy and Felicia and carried them to the raised patio near the bar. Blushing from her ears to her toes, Felicia tried her damnedest to remember that she was *enjoying* being a diva. Faking ease with being at the center of Maddy's insane antics, she glanced around for a friendly face.

Where had Willard gotten off to?

"Tony Rossi!" Maddy exclaimed. "Just the man to help kick off our new adventure."

Felicia's gaze zinged toward the door and the least friendly man at the lodge.

Assessing. Guarded. Sexy as all hell. More than a little uneasy, as he took in every inch of her and the flesh her suit was shamelessly revealing. But Tony Rossi—friendly?

What had she been thinking, thumbing her nose and resort wear at this guy! But she refused to look away as he strode toward the patio. What did she care what this guy thought?

Except she did care, damn it.

Bad, rebellious diva.

Bad!

"You two are creating your own little adventure?" Rossi's mercurial gaze shifted to Maddy.

"A contest between the sexes, to start the day right. Let's see who seduces who first!" Maddy played to the crowd. "Man and woman at their most primal, here in the rugged wilds of Colorado. Isn't that the hype you've been peddling, Mr. Rossi?"

"Primal…cool!" Samantha handed Felicia's and Maddy's things to a stranger. "But don't start yet. Let me round up a few photographers."

She raced away.

"I don't suppose it would do any good to try to talk you out of this." Tony's focus stayed on Maddy.

On business.

All business.

Something Felicia was an expert at. Which was how she knew she could slip away and Tony would never notice—not with his latest PR crisis to finesse. And as far away from the man as possible was exactly where Felicia and her skimpy bathing suit suddenly needed to be.

"Why would you want to talk me out of some harmless fun?" Maddy caught Felicia slinking off and shot her an accusing glance. "Come up here, handsome. Give it a try."

She tugged Tony onto her makeshift stage. Feminine squeals erupted.

"Try me!" A curvy redhead in a bikini called out.

"Don't let him get away, Maddy," added the brunette beside where Felicia had stumbled to a standstill. A woman whose enormous breasts were bursting out of her tube top. "If you don't want him, we do!"

"What do you say, Mr. Rossi?" Maddy challenged. "I wonder what it would take to shake up a fine specimen of a man like you."

"You can shake him!" someone behind Felicia yelled. "Rock and roll!"

"Let's say we let Mr. Rossi show us what he looks for in a woman?" Maddy's attention shifted to where Felicia stood, transfixed amidst the rambunctious crowd, her escape forgotten at the thought of any of the bimbos around her getting their three-inch nails into Tony. "What do we think about a blind kissing contest? Is Weekend Pass magical enough, that even a busy man like Tony Rossi can find the kiss of his dreams?"

THE KISS OF HIS dreams?

Tony's hold on the day slipped another inch from his grasp.

Felicia had disappeared. He caught himself searching the ecstatic crowd for amazing legs and sky-blue eyes and reddish-gold hair. Not to mention the nonsense bathing suit that had made her sexy nightgown seem downright frumpy.

He forced himself to turn back to Maddy Lov and the business at hand. Maddy was holding up a monogrammed linen napkin, presumably for him to use to cover his eyes. Pain in Tony's ass or not, she'd just given him a public forum to drive his PR message home to the rowdy pool partiers. He'd be crazy to pass up the chance.

"Well?" she pressed. "Does Weekend Pass's peddler of romance really buy into what he's selling? Can *anyone* find their heart's desire here?"

"Let's find out." He stepped down from the patio and tied the napkin around his forehead.

Squeals erupted. Female bodies pressed closer.

"All right, Mr. Rossi," Maddy cooed, more for the crowd than for him. "It's time to find the kiss of your dreams! Gentlemen, give the ladies room."

A spin and a shove later, and Tony was on his way to kiss a total stranger. Just part of the job, he reminded himself. Whatever it took to close the deal.

Except Felicia Gallo's lips, not the Walker account, were where his mind veered. The white-hot desire that had sparked from every stroke of her tongue. His. Her body. His.

He held out his hands. Reached. Did his job. Made contact with soft, feminine flesh. Pandemonium echoed around him as he made a show of caressing perfumed arms and shoulders, weighing his choices. He tried not to put his hands on anything he could get sued for later, while he applied himself to at least appearing to be enjoying himself.

Then it happened.

The same zing of electricity that shocked him each time he touched Felicia.

She hadn't run after all, the little minx.

Tony felt himself smile—really smile—for the first time in a long time. Clenching his fingers around Felicia's shoulders, he pulled her closer.

Her skin and hair were just as soft as he remembered. Her gasp of shock was the intoxicating sound that he'd dreamed about all night.

"Look what I found," he said.

CHAPTER SIX

FELICIA WAS DROWNING. Held tightly in the arms of the man she'd meant to provoke when she'd headed for the pool in her outlandish getup, she'd never felt more lost. And the throng of spectators surrounding them were enjoying the show too much to throw her a lifeline.

This weekend was supposed to be about having mad, care-free fun. Not craving more of what would only get her hurt.

But there was clearly no carefree for her with Tony. No keeping her cool, while she tantalized this man. No easy in-difference to throw back in his face. One glance from those eyes that heated whenever he looked at her, one of the almost soundless moans that escaped his control each time they kissed, and she would always need more.

His hands slid from her shoulders to her bare back, trailing down her spine to cup the skimpy bottom of her swimsuit. And then, even more wasn't enough. Closing her eyes, she forgot about self-preservation. About everything but the re-ality of having her hands on Rossi again. And knowing he couldn't keep his off her.

The strength of his chest. His arms. The thundering pulse pounding along his neck—proof that he was as swept away as she was. Not aloof and disapproving. Not unaffected and all-business and immune, after all. He'd picked her out of a crowd—her—and he was kissing her as if he'd never stop.

She ran her hands through the thickness of his hair. Then her fingers brushed the edges of his blindfold—and every warm, dreamy thing inside her froze ice cold.

Eyes wide-open that morning, this man had made it clear she wasn't enough to tempt him ever again. The amazing way he'd made her feel after last night's dinner hadn't meant anything to him. He was kissing a stranger now, not *her*. She hadn't kept Tony's interest for longer than it took for him to hit on someone else. *Anyone* else. Just like her ex.

"No." She stiffened to move away.

Tony held on tighter.

His next kiss weakened her knees but not her resolve. She broke free of it, even though her hands refused to stop clinging. She didn't want this. She couldn't want one more man who didn't want her the same way in return.

"Let me go!" She reached for the cloth covering his eyes.

Still blind, he grabbed her hand. Brought her fingers to his lips.

"How can I let go of the kiss of my dreams?" His voice was even rougher than in her fantasies.

Better than anything she'd ever known. Like dark chocolate fudge on top of the perfect brownie sundae. She wanted to lick up every drop.

It was the final straw.

"Screw you, Rossi!" She ripped the ridiculous napkin from his face, then slapped that rock-solid jaw before he could blink her into focus. "Dream about that!"

Half of their onlookers booed. The other half degenerated into another clapping frenzy.

"Looks like true love to me!" someone yelled from the direction of the Jacuzzi. "She's a hellcat, Tony. Don't let her get away."

"I'll dream kiss you if she doesn't want to," offered the brunette gawking beside them.

Tony's grip on Felicia's arm prevented her from storming off.

"More!" the crowd chanted. "More!"

"Screw me?" His fury engulfed her. "Why the righteous indignation, *Fe?* You grabbed my ass, the second you stepped out of the car from the airport."

"What about you, you miscreant," she hissed. "You felt me up yesterday. Twice! Then this morning you laid down the law about the proper deportment of Weekend Pass VIP guests— on your way to making it with the next warm body you got your hands on!"

Perfect.

She sounded like a jealous, jilted lover. Felicia's very favorite thing to be!

But she'd hit her mark. The mighty Tony Rossi looked chagrined. Confused. He moved her toward the exit, silent and brooding once more, snagging her mink from a chair by the door.

"I'd say that's about as elemental as it gets," Maddy shouted over the craziness. A quick glance her way earned Felicia a "You go, girl!" thumbs-up. "Who's next? Let's kick it up a notch!"

Felicia could feel Tony's frustration ratcheting to a whole new level, thanks to the rock star's taunting. He yanked her into the hallway, tugged her into her fur, then marched her toward a side room.

"Stop dragging me around!" The warmth of her coat felt marvelous in the chill of the hallway. But she didn't for a second believe Tony's concern had been for her comfort. "If you're so damn embarrassed to be seen with me dressed this way, then maybe you should cut back on the public foreplay!"

"Embarrassed?" He opened the door to what turned out to be a linen closet filled with fluffy towels and the subtle sandalwood scent Felicia had noticed at the pool. "Lady, I'm far from embarrassed." He pushed until she stumbled inside, his little-boy scowl threatening a matching tantrum any second. "And cutting back never crossed my mind."

TONY FLIPPED ON THE closet's light and shut them both inside. Enough was enough.

"Let me out of here!" Felicia reached for the door, but he blocked her with his body. Bit back a groan when her hand brushed his thigh.

"So you can keep driving me to distraction while the entire lodge watches? We need to get a few things settled, Ms. Gallo." *Screw him?* Clearly the lady had no idea how close to the edge she'd pushed things. "A bikini and a fur coat? Prancing around with Maddy Lov! What were you trying to prove?"

"I don't prance, Mr. Rossi." Felicia's back arched in indignation.

Maybe if she would just back down. Behave. Get out of his way. His head... Maybe then he could let them both out of the closet, before he made a mistake bigger than picking *her* kiss out of an anonymous crowd. But instead of retreating, Felicia's deep, calming breath made her breasts strain against the triangles of white fabric barely containing them.

"And for your information." She shimmied out of her coat, blatantly challenging him, the way he was beginning to expect at every turn. "This is the chicest one-piece suit of the resort season. It's sold out everywhere."

"*One* piece, only because the designer stitched dental floss between the top and the nonexistent bottom."

Leaving the flesh in between bared for Tony's eyes and hands to feast on. His and every other guy's in the place.

He should get out of there. He'd won the latest round with

Maddy, but he was backtracking with Felicia. Losing his focus, when there was an impossible amount of work left to oversee.

"What do you care?" Felicia was in his face now, almost eye to eye with him in her four-inch, leopard-print heels. "You're just worried about your grand opening. In case you didn't notice, I wasn't the one egging you and everyone else on back there. Forget me. Push Samantha and Evelyn to rein in Maddy Lov."

"*Forget* you? I expected Maddy to be out of control, but you…" He had to touch her, then he had to pull her closer. Then he had to kiss her, while his hands clenched around her tiny, toned waist. "I swear, if I see another man touch you in this getup, I'll kill him. Blindfolded or not, I'd have known it was you back there, as soon as I put my hands on you. You're…"

"I'm what?" The vulnerability he'd seen for just an instant in her suite and during her poetry reading was back.

He stroked the back of his hand across her cheek, willing away the sheen of tears gathering in her eyes.

"I don't know," he admitted to both of them. "What are you? Poet? Temptress? Romantic? Maneater? For the life of me, I can't figure you out. But you're making me jealous as hell, and I don't get jealous. And…"

"And?" She was trembling. Then her tears disappeared behind sizzling blue anger. "Whatever I am, you and your *jealousy* could barely stand the sight of me a few hours ago. Your loss, Mr. Rossi. I've wasted my last kiss, my last dream, on you!"

"Dreams?" Tony's body grew painfully hard. His vision narrowed to her mouth. "You dreamed about us?"

…the kiss of your dreams…

"*Romantic* fantasies," she breathed against his lips. Then she reached around him for the door handle. "Exactly what you're telling the world Weekend Pass is the ultimate desti-

nation for. Not that you can stand to be anywhere near romance, or me, for real. I guess my dental floss and I will have
to find someone else to make my weekend fantasies come
true…"

"Like hell." He grabbed her arm. Held it at her waist.
Refused to let her go, as he tipped her chin up with his other
hand. "You wanted a weekend meltdown, Ms. Gallo? You got
one!"

CHAPTER SEVEN

FELICIA'S ATTEMPT to struggle free lasted all of two seconds. Feeling Tony lose control again was too good to pass up. Next thing she knew she was wrapping herself around him. Crawling up his body while his hands supported her bottom.

He turned and pinned her to the door. Her breasts rubbed erotically against his chest. First through their clothing, and then freely as he tugged down her bandeau top and cupped her with strong, callused fingers.

Followed by his lips.

Felicia arched into the bite of his teeth on her nipple.

Shouts and screams from the pool filtered into their secret world, drowning out the keening sound she made. Everything inside her dissolved into blazing, molten need.

"More," she begged.

"Hard or soft?" Tony demanded. "Because right now, I could—"

"No soft," she panted, yanking at the buttons holding his silk shirt together. "Not here. Not with you."

She was shoving his flannel sport coat off, her lips finding warm muscles beneath his open shirt, when a rip and a tear opened *her* to the man supporting her weight.

"Hard, it is." He pushed aside the tattered remains of her suit, his fingers spreading the cheeks of her bottom. He pressed deeper between her thighs, until she could feel the hard flesh below his waist throbbing, needing, through the fabric that separated them.

"Please." She wiggled closer.

Her hands dropped to his belt.

He moved them to the door beside her head. Made fast work of his pants, desire that bordered on anger hardening the gaze that never left hers. Then he held himself poised at the brink, restraining her hips while she panted and nibbled the line of his jaw, her body fighting to close that final inch and merge with his.

"Please." Her head fell back.

His fingers threaded through the riot of curls the pool's humidity had made of her hair. Then he softly licked the corner of her mouth. Tender. Surprising. As vulnerable in that moment as she was.

"Hard, Ms. Gallo?"

"Y-yes." She'd never heard anything more erotic than the need in his voice. Never wanted the rush, the shock, of a man's body inside hers more.

Chuckling, denying them both, he pressed against her entrance, then receded. Pressed just a little deeper, holding her still, not letting her take more. He was naughtiness in the flesh. Wicked and playful and kind in a way that drove her need even higher.

"Are you sure?" A bead of sweat trailed down his cheek. Holding back was costing him, too. "*Are* you the bad-girl socialite, Ms. Gallo, or a softhearted romantic?"

"If we're going to do this, shouldn't you call me Felicia?" she panted. She let her dreams be her guide and licked a path up the salty skin of his neck, until her teeth could nip the softness behind his ear. "Who are *you?* The badass you pretend to be? All cold, hard business, and you don't care what it costs you? Or is there a heart underneath, after all? Which is it going to be, Mr. Rossi?"

He blinked, then smiled at her challenge.

"Call me Tony." His hips met hers as he pushed inside. One long, sensuous stretch of friction and skin-on-skin and aching hardness that tortured her, rather than giving her the relief she craved. "Hold on tight, *Felicia.*"

She gasped at him calling her anything but Ms. Gallo, then again as he pulled back and thrust home. His hand behind her bottom cushioned her against the door. His pace increased. Salty drops of exertion trailed from his hairline. Sparks flew behind her eyes. And still he pushed harder, faster, deeper.

"Please," she begged. "More."

"Yes. Damn." He buried his face in her neck. "Where did you come from, lady?"

She had no answer for him. No words. Nothing but the sense that she'd come from nowhere, had nowhere to go. There was just now. Freedom. Abandon. No limits. No regrets. Just this. Him. Her. Letting go of everything else, in a way she never had. And feeling wicked and real with a man who was craving every second of it, just as much as she did.

She pulled his head up until she had his mouth. Joined their tongues in a fantasy dance of their own. Squeezed her legs around his hips and rocked into the sensation of being consumed.

"Ah…" Teetering on the pinnacle, wanting it to last, she tried to shy away from the overwhelming tension. The wildness of it.

Too much.

Too real.

"No." He held tight. Buried himself as deep as he could. Deeper. Rocked bolts of electricity into her, while her hips met each thrust like an addict. "Take it, Felicia. Give. Look at me. Sweetheart… Let go…"

Sweetheart…

It pushed her over, hearing such a gentle endearment amidst the fury of their lovemaking. She lost her heart to him, right then and there.

"Please," she begged.

"Say my name," he demanded. His hips pistoned faster. Driving her higher. His jaw clenched. "Who are you with, Felicia? Who has you now?"

"You do… Oh…" The spasms grew stronger. Her body exploded around him, drenching them both in pleasure.

He groaned. Pounded her into the door. "Say my name. Let me hear it, while you—"

"Tony…please!" Her world was a rainbow of color and unbearable pleasure. Craving. Releasing. "Tony! Don't stop. Don't ever stop…"

He anchored their hips together. Slapped a palm to the door. Came undone. His release sounded as good as it felt, his breath gushing on groan after groan, as he throbbed inside her.

"Tony…" she whispered. "Don't stop…"

"Never. Never…"

His hands smoothed over her body. Her legs wilted to the ground. She held tight to his shoulders, needing the reassurance of contact as the rest of their bodies separated.

"Shh…" He planted a chaste kiss on her temple. "Just let me hold you a little longer."

She hadn't realized she was trembling. Because her mind was already racing ahead, the numbness receding more with each passing heartbeat. The reality of what she'd done, what was bound to happen next, settled deep. Almost as deep as Tony's touch had. Too deep to pretend she wasn't in serious trouble.

"I…" She cleared the sound of soul-shattering release from her voice. Reached down and sorted out the bottom of her swimsuit. It was hopelessly damaged. She pulled the top together as best she could. Fumbled for her coat. "I think I'm okay."

Tony hesitated, then let her inch away.

"Felicia," he started. He ran a shaking hand over his face. "I—"

"It's okay." She couldn't stand to hear it. Not from him.

How they'd made a mistake. How it had been *great,* but he just couldn't see this going anywhere.

More cheers went up from Maddy's damn contest. Tony glared over her shoulder, as if he could see through the closed door that was helping her stay upright.

"You should get back out there," she offered. "Lord knows what Lov's got everyone doing now. Body shots come to mind."

"Felicia…" He didn't move, when he should have been racing out the door.

Tony Rossi—not such a badass, after all.

Nothing was worse than the guy who was dumping you feeling sorry for you at the same time.

"What are you, a moron!" She'd rather have his anger than his pity. "Go do your job, instead of doing me."

She slipped into her mink.

"You're off the hook," she added, when he just stood there staring, shirt hanging, pants halfway down his rock-hard thighs. "I'll fly under the radar for the rest of the weekend… I've had my fill of melting down. You don't have to babysit me. I'll show where I'm supposed to, and I'll behave myself."

Seconds ticked by like hours. Tony couldn't seem to form a response to her rambling. He almost seemed hurt by her brush-off. And that, more than anything else, finally pissed *her* off.

"Asshole," she muttered as she spun and opened the door, intending to walk away with her head high, letting Rossi know she was unfazed by whatever game he was playing now.

No matter what his body had promised, he didn't care. Not about her. Believing anything else would only get her hurt more.

The shock of a flash strobing in her face stunned her motionless.

"Ms. Gallo!" a lady with a handheld recorder said, a reporter she'd talked with at last night's dinner. More lights flashed. A man with a digital camera was happily shooting away over the woman's shoulder. "Is Tony Rossi really the kiss of your dreams? Do you credit winning your romantic getaway at Weekend Pass with bringing the two of you together? Or was it Maddy Lov's wicked kissing contest?"

"What?" Felicia shielded her eyes with the hand that wasn't holding her coat closed. "We're...Mr. Rossi and I aren't together. It's not—"

"What it looks like?" the reporter finished in disbelief.

"It looks pretty sensational from here." The creepy-looking slime laughed, still snapping pictures.

"That's enough!" Tony finally said.

Felicia turned, the camera's shutter clicking away. No wonder, because there Rossi stood, buttoning up the rumpled, sexy mess they'd made out of his clothes.

"How about you, Tony?" the reporter asked. "Did Maddy Lov help you find the kiss of your dreams, or was it Weekend Pass?"

Tony swallowed instead of answering. Tucked in the front of his shirt. He'd pulled on his game face. All business again. No heart. He glanced at Felicia, but not long enough to count as legitimate eye contact. Of course, the paparazzi snapped up every frame of his indecision.

Perfect.

The man had saved his rejection until it could be immortalized on the Internet.

"Asshole." She headed for the elevator, stiletto heels, slutty bathing suit that no longer had even dental floss to hold it together, and all.

"Felicia!" the asshole called after her.

She ran then, leaving Tony to deal with the fallout from their temporary insanity.

Leaving him period.

She could avoid the man until the Town Car arrived tomorrow to take her back to the airport. She *would* avoid him.

She'd officially had enough of *not being enough* for the men of her dreams.

"AT THE CURB AS soon as the woman got here?" Matt Walker's shoulders shook in silent laughter beneath his Burberry coat. Tom and Alice's son flanked Tony near a snowdrift, both of them watching the lodge's top pro give Felicia and Willard and several other guests a beginner's ski lesson. "At the pool this morning? Getting busy in a linen closet! Damn, Rossi. Your résumé said you put everything on the line to close an account. But I don't think my parents expected you to put out quite this much."

Tony grunted, distracted by Felicia taking her turn down the bunny slope—swooshing past them on unsteady skis, while a gaggle of press clicked away. She made a point of ignoring him, even though he'd been there for fifteen minutes. He'd told himself he'd come to keep an eye on the press, and to talk up the other couples' activities he wanted covered throughout the day.

So why had he been so relieved that Felicia had dragged Willard to the lesson after all, instead of one of her many admirers from the pool?

Matt's sarcasm finally filtered through the mush that sex with Felicia had made of Tony's brain.

"The gossip sites have blown this morning out of proportion." Tony headed for the lodge. Heaven knew what Maddy and the A-Bombs were up to now. "I hear you weren't exactly a passive, pool-party bystander yourself."

"But *I'm* not the mastermind behind Weekend Pass becoming a lovers' dream getaway." Matt sidestepped a patch of ice, as well as Tony's intel that the Walkers' son and another one of the contest winners had been sucked into Lov's antics that morning. "You're the face of what my folks want this place to be. And now your face is everywhere—you've made sure romance is alive and kicking at Weekend Pass, even if you had to fake it with a stranger to get the job done."

"That's not what happened!" Several heads turned toward Tony's outburst. He rounded on Matt and lowered his voice. "I wouldn't have set Felicia up like that."

And you weren't faking a damn thing, his conscience silently added.

"Felicia? What happened to 'Ms. Gallo'?"

"I wouldn't have dragged *her* or any other woman into this media mess. Yes, I'm responsible for the romantic trappings and the hype around here. But that doesn't mean I'm buying into a word of it, or peddling it personally."

"Too bad the press doesn't know that, man." Matt held up his hands at Tony's growl. He toed at the snow under his boots. "Hey, I'm just telling it like it is. It's a competition now. Whose Weekend Pass is the real deal—your romantic retreat or Maddy Lov's all-night-long partying? And the photographers are eating you and Gallo up, whether *you're* buying into what's happening between you two or not. According to the blogs, you and your Felicia are a nose out in front. Romance might just trump rock and roll after all."

His Felicia?

Tony's mind rejected the concept, even though his body

had gone to Def Con 1 as soon as he'd spotted her in another body-molding ski suit—black this time.

"There is no competition," he insisted. "Not involving Felicia."

And she wasn't *his* anything. The woman wouldn't even look at him now. Not after he'd hesitated after stumbling out of their closet, not able to admit in front of God and everybody what being with her had meant to him.

"Probably a good thing. I don't remember reading anything in the contest guidelines that said being your foil for the paparazzi was part of the prize package. I know Liz wouldn't shine with being used that way. She—"

"Liz?" Tony headed up the deck and through the glass doors that lead into the solarium attached to the lodge's three-story lobby. "So where exactly do things stand with you and Ms. Song?"

Matt kept pace with him, both of them stomping off snow on the provided mats, instead of scattering it across the lobby's red oak floor.

"Did you ever feel like you knew someone instantly?" Matt finally asked. "You know, with just one touch? Then you realized you didn't really know anything about them at all?"

Tony's scattered thoughts first ran to him and Felicia. But he kept his mouth shut long enough to realize Matt was talking about whatever he had going on with *his* contest winner.

"I don't believe in knowing a woman," Tony insisted. "Not beyond whatever she chooses to show you."

"Lord!" Matt clapped him on the back. A gesture he'd inherited from his father. "Don't let a reporter hear you talking like that until the weekend's over. Planned or not, this *thing* you and Gallo have going is the new face of your PR plan. Enjoy it while it lasts!"

Matt walked toward the lodge's offices, still laughing.

Whose Weekend Pass is the real deal?

There was no plan....

Tony had never wanted real. Not in relationships. Thanks to his parents' dysfunctional example, wanting *real* felt like the worst kind of setup for disappointment. And he'd never met a woman who could make him want more than a night or two of mutually gratifying pleasure.

Except Tony had personally greeted Felicia's Town Car, when he hadn't any of the other contest winners. When she'd e-mailed a week ago that she was too cold-natured to want to trek back and forth from one of the secluded chalets, he'd rearranged bookings so she could have their best top-floor suite in the main lodge. He'd memorized her poem. Her picture. Her bio. Almost as if he *had* subconsciously planned what had happened.

So why had he been such an ass since she'd arrived? Judgmental, because she'd behaved too much like the kind of woman he'd sworn never to want. Frustrated, once the sensitive, beautiful soul that had captivated him long-distance began to emerge. Then she'd thrown animal fur and Lycra into the mix, and he'd completely lost his ability to see anything but red. Testosterone red.

And the blue of Felicia's eyes, shining with mischief, bewitching him until he couldn't help but take what he'd wanted. What she'd made him need. What she'd given back with more beauty than he'd ever known. A hot, irresistible chameleon revealing one amazing color after another.

The press would keep hounding both of them, and he wasn't sure which was more unsettling. Knowing he'd have to keep his distance, so no one would pick up on how much Felicia despised him after that morning. Or knowing he couldn't, because being near her had become an addiction he had to feed.

Hell, he'd spied on her ski lesson! He'd talked Matt into riding shotgun. *Him,* Tony Rossi. Hiding behind another guy. Off balance and ignoring the job, so he could stalk a woman who'd written him off.

Willard walked by, his arm around one of the men who'd been worshipping at the altar of Lov since the singer's arrival. The guy had also joined Willard and Felicia's ski group.

"Go get her, bad boy," Willard said to Tony. He and his buddy stopped a few feet away. "Maddy's online poll says you and Fe have a fifty-fifty shot at making a go of it. Go nail yourself a hottie. I have."

He cupped his friend's posterior. The guy laughed, and the two of them headed toward the lobby coffee shop, arms around each other's waists.

Fifty-fifty odds?

Tony only dealt in sure things. Only focused on the challenge at hand. The job that would never let him down, because he was always in control.

But he'd hurt Felicia that morning. He was certain of it. It shouldn't matter. She'd come to Weekend Pass for a wild time. She'd hooked up with Maddy Lov. Tears or not, Felicia had given as good as she'd gotten. And she seemed to be fine now.

Except, he wasn't buying it. The romantic dreamer inside all that sizzling beauty was suffering. Because of him.

He knew each place Felicia was scheduled to be throughout the day. And damn if he wasn't mentally rearranging his schedule to make room for keeping her in his sights.

CHAPTER EIGHT

"FELICIA—THIS WAY!" a reported called.

Another shoved closer, while photographers snapped all around her. Ribbons of harsh light flashed between the fingers of the hand Felicia held in front of her face.

"Ms. Gallo, are you and Tony Rossi quits already?"

"Has Weekend Pass's magic failed? What about the kind of romance your poem talked about? Do you still hope for Mr. Right?"

Romance?

Mr. Right?

Were they serious?

The questions had escalated all morning. The more Felicia refused to answer, the harder the reporters pushed.

"Come on, boys." Maddy Lov appeared at Felicia's side, emerging from the lodge's restaurant. "Every diva needs a break from her public. Give us twenty, and I promise you some juicy pictures for your afternoon deadlines. How about I meet you by the whirlpool at one?"

A few more camera clicks and an enthusiastic hug between Maddy and the closest reporter, and Felicia's unwanted admirers scurried to do their idol's bidding.

Maddy flashed her a hopeful smile.

"Does that make up for this morning?" She grimaced. "At least a little?"

"You mean the fact that you and your poolside fun are responsible for those leeches trailing me all over the lodge?" At one scheduled event after another, Felicia had forced herself to smile and simper and have fun, damn it—as if her closet misadventure with Tony had never happened.

"No." Maddy's contrition disappeared. "I mean that I didn't do a better job of keeping the press busy while you and Tony figured some things out. The rest is on you. And don't tell me it wasn't worth it. 'Cause I'm not buying it."

"Worth what?" Felicia sputtered.

"Throwing caution to the wind and living, girl!"

"You've been talking to Willard again."

"Haven't seen him all morning." Maddy led her into the restaurant. "My bet's on him having better things to do today than gossip with me. You look like a girl who could use a stiff drink."

Maddy motioned to a booth and the steaming cup of hot chocolate she must have just ordered. She sat and slid the mug across the table, where she clearly expected Felicia to join her.

"No, I can't take your—" Felicia sputtered.

"The longer you stand there, the longer everyone's going to stare." Maddy raised her hand for a passing waiter, who screeched to halt, instantly enthralled, then scurried off for more hot chocolate.

After a quick scan of the airy room, Felicia accepted her limited options. She could make a scene, bailing out on Lov's generous let's-be-girlfriends offer. Or continue to prove to everyone but herself that she was fine—just fine—no matter what outlandish thing happened next.

She sat, staring at the whipped cream melting on top of the sugary concoction in front of her.

"Nectar of the gods." Maddy smiled at the waiter who deftly deposited her new mug, then she lifted it and took a sexy sip. She licked the cream mustache from her upper lip.

A man staring at them from a patio table outside nearly fell out of his chair. He righted himself and turned back to his buddies, who were laughing themselves senseless.

"Drink up," Maddy insisted. "Better yet, let a drop of cream land on your chest and make a production of wiping it off." She sighed. "I'll be your slave for the rest of the weekend."

Felicia snorted, choking on her first scalding taste. And damn if the topping didn't splash over the rim and land on the cleavage above her dress's plunging neckline—her third outfit change of the day, for the dance lessons she'd just finished. She picked up her napkin to deal with the cream.

"Don't you dare!" Maddy grabbed the cloth away. "Take pity on a tired diva and play it up for the cheap seats in the back. Use your fingers, girl. Give your fans the show they're paying for."

"*My* fans?" Felicia wrinkled her nose at the ridiculousness of the statement.

But what the hell. She'd made love with a near stranger in a closet that morning. Publicly licking cream off her ta-tas was G-rated by comparison. Maddy yawned, as if in agreement, propping her elbow on the table and her cheek on her hand.

And that's when Felicia got it—*she* wasn't the only one who'd been pretending to thrive on media chaos all morning.

"You're a total tease!" Felicia applied herself to entertaining the hoards of rock idol worshippers who tracked Lov's every move. With one finger she traced down the trail the sticky dollop of confection had left, around the slippery underside, and lifted the cream free. "Do you really do stuff like this every day of your life?"

Maddy's eyes sparkled as Felicia licked the topping from her finger, then sucked the tip into her mouth. Felicia glanced around to discover that every male eye was indeed focused on her shameless display, not the love goddess sitting across from her.

"Do I enjoy expressing my sexuality?" Maddy checked out their audience as casually as if she were watching the snow report muted on every public TV in the lodge. "Do I embrace being noticed for the smoking-hot woman I am? Hell, yeah, sister! The question is, why don't you? Why don't you try really buying into your sexy hype for the rest of the day?"

Felicia swallowed, yanked her napkin back, and made fast work cleaning up the last traces of her mess.

"Hype?" She managed her second sip of chocolate without making a spectacle of herself.

The other woman's fingernail lazily toyed with her drink's topping. "You're a knockout, who should be enjoying the way that model-thin figure of yours looks in everything you wear. And I'd appreciate any help you can give me, distracting folks so I can breathe every now and then. But your body language doesn't exactly scream *I'm fabulous!* to me, no matter how incredible everyone else thinks you look."

Felicia smoothed her hands down soft, chocolate-brown wool, until they reached the daringly high hem of the skirt that barely covered her bottom when she sat. As the day had dragged on, she'd grown less and less comfortable in her own skin—and the trappings she'd bought to display herself in. In fact, the only times she'd felt truly *fabulous* all weekend had been the moments when Tony Rossi's hands and mouth and body had been worshipping hers, as if he'd never held anything as amazing in his arms.

"This—" Felicia motioned to her Marc Jacobs dress. "It's not really me."

"Well, it should be." Maddy studied her with a critical eye. "With a body like that, and the killer mind you've got going on underneath, you were born to drive men crazy, Fe."

"I do. In a boardroom. In business. Just not—"

"In bed? In your dating life?"

"Dating?" Felicia hadn't meant to gasp the word quite so harshly. A quick scan of the room confirmed that, of course, too many people had heard and were listening for more. "Men aren't exactly fixated on me in my real life," she said in a quieter voice.

And *why,* exactly, was she spilling that fun fact to one of the most sought-after women in the world?

Maddy nodded a girlfriend's understanding and took a long sip of her cooling chocolate. "Me, neither."

"You're an MTV goddess!"

"And when I do make it back home every month or so, I'm just as alone as you are."

Felicia didn't bother denying that's exactly how she felt. Even now, with a lodge full of *admirers* trailing after her.

"Why do you think I'd rather be on the road doing fun gigs like this?" Maddy asked. "But after working so hard playing *All Lov, All the Time,* who's got the energy to get into it for real? Not to mention that the persona can be pretty intimidating to most guys."

Felicia stared, stunned. "But you're—"

"Working my ass off creating an illusion for the cameras, just like you." The other woman winked. "Don't get me wrong. I love it, at least for now. I wouldn't trade my job for anyone else's. But it would be nice every once in a while to have someone real and solid to cuddle up with at night. To wake up next to in the morning. I'm going to have that one day, when I'm ready for it."

"Yeah. Being ready for it…"

"It sure beats letting some dick make you think a brainiac can't look and dress and behave the way you have this weekend." Maddy Lov, shaking her head like a disapproving mamma, was a startling sight to behold. "I pumped Willard for information last night. You're too damn smart to buy into your ex's bull. The press thinks you're a diva. You have every man here on the hook. But *you're* the one who's the tease. Stop phoning it in and decide what you want."

"Yeah. Deciding…"

Instead of not feeling like enough, and telling herself it was because of Phillip's cheating. Or a bad breakup. Or Tony Rossi's fleeting interest in her.

Not being enough outside of her safe little world of work was in her head. It had become her comfort zone. Her excuse for not risking more.

"Something tells me," Maddy mused, "that there's no shoving this Weekend-Pass Felicia you've been playing at back down inside."

The Felicia who'd been what a man like Tony Rossi had needed, at least for a little while.

Did she really want to walk away from that? Or did she want to challenge him more, until he admitted what they'd made each other feel?

"He's been watching you this entire time, by the way," Maddy said as she stood.

"What? Who?"

"A very frustrated man who's followed you around like a puppy all day, ever since you shagged him near the pool."

"Tony?" Felicia felt her face blush crimson at Maddy's laugh. "How did you know we—"

"Everyone knows about your closet rendezvous. It's all over the Internet." The rock star gave Maddy's shoulder a commiserating pat. "That part sucks. But I'll do the best I can to shift the gossip back my way. You've got enough to worry about. For the record, my money's on you figuring out what you need, before the sun sets on today's slopes."

Felicia turned from watching Maddy leave to seeing

what the woman's body had been hiding up till then. Off
to the corner of the restaurant, in the only shadowy place
there was with the sun streaming through the wall of windows that fronted the patio, sat Tony Rossi. His gaze locked
with hers.

His expression sent Felicia's skin tingling everywhere at
once, especially where she'd let the whipped cream slide
down her chest.

Need.

The man's gaze communicated the same frustrated need
that had been building, bubbling, inside her, no matter how skill-
fully she'd ignored him. And her. And what she secretly wanted.

More, she'd begged him.

She hadn't gotten nearly enough, and from the looks of
Tony, neither had he.

She was still pissed at him for not at least trying to lie to
the press outside the linen closet. For not being the kind of
gallant guy a woman dressed like her, who'd been behaving
the way she had all weekend, shouldn't want. Not once the
hot sex was over and it was time to tap, tap, tap away on her
Christian Louboutins.

But she *did* want him. Both the tiger who'd tamed her, and
the Prince Charming who'd tenderly wiped away her tears.
Just like deep inside, she needed to be both a diva and a
hopeless romantic. She sat taller in her booth and stared back,
daring Tony to engage, instead of continuing to lurk at the safe
distance he'd kept all morning.

Did he want more than hot sex? Did he want gentleness,
too? Could a man like Tony Rossi let himself believe in the
romance he'd seemed to crave for at least a few minutes last
night, when she recited her poem?

Or would he have avoided her entirely all weekend, if she
hadn't been dressed like a sex kitten and purred all over him?

She blew him a soft, romantic kiss. An unspoken challenge. Then she stood to leave.

And for the first time since arriving at Weekend Pass, she prayed Tony would follow her.

CHAPTER NINE

"DONNA REED MEETS Heidi Klum!" Willard's smile of approval dimmed with just a hint of concern as he fluffed Felicia's hair from behind. "You're transformed."

"Well, you did tell me to lose myself in the weekend." Felicia realized she was frowning at her reflection in her bedroom's vanity mirror and told herself to knock it off.

Willard preened behind her. A stylist had supervised her hair and makeup and clothing choices for the upcoming "Face of Romance" interview and photo shoot. Willard, of course, had supervised the stylist. He tilted his head and gave her a naughty squint.

"You know, I spent the morning getting busy with a hunky blonde, too. But *I* had the good sense not to get photographed doing it."

Felicia bit her lip, then shrugged off her embarrassment, the way Maddy shrugged off the crazy things she did. The weekend, the risks Felicia had taken, were a part of her. Not all of her, but an important part she was determined to take back home to New York.

She smoothed a hand down her turquoise St. John suit—a conservative choice for the interview and pictures that would formally reflect on Weekend Pass's—and Tony's—grand opening success.

"I wasn't photographed *doing* anything."

"Except running away from the hottest sex of your life."

Willard had let her slide all day. Her reprieve from explaining herself was clearly over.

"Five minutes…" the photographer called from the den.

Her friend's timing was impeccable, as always.

"Last night," he pushed, "you told me you wanted nothing else to do with Rossi."

"I guess he was something I needed to get out of my system, so I could enjoy the rest of the weekend."

"You 'bout done, then?"

"Yes…" She caught herself biting her lip again. "No. I…I don't know."

She'd exited the restaurant feeling energized by her decision to leave the ball in Tony's court. Then the paparazzi had swarmed again, outside the office where she'd done her guest blog. She hadn't had a moment's peace to think before now, but that hadn't stopped her mind from swinging back to Tony, again and again. "I'm not sure what to feel anymore."

"You've put on a pretty good show of knowing all day. It was brilliantly played, refusing to acknowledge the gossip and intrigue. Just going about the business of making every man in the lodge fall in love with you, including that poor bastard Rossi."

"He's not—"

"Of course he is, just like you've fallen for him. You're both intelligent and intense. Stylish, but couldn't care less about the impact you make, as long as it gets the job done. Neither of you knows how to back down, once you're riled. One touch, and you were hopeless for each other."

"Really? Is that why we've kept our distance all day?"

"Rossi showed at every event on your schedule this morning, and he's the busiest man in the place."

"He never said a word to me."

"Actions speak louder."

"Then brace your matchmaking self, because my reign as a diva is almost over. Tomorrow's just breakfast and a few more photos with the other winners, and then…then you and I head back."

But back to what?

It felt like the most important question of Felicia's life.

Maddy had been right. What Felicia needed was to stop going through the motions, both in Manhattan and at Weekend Pass. No more meltdowns. No more pretending.

"Tony doesn't love me," she insisted, no matter how much she wanted to believe he could. "Whatever we might have been feeling for each other is pretty much messed up now."

"Maybe you need the mess you've made here," Willard reasoned, "more than the perfection waiting for you at home." He smoothed the loose curls tumbling down her shoulders. "Maybe you need more, Fe. You sure as hell deserve it."

More…

More mess that made her feel alive. And more Tony. Except, when she'd left him at the restaurant, he hadn't followed. And he hadn't shown up anywhere she'd been since.

"Don't you have a little more of *Roger* to see before we're finished with our weekend getaway?" she asked her friend.

"We're planning to hook up at dinner, but—"

"Oh, no, you don't." She pushed him toward her bedroom's closed door. "You're done babysitting for tonight. Go find your handsome man. Enjoy yourself. Take notes, so I can live vicariously on the flight home."

"Fe—"

"Go, Willard. I can handle a reporter and a photographer without a lady-in-waiting. I'll find you at dinner."

She was giving him her "girlfriend" smile. The one you smiled when you didn't quite believe what you were saying and neither did your best friend. But a good girlfriend pretended to buy it, regardless, because that's what you needed.

"I'll be looking for you." Willard gave her cheek a quick kiss. "So will every other man in the place. They'll be lining up to eat out of their resident diva's hands."

"Go."

She pointed an imperious finger toward the door, instead of clinging and begging Willard to stay.

Because the only man she wanted eating out of her hands had clearly moved on for good.

"I DON'T NEED ANY MORE surprises," Tony groused into his cell phone. "What do you mean you don't know where she is? She's your VIP and has a freaking circus following her all over the place. Find Maddy and keep her in check. I have my own events to keep track of."

"Everything's going fine," Samantha insisted back. "I know Maddy's a little out of control at times. Still, between her press and yours, the lodge's Web site and Lov's blog are scoring record numbers of hits. This might not be the way you wanted things to turn out, but—"

"No." Tony punched the elevator's up button. "No *buts*. I assured the Walkers that using free press was the way to go, because resort bookings are seventy-five percent word of mouth. But they want their lodge to be a welcoming, romantic retreat. Not somewhere fraternities think would be a *bitchin'* hotspot to blow off steam!"

"That's why they brought you in, and you're doing a great job!" Samantha enthused. "But the singles events—"

"Are out of control."

"Evelyn and I are on top of it." Turf war crept into his colleague's voice.

"Then why do I keep having to pull away from my schedule, to babysit your star? A-List wanted Maddy Lov here. A-List controls her. That was the deal. The woman's a menace. Left to her own devices, it's only a matter of time before her antics do permanent damage to Weekend Pass's reputation. Your job is to make sure that doesn't happen. If that means you and Evelyn stay attached to her hip, do it!"

He slapped his phone closed. The elevator shut, and silence crowded in. Silence and the truth.

He'd lost control with Samantha, when he never lost control on the job. Not even with the A-Bombs, whom he'd managed to work around just fine up till now. Samantha and Evelyn were more of a hassle than a threat to his plans. And Maddy Lov, despite her antics, wasn't nearly as dangerous as he'd just made her out to be.

He was pissed at himself, not anyone else.

He was the menace to his success at Weekend Pass. Himself, and this ridiculous connection he felt to Felicia that he couldn't shake. He'd been avoiding Tom and Alice all day, and whatever they would want to know about his poolside kissing contest fiasco. Instead of staying focused on his job, his mind kept sliding into wondering what Felicia was doing. To needing to check on her. Again and again, to make sure she was okay—even if he'd never allowed himself to actually approach her.

Then he'd watched her leave the restaurant, all smiles and confidence, blowing a kiss his way after vamping it up with Maddy for all the other men there. And he'd told himself enough was enough. Felicia wasn't a woman who could need him the way he needed her. It was time to move on.

Except, none of the PR professionals the Walkers were paying a fortune currently knew what Maddy Lov and her full-tilt-boogie sideshow were up to. And where was his focus? Checking in on a romantic photo op and interview he'd set up with one of the nations top women's magazines. A gig that was no doubt running on autopilot.

So much for *enough*.

The elevator slowed and opened onto the third floor. Tony hesitated so long, the doors began closing. He pushed the hold button at the same time that his phone rang. He flipped the thing open.

"What!" he barked without checking the display.

"Where the hell are you, man?" Matt demanded. "Maddy's pitching a fit about something, and she's supposed to be singing any minute."

"I'm checking in on the *Women's Life* 'Face of Romance' shoot. Get A-List to cover Lov's temper tantrum."

"And they're where, exactly?"

"I just got off the phone with Samantha. She's on her way. I haven't seen Evelyn all day."

"But—"

"I'll be down in a minute. I have to check on something first."

Someone.

He ended the call in the middle of whatever Matt was saying next, then marched down the hall. He was getting this done—*closing* whatever this was between him and Felicia— for good. It was time to get back to work.

The sound of familiar feminine laughter, as gentle and sultry as spring rain, filtered through the suite's door. Tony's body hardened in a blistering rush of need. His hand shook as he curled it into a fist to knock.

Right.

Refocusing on his job.

Cold, hard math.

That's what this was about.

CHAPTER TEN

"GO CHANGE INTO something flirty and glamorous, love," the shoot photographer was saying, as an assistant answered Tony's knock and waved him into Felicia's suite. "We'll finish up in a jiff, so you can hurry your fabulous self downstairs to your fans at dinner."

"Oh! Mr. Rossi." The female reporter Tony had prepped several hours before rushed across the sitting room. "We just finished the first round of photos and the interview. Ms. Gallo is wonderful. Smart and sexy and an incurable romantic. Everything I expected her to be after reading her poem."

Tony heard the woman, but he couldn't drum up a response. He was too distracted watching Felicia disappear into her bedroom, dressed in a skirt and jacket that had been tailored to fit her lithe body. A body his hands ached to mold just as closely.

"Mr. Rossi?" The reporter—Gloria something or other—said. "Could I get some comments from you on the record, to supplement Ms. Gallo's interview?"

"Comments?"

"You know—how you think the Weekend Pass's grand opening and love sonnet contest are working out? *Is* this really the romantic couples getaway to die for? That sort of thing."

The business part of Tony's brain clicked into gear, and he

began answering her questions. But when Felicia reemerged from the bedroom, every sensation above his waist shut down midsentence. The wispy rose-colored dress she'd changed into floated around her body. The neckline and hem were still a daring nod to whatever high-end designer had created it, but the woman wearing the ensemble exuded more than sex appeal. Felicia Gallo had transformed herself into the embodiment of the romantic spirit Gloria was raving about.

At least until Felicia's gaze connected with Tony's. Then her easy confidence crumbled. Insecurity replaced it. Hurt.

Tony felt it all like a punch to the gut. He'd come to get closure for himself—so sure she'd moved on from that morning. He'd never been more certain that he was wrong.

"Okay, love." The photographer had been resetting across from the roaring fireplace. He'd arranged a silk throw on the floor in artful disarray. There was a box of chocolates nearby and an open bottle of wine. He poured a glass and handed it to Felicia. "Enough with the couch. Make yourself comfortable in front of the fire. These are candids of you enjoying the scrumptious perks of your romantic getaway win! I want to see what that golden hair of yours looks like in firelight."

"Has the contest promotion been everything you'd wanted for the lodge?" Gloria asked.

"It's had its surprises." Tony winced as Felicia smoothed a self-conscious hand down her dress, then sat on the throw.

Self-conscious didn't suit a woman who could boldly taunt him one minute, then come apart so sweetly in his arms the next.

"Surprises?" the reporter pressed.

Tony made himself look at the brunette who barely came up to his shoulder, which of course reminded him that Felicia's curvy legs were almost as long as his.

"The Walkers have created an ideal retreat," he answered, running down his list of talking points. "A magical place that brings out the best in everyone who visits. We expect each of our contest winners, and each of our guests, to find their own way during the grand opening. To let Weekend Pass's energy and the magnificent mountain vistas cultivate the romance inside them. Those are the best kinds of surprises, don't you think?"

He'd turned back to watch as the photographer clicked frame after frame of the vibrant, magnetic woman sitting before the fire. A woman whose shine and energy had dimmed when she'd looked at Tony. Felicia had been one shocking surprise after another. And his doubt that she could really be feeling the same things he was had made her unsure of herself.

"Relax, gorgeous," the photographer cooed. "Give me more of that captivating woman our readers want to see."

Tony realized Gloria was staring at him, not Felicia. Then her attention shifted to the woman *he* was staring at. The reporter had no doubt seen and read plenty online about his and Felicia's poolside passion. She could be warming up to ask any number of damaging questions.

"And what are *your* favorite kinds of surprises, Mr. Rossi?" she wanted to know instead.

Felicia looked over, her eyes liquid blue as they reflected the firelight.

"I don't let myself be surprised often," he heard himself admitting loud enough for everyone to hear. "But—"

"That's it, gorgeous," the photographer enthused. "Like you're looking into your lover's eyes…"

"But I have to admit that even *I* have fallen under Weekend Pass's spell."

Or was it Felicia Gallo's spell?

"Magic, huh?" Gloria asked as Felicia's eyes widened in shock, then narrowed with doubt. "So the Walkers really think the lodge can conjure love and romance for couples, over just a single weekend? Even amidst all the partying that's been going on around here?"

"If the connection between the two people is right, anything's possible." Even him trusting in love. Tony's talking points were forgotten. So was his commitment to hurry down to help Matt. "Weekend Pass can absolutely bring a couple together, no matter the odds against them. I challenge your readers to try it for themselves, then to tell me if they don't discover what I have over the past few days."

"Wow!" Gloria shut off the minirecorder she'd been using. "You really know your stuff. I'm a believer, and *Women's Life* readers will be, too." She smiled as she packed up the purse sitting beside her on a high coffee table. "Especially after they get a look at the pictures Chase is taking. Nothing sells a story on romance, or a resort locale, like a beautiful woman who's hopelessly in love."

Tony was too stunned to respond as Gloria gave his arm a you-poor-besotted-guy nudge and let herself out of the suite.

"Right!" Chase said behind Tony. "I think that's it."

The guy was already packing up.

"Got to get downstairs and set up for dinner, before the crowd converges," Chase explained, misreading Tony's shock. "But don't worry. Gloria and I have Weekend Pass and your lovely lady here covered beautifully. Your bosses will be thrilled with the way the article turns out."

Tony's phone rang before he could respond.

Tom Walker, the display read.

"Rossi," Tony said into the receiver, turning his back to Felicia while the photographer bustled by and out of the suite.

"How are things with the shoot?" Tom asked.

"I just got here, but the magazine staff seemed pleased. We'll know more when we see the copy, but I think you've got yourself a home run on your hands."

"Thank God, after this morning's fiasco with Ms. Gallo. Alice mentioned that she and you talked before those pictures were taken of you and Felicia. That you'd insisted that you had everything under control. Then… Well, it's good to have you back on your game, Tony."

The unguarded things Tony had just said to the reporter, Gloria's glee in observing the sparks still flying between him and Felicia, replayed in Tony's mind.

"Yeah," he agreed with his boss. "We'll talk more over dinner. I should be down in a bit."

"No rush," Tom assured him with a weekend of weary in his voice. "I'm helping Matt run interference with A-List issues. I'll be late myself."

Tony stared at his closed phone for several seconds, assuming that after Chase left, Felicia had escaped into her bedroom to change. It was nearly impossible, but he convinced himself to walk toward the door. Felicia deserved time and space to figure out what she wanted next.

"Is everything okay?"

He spun to face the gorgeous woman who hadn't left after all.

"What?"

"The Walkers' grand opening. The success of the love sonnet promotion." Felicia motioned around her. "All of this. I heard you talking with Gloria. I know how important this weekend is to the Walkers. If I've done anything to jeopardize that, I—"

"You've been like a breath of fresh air, blowing through this place." Blowing through him. Tony stepped toward her. He didn't stop until he could see the pulse fluttering at the base of her throat. "Don't worry about it."

"But this morning. I didn't…." She stared down at the hand he hadn't realized he was holding.

"Neither of us did. It was a mistake…" He didn't quite catch the words before they were out of his mouth. Felicia flinched, but he caught her hand before she could pull away. Grabbed the other one. "I didn't mean us…what we did. That was unexpected… But it was amazing, and I didn't handle it well. The press waiting outside… I didn't expect them there, and then I didn't know what to say, and I made a mistake not speaking up. Making you think I regretted being with you."

"I understand." And she did. He could tell.

At least, she understood who he'd been before she'd slipped under his relationship radar and into his heart. He let her hands go, so she could escape if that's what she really needed to do.

"Your job is to protect the Walkers' investment," she continued. "Their business is on the line, and I'm not exactly what anyone expected. Being caught with someone like me—"

"*You're* amazing," he blurted out. A sentence he'd said to a woman about as often as he'd said the words *I love you*—which was exactly never. "You're everything we thought you'd be when you were chosen as a contest winner, and about a hundred more amazing things. You were right. I *was* an asshole for judging you yesterday, without getting to know you first. For thinking I knew who you were at all, just because you were glamorous and sophisticated and sexy. But that's my—"

"Job." She nodded. "Yeah. I understand."

And she did. He could tell.

And somehow he was holding her hands again. Her fingers wrapped trustingly around his.

"How can I feel this way?" she asked. "I never feel this way. Work is where I'm comfortable, just like you. Not breaking all the rules."

"Whose rules?" He drew her closer, needing the way she couldn't resist his touch.

"You have a few of your own, as I recall. At least for how things with me and this weekend were supposed to have gone."

"I'm an idiot."

"You're a very smart man." And it sounded as if she liked that about him.

Not just his edgy wardrobe or his successful career, or the looks that other women swooned over. But his mind. *Him*. She saw him. She had from the start, even though she looked like exactly the type of woman he'd always assumed couldn't see past what his success could buy for her.

"Did you hear me tell that reporter that I've fallen under Weekend Pass's spell?" he asked.

That he was finally letting himself want what was happening between them?

"Spell?"

"What did you call it? A meltdown?" He leaned in and kissed those soft pink lips. She tasted of expensive chocolate and fine wine—an erotic mixture that suited Felicia perfectly.

What would she taste like naked and bathed in firelight?

She kissed him back, her moan managing to sound both needy and demanding at the same time. It was the same sound she'd made when his body had been joined with hers that morning. When, for a brief moment, he'd let her all the way in.

Now it felt as if he might never be able to let her go.

FELICIA WAS LOSING HERSELF in Tony, in his kiss.

Then his cell phone rang.

She stiffened and stepped away. The roller coaster her emotions had been on all day dived to a new low. Doubt flooded in—doubt she'd been so determined to purge when she'd walked away from him the last time. She either meant more to Tony than his job at Weekend Pass or she didn't.

The phone rang again.

"Answer it!" She propped her hand on the hip of the one new dress she felt completely at ease in, even if the soft, clingy cashmere showed off way too much of the goodies underneath. "Whatever you've got left on your PR plate for tonight, you should definitely be getting to it. But I think I've had more than enough *joining in* for one dream vacation."

Tony gave her hostile stance a thorough once-over. Then he stepped closer instead of away and plucked a piece of chocolate from the box of Belgian delicacies that had come complimentary with the suite. His strong white teeth bit into the sinfully dark truffle. He held the second half up to her mouth. Licked at where a dab of gooey filling clung to his bottom lip.

Her mouth dropped open in pure lust. He pressed the tempting morsel inside, as he pulled his still-ringing phone from his pocket and thumbed the thing off.

"No more PR. No more distractions that keep us from figuring out what this is."

Felicia swallowed chocolate and the desperate need to believe him. The man was a professional closer. He knew how to convince a client and a customer of anything. But he also knew exactly how to drive her body crazy. How to make her want, even while he annoyed the hell out of her.

"You must have commitments for the rest of the night," she challenged.

"All that's going on right now is dinner. The choices are steak, quail or salmon." He held up another candy for her to sample. "I can think of things I'd much rather be…" if he said *eating,* she was going to faint, right then and there "…*enjoying,* besides a roomful of half-drunk strangers."

She nibbled, and he groaned. He licked the chocolate where her mouth had been, then sucked it inside. Her knees went ahead and buckled. Of course he caught her, his hands circling to draw her closer. Closer still. Until the hard evidence of exactly what he'd really like to be sampling was pressed to where her body needed him most.

"How 'bout trying this again, Felicia?" he dared her. "How about we keep trying, all night if we have to, until we get it right?"

CHAPTER ELEVEN

IF AT FIRST YOU don't succeed, try, try again….

Felicia had always known being a Type A personality had its good points. But never had perfectionism felt so good. Tony rolled to his back, bringing her with him, their bodies still connected, rocking, each motion in time with the other. Skin to skin, until they couldn't get any closer.

And still he wasn't through.

He pushed up until he was sitting, cradling her in his lap. The fire's reflection licked at the passion in his gaze. Deepened it even more. He ran shaking fingers through her hair. Tony Rossi. *Shaking*—for her. He kissed her gently, then fiercely, then gently again.

Her calves settled on the cool surface of the silk throw. Her bottom wiggled against him. Sweet, intoxicating friction was her reward. His fingers bit into her thighs, encouraging her to ride.

"Felicia," he murmured, his face buried in her hair.

Her body clinched around him. "Say it again. Say my name again."

He arched her backward, kissing his way down to one breast. "Take me, Felicia. Take what you need."

She pulled his head closer, the last of her doubts about what came next evaporating. Rocked harder.

And she took.

What she was feeling was the most dangerous insanity she'd

ever known. But she was flying over the edge, not tiptoeing. Embracing the wicked, sexy diva inside her that the man in her arms couldn't get enough of.

No limits.

No regrets.

"WE MISSED YOU BOTH at dinner last night," Alice Walker said at Felicia's suite door the next morning.

"I don't suppose you and Tom were the only ones who noticed?" Tony motioned her inside.

He'd only bothered with his pants when he'd gotten out of bed to make coffee, reluctantly leaving Felicia and her warmth behind.

"Noticed what?" Alice took the cup of coffee Tony offered. "The conspicuous absence of the weekend's *it* couple? You two were the talk of the evening. The rumors grew even more colorful, once that *Women's Life* reporter began doing shots of tequila with Maddy. This morning's Internet blogs are awash with 'Tony and Felicia's' weekend exploits."

Tony winced, then poured his coffee into the sink.

"Give me a few minutes to get dressed," he said. "Another fifteen to shower and change in my room, and I'll start on damage control. There's got to be some way to turn this still. To—"

"Turn what? The gossip rags are declaring it true love, thanks to that magazine photographer and reporter who saw you two together yesterday afternoon. Well, them and everyone else who watched you trailing around after the woman, and Felicia trying her best not to look like she noticed. Seems Tom and I were the only ones who weren't in on it."

"In on what?" Tony hadn't exactly figured the *what* out for himself yet.

"Your whirlwind love affair." Alice's smile was pleasure and relief in equal parts. "You had us worried, I'll admit. But things couldn't have turned out better if you'd planned them this way. Love at first sight. The two of you sparring with each other one minute. Then passion and the lodge's mystique taking over, refusing to be denied the next. You couldn't have delivered a better PR outcome if you'd written a script and played it out."

PR.

Work.

For a few hours he'd forgotten that the job was what he was all about. As long as he'd held Felicia in his arms, nothing else had existed.

"It *was* real, wasn't it?" Alice asked, echoing the question that had pulled Tony from bed.

The real reason he hadn't been able to lie next to Felicia in the gray light of morning.

"Does it matter?" he asked. "If Weekend Pass is going strong, and you have the romantic reputation you paid for, then there's no harm done."

No harm to anyone—especially Felicia. If she woke up looking for an out, he owed her as smooth an exit as possible from the fiasco he'd turned the Weekend Pass account into. A chance to make up her mind about them, with no more interference from flashbulbs and reporters' questions and the rabid interest from the other guests.

Even if space made it easier for her to move on.

"You all right?" Alice asked.

Tony realized he'd been staring at his empty cup, his back turned to his boss.

What if Felicia's returning the kind of love he'd never let himself want before was the one deal he couldn't close?

"Yeah, I'm fine," he forced out. "I'll be downstairs in fifteen, okay?"

Alice nodded, her expression unsure as he showed her out.

Tony slid into the rest of the clothes he'd left by the fireplace and told himself to go. Not to head back to the bedroom to watch Felicia peacefully sleeping beneath their sex-rumpled sheets.

Whether or not Felicia really wanted to love him had to be her decision, with no pressure from him.

He wrote her a quick note, outlining his first couple of commitments that morning so she could find him when she was ready. Another agenda—this time to bring her to him, instead of keeping her at a distance. That was, if *closer* was what Felicia wanted.

How about we keep trying…until we get it right….

He let himself out of the suite—looking toward her closed bedroom door one last time. Ahead of him was another day of making clients' dreams a reality. And according to Alice, it would be his most successful account closing yet. But the exhilaration he normally felt at the end of a contract was a no-show.

The rightness of what he and Felicia had shared last night was a trap he felt closing around him. He'd given a goddess his heart to break.

Tony pressed the elevator's down button.

What if Felicia decided that the weekend was all she really wanted?

CHAPTER TWELVE

"JUST BECAUSE YOU'RE doing the walk of shame and slinking away, doesn't mean you have to go all Jackie O on me." Willard sighed, but he didn't look up from whatever he was texting to whomever on his iPhone.

"I'm *not* slinking." Felicia gazed at the icy world whizzing by outside the cab's window. Despite the taxi's heater, she felt cold everywhere, especially where Tony's words of passion had touched her heart.

"True," Willard conceded. "Sneaking out in a taxi isn't exactly slinking. But you'd really be shoving it back in that bastard's face, if you'd made him call for the Town Car that brought you here."

"I thought you'd be proud of me. I went all out. I let my inner diva run amok, and I made the hottest guy in the place my love slave."

"Proud?" Willard pressed Send with a vengeance, then looked up in concern. "You got your heart broken, darling."

"It's just the fallout from a crazy weekend," Felicia insisted. "Not a broken heart."

"*You* don't fall for a guy like that and just walk away, Fe. I don't care how much I pushed you, you wouldn't have slept with the man again last night, if you weren't putting everything on the line—all of you."

"Well, clearly *that* was a miscalculation. And now it's over. No blood, no foul."

"Seems Tom and I are the only ones who weren't in on it," Felicia had overheard Alice Walker saying to Tony.

"In on what?" Tony had at least tried for confused innocence.

"Your whirlwind love affair…. You couldn't have delivered a better PR outcome, if you'd written a script and played it out…. It was real, wasn't it?"

"Does it matter? If Weekend Pass is still going strong, and you have the romantic reputation you paid for, then there's no harm done…."

"No harm done," Felicia repeated to her friend. Her frozen heart clenched at the casual way Tony has dismissed her new start—her faith that he would keep her love safe.

He'd been acting all day yesterday. He'd probably even staged his conversation with the *Women's Life* reporter, knowing Felicia would overhear.

"Oversize sunglasses are no good," Willard informed her. "I can tell you've been bawling your eyes out, ever since you dragged me out of Roger's bed and tossed me and our things to the curb."

Willard's phone chirped. He studied the message, then immediately began texting back.

"Who are you talking to?" Felicia grabbed the thing and read a few lines of the last incoming message from a contact named Diva.

…don't worry. I'll make sure Rossi pays. RAT BASTARD!

"Willard…" What had he done?

"I don't care what you say." Willard yanked his phone away and went back to typing. "Or what kind of bind Rossi was in promoting the lodge's grand opening. That golden boy hurt you. He publicly stalked you until you let yourself trust him, then he used you. Just because *he* was willing to put out for his clients didn't make it okay for him to drag you into it."

"Put out?" Felicia's stomach rolled, even though it was empty of everything but the wine and chocolate from yesterday's photo shoot.

"Bad choice of words." Willard's pout was a plea for forgiveness. "But you disappearing into the friendly skies is too easy an out for the guy. Maddy agrees."

"Maddy!" Felicia rubbed the migraine beating away at her left temple.

She wanted to forget Weekend Pass existed. Meanwhile, her friend was still waging war on her behalf across the information superhighway.

"You're going to be fine, gorgeous." Willard finished his Diva message and set the phone aside. He cuddled Felicia close, so she could rest her throbbing head on his wide shoulders. "The weekend wasn't a total loss. Now that your sexy self is unchained, you can go back home and find someone who'll treat you like the goddess you are."

Felicia snuggled into her friend's warmth and swallowed the truth. She'd been holding it in, ever since Tony had left after talking without Alice Walker—leaving Felicia nothing more than his morning agenda, so she'd have no trouble finding him and the press that was gobbling up the gossip about their "whirlwind romance."

She didn't want someone else. She wanted Tony—as much as she wanted to hold on to the goddess he'd helped her unchain.

But he hadn't wanted her, not really. Not the *real* Felicia, who had to show up at the office tomorrow for a nine-o'clock client meeting and spend the morning in the stuffy boardroom that had become her life.

Maybe Tony *had* wanted her heart last night, at least for the few hours he'd let himself believe in the love they were making. But a cynical man like him hadn't known how to keep it. How not to break it, as he used their love to his best business advantage.

So somehow Felicia and her inner diva would just have to find a way to move on.

TONY BANGED ON Felicia's suite door, too frustrated to care who was around to hear.

Where was she?

The morning had been endless, without having Felicia with him, close enough to touch. He needed her wicked laugh and sassy smile, combined with the gentle love that had shone in her eyes last night....

The hell with giving her time and space.

Had she been pissed that he hadn't woken her? Maybe she hadn't gotten his note.

Or was she avoiding him, trying to think of the best way to disentangle herself from what they'd started?

"Felicia," he called, knocking again.

"Your little prop's spread her wings and flown the coop," an accusing voice said from the direction of the elevator.

"What?" Tony spun to find Maddy Lov waiting for a ride to the lobby. Some of her staff had a suite at the other end of the hall.

"I can't believe I pushed her to go for you." The rocker shook her head in disgust. "I thought you two were perfect for each other. Then again, I thought *you* were the real thing, Rossi. Guess you're even more of a snake oil salesman than everybody said."

"What are you talking about?" Tony's anxiety pounded into full-blown panic. "Where's Felicia? I haven't seen her all morning, and she's not answering her phone or her door."

"I doubt she can hear you from the fifth row of first

class," Maddy commiserated. "Didn't she leave you her daily schedule?"

Tony didn't remember stepping away from Felicia's door, but he found himself towering over Lov—truly furious at her for the first time.

"Where is she?" He spaced each word carefully, because if he didn't get an answer soon, he was going to do bodily harm to an international superstar.

Felicia hadn't left him.

Maddy shook her head. The elevator dinged open, closed, took off for the lobby without her, and she was still shaking. Tony inhaled deeply and clenched his fists to keep from wrapping them around the woman's neck.

"She's halfway between here and New York by now," Maddy finally said. "Guess that means you'll have to have a second heart-to-heart with Alice Walker this morning. I'm sure she'll want to know how you're going to keep the romantic reputation of this place *going strong*, now that the lover everyone saw you panting after has jilted you."

"Jilted me? New York?"

Felicia was gone.

Not just from his side, but gone from Weekend Pass. From his life. His fists unclenched. Numbness spread everywhere. He leaned a hand against the wall to steady himself.

"Don't even try sad sack with me." Maddy gave an angry laugh. "Felicia told Willard everything she overheard this morning, and Willard texted all the gory details to me while they were hightailing it to the airport. You deserve whatever shit storm the Walkers throw at you for—"

"The Walkers?" Tony straightened. "What do the Walkers have to do with any of this? They're downstairs enjoying the party. What…" Oh, God. "What did Felicia think she overheard this morning?"

"Think?" Maddy jammed her thumb against the down button. "She *thinks* she heard you and your boss talking over your successful plan to spin Felicia's love for you into PR gold. Something about it not even mattering if it's real or not…"

"Her…Felicia's love?" Tony's thoughts raced past everything else Maddy had said. "She loves me?"

"Love*d*," Maddy corrected. "Past tense." The elevator arrived with a cheery ding. "You're one cold operator," she continued. "I'll give you that. At least I have all the inspiration I need now, when I write Felicia's ballad."

Felicia's poem about love being destroyed by the one person you trusted most.

Tony was still standing there, silent and stunned, long after the doors closed.

CHAPTER THIRTEEN

ROBERTO CAVALLI in the boardroom.

Felicia was pretty sure from the looks she'd received when she'd arrived at work that morning that this was a first for her father's firm. Or maybe her colleagues hadn't known who she was for a moment, with her hair down and her feet shod in four-inch heels and the skirt of her rose-colored, cashmere dress ending several inches above her knees.

Hell, even she didn't recognize herself today. And that felt surprisingly good.

Something had told her when she'd struggled out of her own bed that morning—which she'd shared with Willard, who'd slept over to make sure she'd had as much shoulder to cry on as she'd needed—that the only way to face her first day back in Manhattan was with daring.

Daring. That's what she wanted for her life. She wanted the wicked diva inside her to show off her curves, even when she had to be an intelligent corporate professional. And she wanted her belief in romance to thrive again, even though she'd just lost the second love of her life.

Even though she felt as if a part of her would belong to Tony forever.

Tony Rossi might not have been able to love her, but meeting him had helped her learn how to love herself again. And for that, once she dried her tears and put the weekend behind her for good, she'd always be grateful to him.

She was wrapping up a particularly complex contract negotiating for a string of dry cleaners that would be servicing one of the firm's largest hotel industry clients, when a commotion in the outer office brought her meeting to a screeching halt.

"I have to see her now!" boomed a masculine voice that Felicia never thought she'd hear again. "I'm sorry, but this can't wait...."

Felicia's breath froze. She could only stare back at her assistant and her shocked clients as the boardroom door burst open and the kiss of her dreams barged in.

She drank in the sight of Tony in jeans—jeans!—and the most wrinkled T-shirt she'd ever seen. So much for his rebelliously stylish rep of never being ruffled by anything. Then her gaze shot to the other people sitting at the table. The secretaries and associates crowding behind Tony to watch.

They'd all read the gossip sites, of course. Everyone knew all about her and Tony, even if being the boss's daughter kept them from giving her a hard time about it.

Felicia pushed out of her chair. Whatever the man was doing there, *she* wasn't doing it in front of the people she'd already shocked enough for one day.

"Let me walk you to my office," she said. "And we can—"

"No."

He was beside her in two long strides of those endlessly long legs. More handsome than should be legal. Taller and stronger and more dear to her than any man she'd ever known. But his eyes were red-rimmed and glassy. Dark shadows curved beneath his lower lashes. He looked exhausted.

"What's happened?" She couldn't not ask. "What's wrong? The lodge—"

"Everything at Weekend Pass is fine." One of his hands reached out for her shoulder, then ran through her hair, as if he couldn't stop himself. "I stayed as long as I had to, to wrap things up. Then I hopped a red-eye out here…"

She leaned her cheek into his touch, then caught herself.

"Why?" she demanded.

Why was he here, making her remember things she needed to forget?

"Because Maddy Lov told me what you thought you heard me say to Alice Walker yesterday morning, and…"

Felicia was shaking her head.

Trying to step away.

And he let her.

"I know what I heard." She wasn't doing this, and she definitely wasn't doing it here.

She tried to leave. He pulled her back to him.

"You could have asked me for an explanation," he reasoned.

"When? While you were sprinting out the door, instead of coming back to bed with me!"

Her shout—her CliffNotes version of her weekend fling—blasted through the boardroom like the report of an automatic weapon.

"I thought I was giving you space to figure out what you wanted."

"Well," she whispered this time. "Clearly, what I *wanted* was to be on the other side of the country from you."

"No, you wanted to hide from the truth." Anger vibrated in Tony's voice. "And *that,* I'm not willing to give to you."

"What truth? Was I supposed to follow you downstairs, and confront you about using me, in front of the press that you were using me to impress?"

"No." Weariness settled deeper in his expression. Everywhere but his eyes, which gazed at Felicia with an emotion that was way too good, too real, for her to dare believe in again. "You were supposed to give me a chance to tell you what being with you has done to me. What will happen to my life, my heart, if I can't have you with me from now on…"

He tried to say more, but he couldn't seem to get the words out.

Felicia knew exactly how he felt.

From his pocket, he pulled a folded sheet of paper—a copy of the program from Friday night's welcome reception. He handed it over and waited. When she just held it, staring up at him while her fears—and her dreams—paralyzed her, he took the program back and opened it to the poem printed on the cover.

Her poem.

Beside it, he'd written something of his own, matching her prose line for line. And when he started to read aloud his own words of love, of hope, Felicia was certain she was about to melt into a puddle of romantic, diva happiness, right there at his feet.

She'd bet her salary he had never let himself be vulnerable like this. Not Tony Rossi. But he had, with her, Saturday night—at least she'd thought he had at the time. And now there he was, the stone-cold operator she'd assumed had tossed her aside—laying his feelings for her on the line, no matter who else was listening.

Tony's poem didn't rhyme, and the essence of romance was clearly still new to him. But for each line of hers that talked about loss and needing what was gone, he'd written about hope and loving forever. There wasn't a dry eye in the room by the time he finished, including hers.

"I never should have left you yesterday morning." He thumbed away her tears and gently drew her head close for the sweetest kiss of her life. "Screw my job. And I'll understand if you need more time to figure out what you want this craziness between us to be. But I wasn't using you. I wasn't courting the press through you. I was losing my heart, thanks to Weekend Pass's magic—and yours. I was willing to give up everything for it. I still am. Because if you leave, none of the rest of it will work anymore."

Felicia sobbed and threw her arms around his neck. She kissed him back. No sweetness this time. She needed the fire his poem had promised her. The passion from their weekend. The burning hope that her heart would be safe with his forever.

"I love you, Felicia Gallo." He lifted his head. "I promise I'll never make you doubt that again."

"I love you, too, Tony Rossi," she said, dreaming of the imperfect, romantic confusion that would color their happily ever after.

Amidst the claps and cheers of her coworkers, Felicia shed the last of her need for safety and caution, and opened her arms wide to having crazy fun with this man who wanted all of her, just the way she was.

No limits.

No regrets.

She couldn't wait!

HARLEQUIN® Blaze™

Harlequin is 60 years old, and
Harlequin® Blaze™ is celebrating!

After all, a lot can happen
in 60 years, or 60 minutes…
or 60 seconds!

And a lot sure happens in this
new heart-stopping miniseries:

0-60!

Be sure to catch all three:

A LONG, HARD RIDE by Alison Kent
March 2009

OUT OF CONTROL by Julie Miller
April 2009

HOT-WIRED by Jennifer LaBrecque
May 2009

Available wherever books are sold.

REQUEST YOUR
FREE BOOKS!

2 FREE NOVELS
FROM THE ROMANCE/SUSPENSE
COLLECTION PLUS 2 FREE GIFTS!

YES! Please send me 2 FREE novels from the Romance/Suspense Collection and my 2 FREE gifts (gifts are worth about $10). After receiving them, if I don't wish to receive any more books, I can return the shipping statement marked "cancel." If I don't cancel, I will receive 4 brand-new novels every month and be billed just $5.49 per book in the U.S. or $5.99 per book in Canada, plus 25¢ shipping and handling per book plus applicable taxes, if any*. That's a savings of at least 20% off the cover price! I understand that accepting the 2 free books and gifts places me under no obligation to buy anything. I can always return a shipment and cancel at any time. Even if I never buy another book from the Reader Service, the two free books and gifts are mine to keep forever.

185 MDN EF5Y 385 MDN EF6C

Name	(PLEASE PRINT)

Address	Apt. #

City	State/Prov.	Zip/Postal Code

Signature (if under 18, a parent or guardian must sign)

Mail to **The Reader Service:**
IN U.S.A.: P.O. Box 1867, Buffalo, NY 14240-1867
IN CANADA: P.O. Box 609, Fort Erie, Ontario L2A 5X3

Not valid to current subscribers to the Romance Collection,
the Suspense Collection or the Romance/Suspense Collection.

Want to try two free books from another line?
Call 1-800-873-8635 or visit www.morefreebooks.com.

* Terms and prices subject to change without notice. N.Y. residents add applicable sales tax. Canadian residents will be charged applicable provincial taxes and GST. Offer not valid in Quebec. This offer is limited to one order per household. All orders subject to approval. Credit or debit balances in a customer's account(s) may be offset by any other outstanding balance owed by or to the customer. Please allow 4 to 6 weeks for delivery. Offer available while quantities last.

Your Privacy: Harlequin is committed to protecting your privacy. Our Privacy Policy is available online at www.eHarlequin.com or upon request from the Reader Service. From time to time we make our lists of customers available to reputable third parties who may have a product or service of interest to you. If you would prefer we not share your name and address, please check here.

BOB08R

HQN™

We *are* romance™

New York Times bestselling author

SUSAN MALLERY

Sparks fly when Gracie's legendary youthful bad-boy crush, Riley, returns home seeking respectability. Gracie's determined to keep her distance, but she's quickly discovering that first love is sometimes better the second time around.

FALLING *for* GRACIE

Available January 2009 in bookstores everywhere!